IN THE HOLLOW OF TIME

IN THE HOLLOW OF TIME

THE GALATEA SAGA, I

An Unsigned Manuscript

Cover layout and Interior Design: Creative Publishing Book Design
Cover designs inspired by Michael Rooks and Jeffrey Cassens

ISBN Paperback: 978-1-7373376-0-7
ISBN eBook: 978-1-7373376-1-4

Printed in the United States of America

FROM THE EDITOR

THE DISCOVERY OF THIS manuscript occurred when a generational starship named Galatea II was on an archeological mission to investigate the fate of the ancient civilization of Planet Ulro. The ship being in the neighborhood so to speak of the first human colony in interstellar space, we asked Starship Command to request permission for a landing craft to pay a brief visit to Planet 2314. The request, if granted, would be in exception of a long-standing policy of non-interference with local affairs.

To our surprise, permission was given and arrangements were made for a single representative from the ship to meet the Governor of the planet at the remote site explorers had first landed and eventually settled. For our purposes, the location was of much greater interest than a formal reception in one of the cities of the planet.

What followed was a tour of the site, including a visit to caverns in the hills that the explorers had used as shelter. On the planet those caves are still regarded as a kind of shrine to the founders. While examining a host of Ulro names carved into a wall by the pioneers, three items turned up that had been lost and forgotten. It's the stuff of legend.

First was the original manuscript of this book, *In the Hollow of Time*, now believed to be the earliest narrative of terrestrial life after Ulro.

The second, already well-known in the human diaspora, was the manuscript copy of Ishmael Kahn's *Starship Galatea*, an account of life on the first galactic mission, where he was both eyewitness and designated historian. Electronic memory systems aside, his book is the oldest account of human life in the literature from the first age of space travel.

However, the most curious item of all came third: an unknown manuscript named *History of a Dying Planet*, written by Yori Kashimoto, protagonist of the present book, in the solitude of his later years. Curious, because aside from brief references to his "literary hobbyhorse" in *The Hollow of Time*, there had been no reference to this project, which describes itself as cultural archeology.

At least Kashimoto and Kahn leave no doubt about authorship or the sources of their works. The present volume, however, is mysterious. Having been concealed in the cave with copies of the well-known *Starship Galatea*, in Kahn's own hand, and alongside the manuscript of *History of a Dying Planet Ulro*, only Kashimoto could have put all three there. So the mystery of authorship of this story remains unsolved, but the point matters little since readers, adept at understanding, will follow the tale rather than the teller.

"We feel and know by experience that we are eternal."
—Spinoza

PART I

THE COLONY

The land was ours before we were the lands.
She was our land more than a hundred years
Before we were her people . . .
Something we were withholding made us weak
Until we found out it was ourselves
We were withholding from our land of living.

—Robert Frost

1

A LONE FIGURE EMERGES FROM the enclosed colony
and makes his way over several miles of scorched earth toward
the encircling hills. Where the land begins to rise, Yori Kashimoto follows what must once have been a riverbed. He loves
the solid density of the terrain pushing back against his feet,
even the heat on the soles of his hiking boots—enjoying the
sense of being grounded.

The smooth channel ascending slowly between the jagged
cliffs is strewn with river rocks polished by centuries of water
rushing downward. The nearly black stones are lovely, irresistible to the touch but too hot in the blazing sun. Often on
these excursions when he has found a camp for the night,
he sits on a hillside overlooking the plateau, passing one of
these stones back and forth in his hands, feeling the night-
cool surface and the unearthly weight of the thing. Its sheer
impenetrability presents a brute reality that the wanderer can
measure himself against.

His treks into these hills satisfy curiosity and teach him
to attend to whatever the blinding light of a desert sun gives
to teach. Some two hundred yards farther up the riverbed he
discovers, among clumps of dry weeds, a fissure in the rock just
wide enough to slip through. A turn left reveals a path winding
steeply upward over a surface not worn smooth by erosion. But

the sharp, uneven ground sheltered from the scorching heat must be navigated with care. Eventually, the crevice terminates at a small opening that might be the mouth of a cave.

Poking his head inside, he sees nothing. Hours in the sun have blinded him to the darkness. Proceeding by touch rather than sight, he enters, sets his backpack down, and waits. Spreading himself out, back and arms and hands, against the welcoming cool of the wall, he watches a wide chamber slowly materialize in the dimness. It's a strain to make out the shape of the place. Roughly oval walls fading back and upward into obscurity offer little clue to how big the room may be, but stalactites of various lengths bear witness to the presence of water eons past.

As vision clears, a few details emerge. On the side opposite his resting place strange markings extend from the floor upward into the dark. Approaching them, he touches one of the figures on the smooth surface and discovers that they aren't random and not *on* the surface at all. They are *in it*. Scratched, etched into the wall with a tool. Not figures but words! Impossible words, in Arabic letters! His heart races and breathing stops as he staggers under a sensation of some nameless threat as though nature itself had turned capricious.

Struggling to calm himself, he extends a trembling hand to the wall, and forces the decision that, even here, what looks like stone and feels like stone must be stone. However uncanny, words are words and nature is nature still. Rubbing his hand along the wall, he finds etchings by the dozens, the works and words of human hands where humans have never been. His heart outruns the blind finger as he traces one of

4

the dim figures like a blind man reading Braille. It's a name: Plato! They, these engravings, *all* seem to be names. Names extending right, left, and upward beyond reach, into the dark.

Why the growing sense of terror? If discovering the Chauvet Cave paintings could astound a world, what's to be said about stumbling onto human names in a cave on an unpeopled planet orbiting a distant star on an outer edge of the Milky Way?

For some minutes Yori remains rigid, staring dumbly at the wall in front of him. Then a human voice—where there can be no voice—a woman's voice: "Are you one of the Eternals?"

It's not clear where the sound comes from, resonating from wall to wall. He turns around slowly, straining to find an impossible cause for an impossible effect. Eventually, twenty yards away, nearly opaque in the depth of shadow, he detects a human figure in lotus position, motionless on an outcropping of rock.

"Excuse me. Who are you?" The preposterous ricocheting of his own trembling voice through the cavern adds to his alarm. The startling timbre, pitched in a tone that doesn't coincide with who he recognizes himself to be, serves as a pinch to prove it isn't all a dream.

"Do you live in the surplus of time or from one moment to the next?" Each phrase, uttered slowly, fills the cavern with quiet authority. "Do you belong to the living or the dead?" The words make no sense as they die away into the stillness but leave the barest residue of sense behind.

Instead of replying, he stands spellbound by wonder in the middle of the cave. Long before founding the colony, explorers from the mother ship discovered that there were few indigenous life forms more advanced than flora on Planet 2314. So, what is this? Hallucination? Rational beings underground who have somehow escaped detection? Survivors of a cosmic disaster that dried up the surface millennia ago? Or if the dim scene before him isn't real, is he still sane? Perhaps she, this woman, is a simulacrum and not human at all.

That possibility might strike deeper terror into his heart, but the tone of the voice precludes terror. He's accustomed to "conversing" with virtual presences of people long dead, sitting across the table in a seminar room—at least it's called conversing—but this is not the Academy, and there is no way information systems could find their way into the heart of these barren hills. Besides, no one but he ever ventures outside the colony except on closely monitored research assignments.

If not a simulation, then might she, this "woman," be a life-form from elsewhere, able to assume human shape and imitate his language? If so, she is—they are—uncannily good at it, better than any virtual system he knows, at matching tone with gesture and facial expression. And where would they have found models to imitate?

The eyes now—her eyes—indistinct in the dim light, have the depth of human eyes and convey the obligation to respond as if she were human. He finds it impossible to doubt that he's addressed by a sentient rational being.

At least he responds as if it were true and asks again, "Who are you?"

"Paola. One of the Eternals." The tone is slightly mocking yet she speaks darkly, out of a depth of understanding like that of an old Zen master he once knew in a book. Could she be reading his memory and assuming the role?

"I don't understand anything you say. If you are real, where do you come from?"

"I've watched you, crossing the plateau and exploring the hills. Sometimes you remain for two days and sleep in the open or under the shelter of a warm rock. You are one of the wanderers but not like the others." Whether these remarks are intended to unnerve the student further or to prepare for something still more mysterious—either way they work.

"A student," he replies, as though to clarify his identity.

"What do you study?"

"History." He speaks it hesitantly, this word that feels too light for the occasion, as though the commonplace turns incomprehensible on the end of his tongue.

"What is history?"

He replies cautiously, maintaining his composure. "History is the study of the past, what happened before."

"So, they *still* have nothing to teach at your Academy." The voice seems to convey disappointment.

Once more he stares and begins his conjectures again. Machines can be programed to imitate human feeling, but even the latest programs leave a flatness of affect amid disheartening clichés. If you listen carefully, you can detect the artificiality of nothing understood, when the timing of responses is off, or a metaphor is taken as literal, or the tone doesn't rise or fall at just the right instant. Processing rather than understanding. People may call it artificial intelligence, but for one accustomed to reading care in the face and the eyes of another, it's hard to mistake all that for the indifference of no-one-there. Impossible. Impossible as it is for anyone to be in this place, Yori concludes that if he is not facing a person, he must behave as if he were. So he repeats his question, "Who are you?"

"That's hard to say." She slips from her rock and moves with a grace beyond deliberation toward the darkness at the back of the cave. A human motion, unhurried and soundless in the cloistral silence, but without the distortions of androids. Elegant even in a homespun shift that can only result from long human culture or its effective simulation. But which? And whose?

Without looking back, she gestures for him to follow into a low corridor. The seeker of light hesitates to accept the invitation into the dark, then corrects himself and takes a step forward. When she extends a hand, he stares at it as though it were an unfamiliar, even threatening object. But she waits, leaving the hand in the air until he summons the courage or suffers embarrassment enough to accept. It's warm and familiarly human, that hand, except for an unfamiliar roughness. Then she leads down a steep and winding way into darkness as deep as the unthinkable void before creation.

Yori is accustomed to degrees of darkness and light but not degree zero. The starship is a bubble of continuous light swallowed up in endless dark made visible by a million pinholes of light in the heavens. The colony is another such bubble of visibility, though designed to protect against the assault of too much light from a desert sun.

This is different. Descending into the earth along a labyrinth that twists and turns through vaulted passageways too narrow for two to pass abreast—this is darkness absolute. Impenetrable darkness of impenetrable earth. Yet there are things only visible in the degree zero of light. Sight denied, Yori's attention is drawn to the very capacity to see. And the earth itself is illuminated as something more and something darker than an object one may look at from a distance and make use of. Sitting on top of the plateau or tramping through the hills, he is *on* but never immersed in and belonging to earth. But here, descending blindly through the arteries of the planet, its substance impinges on him as bodily presence without distance.

Though eyes are useless, the way is smooth underfoot and the sounds of rocks moved by moving feet take the measure of the spaces. He can feel the walls move away and hear the width and height of corridors opening intermittently into larger chambers. Everything seems more closely related by being only heard and felt and yet the way down is so meandering that his usually keen sense of direction deserts him. Only a nameless something in the touch of a guiding hand and in the unwitting trust in the authority of a voice holds him within bounds.

Eventually, somewhere in the heart of earth, the way ends in a large cavern where, far above, a cleft in the rock formation offers a meager glow of natural light. After the eclipse of the descent, Yori is arrested by the fact of light itself, though in the dimness he can just make out the shape of the open space. The woman drops his hand and, leaving him in place, moves forward to a central hearthstone where the smoldering remains of a fire lend a domestic touch to the underground chamber.

Slowly the room assumes the shape of a larger oval perhaps eighty feet long and half as wide. There is light enough to study the setting, but it's his hostess—or his captor—who dominates his interest, moving about her simple chores with a grace beyond the reach of anyone he knows. If she is adopting his form by some alien power, then why a form so natural yet so palpably unlike his?

She must be older than he by two decades and quite different in appearance. Unlike his slight, Japanese physique clad in the uniform of the colonial student—black hair, long oval face, wide eyes, pronounced nose, less tall than his friends of European heritage—all quite different from her. The brown eyes almond-shaped, the long, straight dark hair falling to the shoulders, olive skin—all these might be Etruscan in one who is neither tall nor stout but sturdy and maternal in a simple country dress.

In the neighborhood of so much mystery Yori is attentive to every detail. The more closely he observes, the greater his suspicion of depth. Everything about her reveals a scope of human culture for which she could have found no model for imitation in the colony or even on the starship, and she could have known neither of these by natural means.

As the narrow light from above is rapidly fading, he extends his search for clues to the chamber itself. The other caves he passed along the descent into this netherworld sounded empty, but this one, large as it is, does not *feel* empty. A smooth floor and relatively smooth walls with ledges and fissures here and there give the feeling of being lived in.

He takes the liberty of moving about, tentatively exploring natural forms in the shadows. There are piles of coarse fabrics neatly folded on tables of rock along the walls. The singular cleanliness suggests a disciplined but simple life of some duration. Along the right wall he touches outcroppings that might serve for sleeping, and random formations jutting up in the floor like aboriginal furniture.

As the woman occupies herself at the hearthstone, he moves across the open space to the left wall where rows of plants resembling fungus grow in the hollows of the rock as though cultivated. The longer he looks the stronger the impression of a human dwelling space. Nothing has been explained, but the orderliness, along with her earlier speech and behavior, are consistent with rationality as he knows it. That fact helps quiet the turbulence of his spirit, and yet the effect of each art and of the whole exceeds anything in his experience.

"This is the Chamber of the Hearth," she says, as though introducing him formally to a living being. "The Rule of the Hearth governs here." That only deepens the mystery, but she seems oblivious of the effect. Then in response to his question about her identity, "Your question will take time. To learn the answer, you will stay. We will eat together. Then you will sleep here."

These clipped remarks are not invitations. They fall somewhere between indifferent facts and commands. It isn't her terse words that unnerve him and not her manner, but her indifference to such things and her peculiar way of watching and listening. The eyes don't so much meet his as rest on him, not bold, but attentive and indifferent, asking nothing, revealing nothing, as though he were transparent, and she were seeing right through. The uncommon stillness as she moves, her soft gaze, and the hypnotic authority of the voice—all these hold him in awe, neither terrified nor at ease. It's not as though she's a shell with no interiority but as though she's quite human with a more than human interior and more than human perception. Somehow he feels accused. Not as a criminal in the dock is accused but accused in an older sense of being understood by a power that sees and exposes the tendency of his own being.

Without further words, she sets about collecting a meal from materials he doesn't recognize. Vegetable all, chopped and cooked in some kind of oil like a stir-fry. Without asking, she goes through his bag of scant camping supplies and takes seasonings to add to the pan on the hearth fire. The curious thing is that she knows what she needs and is familiar with the uses.

Meanwhile she appears to forget all about him as though enclosed animal-like in the moment, unlike the animal, she is clearly aware of being-in the moment. The quality of her attention excludes everything in the vicinity except the task at hand, though Yori still feels that intelligence saturating the surrounding space. If he were so much as to glance into a crack in the wall behind her, busy as she is, she would know.

With a single gesture she shows him where to sit, and they eat together in silence, he perched on a small rock on one side of the hearthstone, she on the floor opposite, legs crossed like a female Buddha. It's a strange moment where nothing is ordinary, yet a strangely relaxed moment. The grace of her every motion and gesture, the eloquence of every phrase, the tasty food, the orderliness of the cavern itself—all these speak a human language and a culture spontaneous and ingrained. Every imaginable way of accounting for her being unlikely, he might as well believe he's sharing the meal with a chthonic priestess at Eleusis. And yet between himself and her, if one of them is real and the other not, then surely it is she who is the real thing.

The silence of the cavern is also unnerving. He has known only three places in his life: the starship where he was born, the terrestrial colony where he has lived for nearly a year, and the surface of these hills that he visits as often as his studies allow. On the ship and in the colony, there is always a background hum of machinery so that in the hills he relishes the stillness, but this underground world lost in the hush of interstellar space is as silent as its night is dark and eerie to the point of alarm. Her not speaking adds another degree and a different quality of silence that makes his ears buzz. In the middle of it all he meets a gaze across the hearth that openly studies him. The idea dawns that she may know him better than he knows himself, and for that, he needs her.

During the meal she remains nearly as still as the surrounding stones, as though observing him by superhuman power, studying the slow relaxing of a troubled mind. The disinterest of that attention has the odd effect of separating him from himself and leaving an interval between. Or is he moving gradually closer to the moment of trust when he will be able to say here what he needs to say that cannot be said in the colony? Closer as well to the moment when he will be ready to hear things unimaginable in return.

When they have finished the simple meal, she announces, "Now you will stay the night." She gestures for him to bring the rustic utensils to a stone basin at one side of the room where they are washed and restored to their places. Then she lights a reed torch at the hearth fire and leads him to the stone ledge in the far wall. Spreading a straw mat, she says, "Now you will sleep. When you wake, you may ask one question. One only." And she moves away, leaving him in the dark.

It's pointless to try to sleep after all that has happened, and yet his second thought is a flood of light from somewhere above. Waking from a sleep so deep and dreamless that for several moments he can't place himself, he sees the light come to rest on a stone in the middle of an open floor. The first thing that rushes in on a storm tide of memory is the moment of terror before the wall of names. It's a return of the suspicion that nature might be arbitrary after all, but if it were, could he have been there to mark the fact? What lingers, the idea borne in on him with the morning light, is that reality might be discontinuous, broadly consistent but not governed by a reliable chain of causes.

In the middle of a reflection that would never again be far from his mind, the mystery woman approaches with a cup of something that comes hot and fresh. "Now that you have slept, what is your one question?"

Is he intended then to decide in advance what he most wants to know? Having lost yesterday's odd instruction in the swarm of uncanny impressions, he can't think where to begin. "I don't know what to ask."

Without giving him time, she replies, "Another time then." Another casual remark in circumstances where nothing can be casual.

Not daring to contradict her, he lets the moment pass. "I have to get back to the colony. I have a seminar today."

Promptly she relights the torch, puts a piece of blue fruit into his hand, and summons him back through the caves the way they had come. The descent into the dark earth, however mysterious, had been easy enough. But ascent along the same path is anything but easy. The angle is much sharper than the riverbed outside rising from the plateau into the hills. Following her once again into complete darkness secures a discovery only half-understood a few hours earlier. If the denial of sight had opened his eyes to the capacity for sight itself, it is not sight alone. By some means, whether sound or touch or smell, he senses the woman moving silently ahead. He feels the distance between, the angle of ascent, even the twists and turns in the corridors—sensations without organs of sensation—as though the two were connected by a magnetic tether or other immaterial line of communication. Not vision alone then that is clarified by perception withheld, but the possibility of sensation itself as he feels the earth around him expanding or contracting into chambers of various size.

Back in the first cave he stops to rest. In a flood of inscrutabilities so numerous and disorienting that they don't yet add up to experience, he has forgotten about the names. Remembering now, he stops and gestures involuntarily toward the wall. The being calling herself Paola passes him the torch

15

and he walks slowly up and down letting the light fall across the surface. Touching the inscriptions with a finger, he reads one random name after another: Confucius, Shakespeare, Goethe, Michelangelo, Zhuangzi, Euclid, Jesus, Mozart, Einstein, and on and on, astonishment growing with every step. Poets, philosophers, scientists, heroes—a who's who of human achievement.

He bursts out, "But these are Ulro names! They can't be here!"

"Here you're in the hollow of time. Where would you expect to find the Immortals but in the underworld?"

Instead of explaining, she takes the torch from him and walks toward the entrance and the daylight. "You may come when you like. When you do, you may ask one question. Only one. Don't squander it."

Extinguishing the torch, she reverses her steps, and disappears into the darkness, leaving him in a crevice on a lone hillside.

2

REELING FROM THE EFFECT of so many mysteries and so little understanding, Yori begins the descent along the arid channel where a stream had once flowed into a freshwater lake, now the desert plateau. Here and there a few scruffy plants add a touch of green to the brown landscape. One who has seen a verdant world only in reproductions and the contrived landscapes of starship greenhouses barely feels the desert as deprivation. And yet the idea of barrenness accompanies the sensations of solid ground underfoot and endless sky overhead. Given the leisure to think, many things of this sort might have come to mind but, as he stumbles downward, the bewildering events of a day and a night leave no space for such ideas.

The encounter with whatever she was—chthonic prophetess or goddess or other species of alien, tending her impossible underworld of sacred names—has turned his world upside down. Strange utterances, adding up to nothing, have disrupted a safe and secure life and left him unacquainted with himself. And yet why, when he should be happy to have made his escape, why the unaccountable feeling of exhilaration? It's like having been awakened from a lifelong sleep and finding himself transformed by a momentary dream without content. As though he had lived his former life on a monotonous plain, then wandered into unknown heights and stumbled into unimaginable depths of experience. The effect in the yellow morning light is of having been exposed by less than a thought to a precariousness at the source of things. As the heat begins to rise from the surface of Planet 2314, these inchoate sensations gather to a point of conviction: There is a task to be performed but no hint of what the task might be.

As Yori emerges from between two ridges onto the desert floor, the transparent vaults and domes of the colony squatting in the distance appear as a cloud of vapor dissolving slowly in the rising light. Taking its signal from the flat earth, his mind goes blank, and in the hour it takes to reach the northern gate he trudges mechanically along without idea or purpose.

Through an unused airlock monitored only by unused surveillance cameras, he passes into the climate-controlled shell. It may look small from the distance of the hills but inside it's as spacious as a small town. Between his entrance and Government Square where the New Academy is, he passes through several zones that describe the social structure of the settlement. First, a sector that in another place and time would have been called "industrial." It's the part he likes least and usually ignores, but today, being so unsettled, he feels the need to reorient himself to life in the colony.

Ambling attentively through this outermost zone, ignored twenty-four hours earlier, he passes into the neighborhoods of the Providers who make and distribute necessary goods and services. It's a residential circle lined on either side of the streets—more paths than streets—with identical row houses, neat cubes of cookie-cutter uniformity. The colors have been selected to balance daylight heat with nighttime cold rather than for aesthetic effect. Similarly, the neat and clean passageways, that, to the eye of a historian evoke dim memories of the narrow urban streets of medieval Ulro, are reduced here to a tightly woven grid. Occasionally he steps aside to let a small cart pass on its daily round of deliveries. Everything in sight is plain and serviceable, nearer historical Bauhaus than Baroque but more ephemeral. The residences and intermittent squares look different from yesterday. It's as though the life here, for all its high-tech luster, is smaller than Yori remembers. And has lost something of its reality.

After the neighborhoods of the Providers comes the district occupied by the Professionals and the Governors who run the various departments. Their lodgings too are row houses built on the same utilitarian plan except that they consist of two cubes vertically stacked. There are traces of architectural style: shallow front porticoes flanked by shuttered windows on either side and doubled in the upper story. The hierarchical class system inherited from the starship is elastic but firmly based on achievement. In an environment where amenities are limited to need without luxury, the few perquisites of this second residential district are thought to provide incentives to excellence.

It takes only a few minutes to walk from the north entrance to Government Square at the center of the colony. Under a large central dome in the transparent protective shell, public buildings form a quad with a park in the middle. Often Yori has sat on the side of a distant hill at night and contemplated this dome with its geometric arms and swells lying like an organism flat on the desert floor, the only evidence of life being a soft glow against the darkness of the cosmos and a distant mechanical hum in the silence. Now observing these familiar spaces from inside and from an altered perspective for which as yet he has no concept, he considers what the town plan reveals of the life inside: the concentric circles of repetitive production; residential zones with intermittent public spaces; and, here at the center, colonial government.

The design evokes historical comparisons: the small ancient city-states of Ulro built around open agoras or the enclosed castles of rulers; medieval villages surrounding cathedrals like a hen encircled by her chicks; phallic skyscrapers of modern-era cities, upward-thrusting temples of economic power; tumble-down city centers bounded by restless suburban neighborhoods and debased ideals. There is no end to the revelations of unconscious life in the forms of human building.

This Square might look puny to those born in one of the great cities of Ulro, but to space wanderers with their feet on terra firma for the first time in generations, there is much to admire and pleasure to draw from these generous spaces. The garden designed by Yori's friend Véronique Dumas is a magnet, the one meeting place where people gather by day and by night.

Government House dominates the Square on the south. It's the single colonial building with a hint of architectural interest. Cubic in construction, but these cubes have turned Georgian style into rectangles that allude to old Roman values of order and balance in civic life.

On the opposite side of the Square, Department Head-quarters is a lesser version of Government House and provides space for the major administrative divisions. Since education is regarded as the lifeline of the colony, the east and west sides of this all-important square are occupied by the schools, lower and upper. These equally large but much plainer structures house all the teaching services from the "Grammar School" to research institutes.

Crossing the park at the entrance of the New Academy, an extension of the starship academy, Yori spots several fellow students. Among those who are talking together is Lars Hanssen, his roommate and friend since childhood. Yori stops as if to join in, then searches the faces and asks, "Has something happened?"

The question means nothing to them, but to their eyes he appears gaunt and unfocused. Lars—tall, Nordic, authoritative Lars—shows concern. "Nothing's happened. We've just returned from holiday on the ship. But you don't look well. Where have you been?"

They have known one another, these students, all their lives, having lived together at the starship academy almost since infancy. A year ago, after distinguishing themselves and being selected for colonial duty, they moved here for the final stage of their training, but at holidays they are ferried back to Starship Galatea much as students on Planet Ulro once attended university at a distance and returned home for vacation. All but Yori return. He prefers to remain.

Lars chortles affectionately. "I've warned you about spending too much time in those barren hills. You could be suffering from overexposure to the atmosphere."

Yori makes an impatient gesture and walks away. The seminar he's obliged to attend is required of all students who are on track for appointment to the Corps of Governors. The topic is "Issues in the Universal History of Planet Ulro." The rationale for the class is familiar: "Those who cannot remember the past are condemned to repeat it." And today's topic is "The Reasons for Colonizing Space Revisited."

As class gets underway in a comfortable and well-equipped seminar room, the familiar ambiance feels unfamiliar to Yori, and the subject seems unimportant or worse. Instead of giving his usual single-minded attention to the argument, he sits preoccupied and vacant, trying and failing to make connections between the underworld where he has just been and the colony where he now is. Occasionally he hears a dark female voice asking, "What is history?" Heard between these walls, the question rouses a startling recognition: He hasn't the slightest idea what history is and still less its uses and abuses. Even the question is new in a school where received opinions are passed on but rarely challenged.

Under the spell of these otherworldly resonances, the luster is gone from his favorite subject. The deadening repetition of facts without imaginative questions or unexpected points of view reduces the topic to banality. He stares about him, marveling that the students and teacher could have become so dull. To an eye stripped too quickly of illusions, the Academy has metamorphosed overnight from a place for wonder and wisdom to a mill endlessly repeating a past incapable of creation or renewal. His thought is, "We're being trained like dogs in a kennel to imitate our masters. And for what? To afflict the same dull round on our victims in turn!"

Such dark thoughts give new substance to his long-standing preference for solitary wandering in the hills. There, and in the caverns beneath, he has met the unknown for the first time and been startled by questions. The need to return at the first possible moment rushes upon him as a thing already decided. He has left something there, and it would be surprising if it were not himself he has left, and an unknown destiny.

Behind a veneer of old Japanese formality that has somehow survived the intervening centuries, he is a restless soul, haunted by an anxiety that struggles for a name. New ideas rush in with the familiarity of things always known but recognized for the first time. The portion of his anxiety that he can bring into focus has to do with the discipline of history itself, though he hardly knows how. Waiting for class to begin, he acknowledges how unlike his friends he has become, as alien in this seminar room as they all are on this planet. Doubly alien, and not especially surprising. His curriculum was designed for a set of talents that marked him for governing, and so far, he has distinguished himself in his studies. Yet he is dissatisfied, restless and unquiet in mind. By contrast Lars, the engineer, thrives on his subject and delights in accusing Yori of being a dreamer, a loafer, an intellectual tramp, especially on his treks in the hills.

And so the dreamer, occupying his usual place at the seminar table, remains inattentive and abstracted without giving a hint of his state of mind. He is deaf to all but the voice of an imaginary Sibyl in an imaginary netherworld. Deaf especially to the seminar paper on the "real causes" of colonization. The student presentation over, comes the dead spot before discussion. This is where Yori usually jumps enthusiastically in. But today he says nothing.

The teacher is a youngish man whose father, like Yori's, once belonged to the Council of Elders on the starship. He, the teacher, volunteered for colonial service to help preserve the tradition of liberal studies that is always in peril. That alone is enough to make him see Yori as a promising student and to wish to launch him into the elite as quickly as possible. Now, in the silence of nothing to say, the teacher looks curiously in his direction. "You're unusually quiet today, Yori."

The remark startles him out of his reverie.

"What do you think?"

He fumbles a bit. "Sorry. What was the question?"

The teacher looks amused and gives a playfully ironic summary of the argument. "The argument is (1) that the first motive for colonization was economic: to expand scarce resources by importing them from other planets; (2) that the original purpose was compromised by elite administrators who believed Ulro was committing suicide and covertly altered the mission to establish a permanent colony for the preservation of the species; and (3) that the elites therefore subverted the mission by infiltrating it with dreamers who might—they hoped *would*—eventually corrupt the plan."

He studies the aristocratic reserve of Yori's face so like his father's: the cheekbones that seem to prevent facial modulations, the slant of half-lidded eyes that betray nothing of inner passion. Then with a suitable dash of irony he asks, "Are you one of those dreamers today?"

"I hope so!" Yori exclaims without recognizing how close he might be to the outer edge of self-control. However unexpected the outburst, it remains controlled. *I've had enough of these ideological defenses of the status quo. We make up arguments to justify living in an incubator where the aim is to reduce people to bare organisms. The truth is we're leaving the human out. That's suicide in slow motion!"*

If it's a spark the class needs, they now have it. Spark enough at least for one person in the room. The relation between Lars Hanssen and Yori Kashimoto is of a peculiar kind. They began school together at the age of three. During the years when children were gradually weaned from the private family unit and integrated more closely in allegiance to the starship as a collective, Lars' ties with his own parents, who were Producers, weakened, and the two boys spent much of their time outside school with Yori's parents.

Whatever the differences in disposition, the friendship between them was untroubled until four years ago when one was selected to study history and the other engineering. Then a moat began to open between them. By the time they were assigned to immigrate to the colony, they had become rivals of a kind that in other circumstances might have been constructive. But in their disagreements they are as abrupt and violent as brothers. Then after each irruption, their quarrels are soon forgotten and familial affection restored.

Lars jumps in by jumping on Yori. "There you go, weaving arcane theories when there's real work to be done. It's your old trick of throwing up obscure arguments instead of acting to improve things. You make an issue so complicated that no one knows what to respond, with the result that things that should be done go undone."

The contrast between these two bright young men could hardly be greater. Lars' features—fair skin, blue eyes, blond hair, the long, narrow oval face with well-defined bone structure—all give the impression of a diplomatic levelheadedness beyond his years. Nothing like Yori's brooding and mercurial temper. This time Lars is fed up. When he stands up at his place as though to gain advantage over Yori seated, his long legs and erect posture add authority to his presence even as his voice trembles.

"You go off to your hills like an otherworldly desert father to dream up arguments against a colony that's your lifeline. You ought to be here helping make it even better than it is. If everyone pulls their weight, we have a chance of building a utopia that satisfies all human interests for the first time in history."

"Your utopia," Yori answers, "your highest ideal of a city, is a well-organized beehive. Everything in harmony: Collect pollen from the flowers, eat and breed and die. We are not insects! We are capable of wonder. Beehives are not the best places for wonder."

Contemptuous of these attacks on common sense, Lars is also irritated that Yori's reasons and his passion spring from sources that he can't reach. His face flushes red with barely controlled anger as though something in the exchange threatens him. "You think if a person doesn't spend his life asking unanswerable questions, he's wasting it. I *wonder* all the time. We all do. We wonder how to do good things for people, keep them safe, provide water and food and education and medical care."

"That's not wonder. That's planning. Calculating relations among things already in sight. Wonder limited to interest is wonder shut down. I'm not looking for your practicalities or the short answers that silence questioning. I mean to face the unknown beyond any aim in view."

Lars gestures as though to interrupt, but Yori talks him down. "Have you ever heard—ever really listened to—the wise question, 'How can we live without the unknown?' That doesn't mean the back side of the galaxy that we don't know *yet*. It means living on the threshold, *needing* to live on the threshold of the unforeseeable, in ourselves as much as in the universe. It's who we are . . . or might be."

By this point the exchange in class has spiraled into a long-standing controversy that the teacher must be enjoying since he makes no move to end it.

Lars slaps the table in front of him with the palm of his hand and barks, "That's bullshit! We have water to purify and food to grow. We don't have time for fuzzy-headed mysticism. When you have these intellectual seizures, you should get up and do something useful, not go off to your wilderness like a dreamer inventing arguments to destabilize the colony. It's time you thought about the consequences of vilifying the power that keeps you alive and makes you comfortable!" And he ends with the complacent smile usually reserved for children.

When on these rare occasions Yori matches his friend's personal tone in argument, Lars tends to back away with a patronizing smile that pushes things to a still more personal level. But this time Yori counterattacks:

"Your faith in material progress protects you from the 'mysticism' that makes you human. Let's imagine that your machines were slowly killing the human spirit . . ."

Lars tries to interrupt and is waved aside.

". . . I know that's unthinkable for you, but what if? Try wondering for a moment. Perhaps you have no eye for the symptoms of the disease because your confidence in better widgets and better mousetraps excludes them. But what if a whole culture were spinning downward toward extinction? You're inside. How would you know? Organization and efficient systems are your cure for all ills. But they could be symptoms of the disease. If we were strangling on those efficient systems, how would you know?"

Then instead of waiting for Lars to answer, Yori gets up and marches out of the room. If he were a few years older, he might take a moment to reflect on the consequences of burning bridges. Bridge burning is one thing in large and diverse worlds where, if things don't work out, you can join the Foreign Legion. Quite another thing to revolt against the only order between you and nonbeing on the backside of the Milky Way. But Yori is bright and seventeen.

3

WITHIN FOUR DAYS YORI is off again to the hills. Crossing the barren plain with his eye on the riverbed that curved away beyond the distant ridges, he is reminded by the emptiness that there is no world here, only the stuff from which a world might be made. A bit later, on rising ground, he searches for the fissure that leads to the cave of names and passes once more from blinding light into the blinding dark where he must wait to see.

Irrationally surprised not to find the woman named Paola sitting where she sat before, he picks his way gingerly downward through the series of caves, aware that one wrong turn and he might be lost forever. In his first descent, an ordinary mode of experience had registered on him with a new intensity: the sense of smell. Now, without prompting, his nose detects the difference between the still air in tunnels with dead ends and the slight whiff of fresh air passing from chambers below toward the surface.

By following his nose and with no ill effects beyond barked knuckles and a bruise on the head from an unexpected turn in the path, he suddenly emerges into the Chamber of the Hearth. And finds it empty! Though the hearth still smolders, pointlessly, a wave of dejection spreads through him. Aimless searching reveals a second passage leading still deeper into the hill, so he lights one of the grass torches at the hearth and follows that path. This way is easy but, despite the evidence of the hearth, fear begins to rise in his breast that Paola may have been a phantom after all.

Three caves farther on he comes upon her sitting beside the first natural reservoir of water he has ever seen. She looks up without curiosity. When eventually he speaks, he is sufficiently calm to speak quietly as though already learning: "I came to ask one question."

When she makes no acknowledgment of the remark, he asks, "Who are you?"

She remains unresponsive, and he sits down opposite her on the stone edge with water between, much as they had sat across the hearth fire a few nights before.

It's difficult to imagine how a first encounter with a natural body of water might feel to a person who has never had the experience. For generations on the starship two things competed as most fascinating: the celestial bodies in deep space and representations of water. Fire aplenty and a bountiful absence of air, but only simulacra of water and earth. The space explorers who "manufactured" water for practical uses were curiously fascinated by photographs and films of the oceans and lakes and rivers of Planet Ulro, but not one could have imagined the effect of sitting beside this little pool, gazing into its opaque depths.

To speak of psychological response would be to miss the point entirely. Instead of letting vision stop at the isolated object, what is needed is a glimpse of the field of shifting relations it belongs to. Not an object colored by a subjective response but a topological field including both. Like the single stone in a mosaic or one note in a symphony. Yori is amazed as significance expands from physical sensation to the genesis of life, and the renewal of the human spirit. All this sweeps over him in one expansive moment without weakening the question "Who are you?"

Eventually the woman folds her hands in her lap in a gesture of ritual preparation as though what she says now will change everything. "I was one of the explorers in the first landing party. You will not know about us. All but three were killed. Starship Command ordered our extermination." She stops and waits for a response: ". . . including your father."

Yori jumps up in surprise and alarm. He who usually absorbs the unexpected with calm is thrown into a tumult by the inclusion of his father . . . his ideal. Until his father had been assigned to that tiny group of twenty explorers, few days of his childhood had passed without time in his company. Then everything had been sacrificed—family, research, life itself—for the mission. Now the news that his death was not accidental after all. Executed! The best man of his generation ignominiously killed. In one second and three words, before reason has time to begin weighing the implications, the phrase "including your father" dissolves the whole motive and direction of his life. Calling up all his reserve stoicism, he protects himself from chaos by laying the news aside and passing to other questions.

Such news, from such a source, across so many years, carries conviction without evidence. It settles several unanswered questions and opens many more. Why has the survivor—if she is—managed this bit of information so carefully? Why had she not told him right off, when they met? If she is who she says, what is her motive? Revenge? Revenge against Starship Command after a lapse of fifteen years? It would be suicide. Did she bring him here to pass on the truth about his father's fate and draw him into a different kind of plot? Or is this some kind of test? To discover his character and measure his loyalties? But why? Whatever her intention, if what she says is true, then nothing is what it seems to be. Nothing known about the fate of his father and the other explorers will have been true! The system he's in training to help administer will have been founded on deception, and the woman sitting in perfect repose on the other side of the pool will be the only reliable person he knows.

He searches her face for clues and finds none. There is no sign that anything out of the ordinary has passed between them. Apparently she has used his uncertainty about her to prepare him to accept news that he might otherwise have doubted. He composes himself sufficiently to say only, "Please go on."

"Both our fathers belonged to the Elders—the Council of Elders—on the Galatea. They were friends. More important, they were allies in ways that no one knew. I knew your father well. He was a brilliant physicist and cosmologist who volunteered for the first landing party. That made us colleagues. You wouldn't know much about all that. That history too, whatever part of it Starship Command knew, would have been sanitized while you were still a child."

She sits quietly as though studying the problem from new angles, then sighs. "But I must go farther back." And so she tells of the explorers' mission, how they fell out of favor with the starship crew and were killed in the Chamber of Names—all but three, she and two others who were away at the time. After the "murderers" left, the survivors lived permanently here in the caves, avoiding detection.

Yori doesn't ask about the others, as he doesn't ask a thousand other questions that crowd in on him. Somehow he knows—rather feels—that particular questions will waste time and lead nowhere, so he waits for her to decide how the story should be told.

"We were held guilty of insubordination and willful subversion of the mission. But we'll bypass all that for now. Our seditious behavior derived from an ancient contradiction embedded in the Galatea itself. Between the crew and the Elders conflict was intrinsic and fated to erupt when conditions were right. It took generations for quiet stresses to become warfare, but it was inevitable, and may have been foreseen, even intended, by the planners. The disagreement was over . . ." She pauses again as though thinking how to put it briefly. "Well, over everything, and it was destined sooner or later to become a life and death struggle. The command structure was essentially military, based on ancient naval authority, and considered in that light, we were mutineers."

There she stops, but the intensity of her gaze has more to tell. At some point in the future, Yori would remember this moment and that gaze as having shown him that the struggle was far from over and that he belonged to it.

She lays that part of the story aside with a barely detectable shrug. "You'll learn all about it in good time. Orders were given, and when we refused to obey, another landing party was sent to liquidate us. People on the ship would have been told nothing. Nothing true."

Yori's face asks a silent question that she answers promptly. "It isn't hard for an oligarchy to manage the disappearance of twenty people several miles below the ship on a piece of space rock where no one else has ever been. There are always androids to execute commands. We know this because they were left to intercept the three of us if we returned.

"We easily evaded them. Contrary to what technicians like to think, androids are profoundly stupid. They deal efficiently where possibilities are finite and commands unambiguous. But introduce ambivalence or imagination and robots founder. My father—he was a classicist—used to say that robots could process everything but poetry, because poetry is human. They could, he said, do anything but fall in love, and therefore they could do nothing. He meant, I suppose, that poetry must be understood and that love simulated isn't love.

"So we easily cheated them, just not soon enough for your father and the sixteen others. We three survivors were out on a research mission at the time. When we returned and saw what had happened, we salvaged what we could and took shelter deeper in the caves. You don't know yet that you have come to the hills for much the same reason we did."

After this longest speech Yori has yet heard from her, she pauses again, as though putting her story in words brings back the full sense of being marooned where rescue would have been worse.

With a sad smile she concludes, "The answer to your question is that I am a space outlaw, presumed dead and forgotten.

A confederate of your late father, Akira Kashimoto, who was a criminal conspirator."

Just at the point where he is ready for the conversation to begin, she breaks it off with no intention of resuming. Getting up from the edge of the pool, she gestures for him to follow back into the Chamber of the Hearth.

During a silent meal, their second together, Yori is entirely distracted by the news that has fractured his world. Slowly he passes from blankness to analysis. In one week: the discovery of Paola and the caves, this account of his father and the deceit at the root of the colony, even perhaps the corruption of the generational space mission itself. In less than a week his life and its foundation, reaching back two and a half centuries, have been reduced to a grand illusion without a future. Life has been false and he, with or without the help of this strange woman, has the task of deciding what to do next.

When she involves him in the domestic tasks first of laying out the utensils for their simple meal then cleaning up and restoring order, he understands that she is also restoring him. As much as to say, "When life turns absurd, get up and put the house in order." Just when he expects the conversation to resume, she announces, "Now it's time to sleep. Tomorrow you will begin to learn how we survive here."

She reads his thought when he looks around as though for the other two "outlaws." "You will not meet them. They are collecting plant species many kilometers to the north."

So he is left doubly in the dark to gnaw on the bare bones of all he has heard. Staring into the distant cavities of rock overhead, he can see one star shining covertly through the opening in the top of the cave, and he imagines himself lying entombed beneath the surface of an unknown planet, abandoned by his own as once upon a time people on Ulro may have felt abandoned by the gods.

When morning comes, Paola does not reopen the topic or allude in any way to the subject that hangs in air still scented with last night's hearth fire. Instead she says, "We need brush for the fire. The brush pile is beyond the pool at the exit of the third cave." She gestures toward the corridor where he had found her yesterday. "The basket is by the door. Light one of those torches."

As he hesitates, "You are an explorer. You'll find your way." She points again. Not a command or even a request, just words that belong to the seamless activities of the day.

He does as she instructs. It's a diversion for a mind still numb. He returns and piles the brush neatly against the wall under the mushrooms. Then, without so much as wondering why, he defers a host of questions that would satisfy curiosity but teach nothing. What he now knows about Paola and why she's here sheds little light. Moving about her domestic chores, she is every bit as mysterious as if she *were* the alien life form or the simulacrum he first surmised. His conviction confirmed that she cannot be rushed, he accepts patience and the obligation to measure up in the face of the unknown. So on this first day, after recovering a past that is a lie and no future at all, he simply endures his private turmoil, attentively watching as she goes about the rituals that make up her strange life.

"This morning I'm going to the garden. You come too. You'll see where we grow food. I'll show you what we do with our refuse, even how we return our own waste to arable earth. Everything here is respected. Everything is saved."

They proceed along the underground path beyond the pool and the brush pile and eventually emerge into an open, sunlit space. It's a wide crevice or small canyon between rock walls that almost meet at the top. The spot is concealed from both scorching heat and surveillance from the sky yet open to several hours of sun each day. Instead of bare rock, the floor is a layer of soil, somehow made arable for neat rows of plants either native to the planet or transplanted long ago from the stores on the starship.

These constitute her garden or "farm." However primitive the setting, Yori notes the orderliness and even the experimental character of the project.

"You bring water . . . from the pool." She gestures in the direction they have just come. "There's plenty of freshwater underground. These caves were once an aquifer." With that, she turns aside to get on with her work.

Yori brings the water, and the question now settled of what order of being she is, he keeps his distress over his father at a distance by watching her tend the plants, trying to gather a unified impression of her and her solitary life. There's no trace of the others in the Chamber of the Hearth nor has she mentioned them again, as though she has lost the habit of responding to other people or doesn't find it worth the effort. Even these sensations make another breach in the boundaries of his mind, as a storm perforates a dam and makes the fields beyond fertile. He has yet to learn the art of channeling such a flood into well-formed questions and new experience.

Meanwhile, responding to some things that would normally not occur to him, he feels an indiscernible force passing between the two of them. Not erotic but some analogous attraction. And not ideas so much as attunement to one another the way musical instruments must be tuned. And that brings another thing to mind: how out of tune he and Lars Hanssen have been of late, how lifelong friends can speak at cross-purposes even when they agree, while strangers may commune at first meeting without words.

Sometime later, after attending to the little things in the garden, Paola returns and sits down beside him. However well he may think he's concealing his inner turmoil, she understands his state of mind. Knows that things merely heard or seen don't add up to experience, that sensations must be handled, weighed, tested with an eye to application and shaped into experience. So she lingers quietly alongside as though time spent in this way is not time lost.

Eventually she remarks, "Before conversation is possible, people must find the place they can share and get the key or the tonality set in their ears."

Silence again. Then, "Today you will learn about a book that was sent by my father and smuggled from the ship by your father at great risk to them both." A wistful expression passes over her face.

"You loved him," Yori responds, grateful for a topic both relevant and distracting.

"Loved one and hated the other. The book was sent after their last meeting on the ship, after Akira had returned from his final consultation with Starship Command.

"We on the ground never knew exactly what happened in those meetings, but disaster followed quickly. The book is called *Starship Galatea*. It was commissioned by the last generation of the Council of Elders. It tells about the mission and the way of life on board, but mainly—this is what made it dangerous—it recounts the struggle of the Council against Command. For several generations, as long as the ship was under the authority of Ground Command on Ulro, the rift was benign. But then, for reasons you will discover, the differences emerged from the shadows into open rebellion and repression."

He waits, hardly daring to breathe, as she decides what needs telling just now. "I won't rehash. Read it all for yourself. You'll also find conversations called Colloquies of the Elders interspersed in the narrative. These are accounts of their debates and much, much more. For fifteen years I have had only two books to live on: the *Iliad*, the one book I brought from the ship, and *Starship Galatea*. As far as I know this is the only copy, and it must not leave the caves. If it were discovered, irreplaceable touchstones of our life would be lost. You may read it only here. When I disappear, the book passes to you."

Once more astonishment renders him speechless. This woman has a way of opening a fissure between the person he was a moment before and the person he may be a moment hence. As though a history could end in an instant and another history—or something other than history—begin in the next.

Rising from the bank where they've been sitting, she leads the way back to the Chamber and in a dimly lit corner removes a small package from a concealed crevice in the wall. As she crosses the room and lays a well-used book reverently on the hearthstone in front of him, he understands that she is sharing her greatest treasure, the source and inspiration for her strange ways of thinking and living.

"You may read the narrative of the starship whenever you like, but the Colloquies are different. They must not be read out of sequence or out of curiosity. That would be misreading. They are records selected from hundreds of Council debates on every subject imaginable over several centuries. But they don't offer truths that can be learned and slavishly followed nor fragments of information about an unchanging past or opinions to be argued. They are portions of eternity. Ideas, bits of the past to be picked over as a child plays with her mother's jewels or assembles rubbish, inventing a new game."

Yori understands the prohibition but nothing of the substance of this speech. A person who by rights does not exist in his world hands a message in a bottle containing secrets of who he is, why he's here, along with intimations of his destiny—how could an ordinary mortal take so much in in an instant, even if he were not barely seventeen? The title of the book alone—the name of the place, if it is a place, where he was born—opens a flood of questions. But instead of asking, he sits staring at the blank cover and feeling the thickness and the weight of the volume.

"My father was Claudio Rucai . . ."

"I knew him!" Yori, startled, interrupts. "Only as a child. He and your mother were friends with my parents. They were often at our apartment."

"Yes." And she gives him the second smile he has had from her. "I remember you when you were a small child. Then only. My father and I parted ways when I was still young."

She leaves the hearth to assume the position on the rock that she seems to prefer when they talk. "Now you may ask any-thing so long as it is essential. But consider carefully. One question only."

He accepts the restriction along with all her other inscrutabilities. Then pours all his wonder into a simple question:

"Why did my father do it? Join the landing party? Defy Starship Command and put all your lives at risk? Why even smuggle the book? If that sounds like four questions instead of one, it isn't. It's only one: What about my father?"

Paola doesn't speak until he is thoroughly concentrated on the single question at hand. Then, pulling her legs up under her, she solicits his gaze with her sloe-dark eyes.

4

"MY FATHER AND I were not always friends." She speaks slowly, not hovering over the phrases, contemplating them one by one, but dropping them like beads for him to follow.

"I was a scientist, and he thought the colony was going to ruin at the hands of 'the engineers.' That was his generic name for the chain of command and all the 'merely useful' people of the kind I emulated after puberty, trying to be as unlike him as possible. That's why he tried to prevent your father from including me in the landing party. And yet, though I hadn't listened to him in years, he must have thought that in time I might listen to the book."

She punctuates her thought with a remorseful silence, staring away into the dark labyrinth of caves beyond the chamber as though wondering whether, considering the enormity of the story, it's worth it to go on. Then she returns to pick up the thread at the beginning. "The answer to your question about Akira is simple, but the question itself is endless. I have to go back a bit."

Again, still ordering her ideas, she makes him wait. "We were twenty: scientists and technicians. Our first consideration was survival. Research came second. The landing party covered every technical aspect of establishing a colony. Your father . . . he was one of us, but he was different. I'll come to that. The thing some of us had no time for was the impractical question 'So what?' Survival obviously, but survival for what? How do you build a good house until you know its aim and motive, what it means to live there? Or a colony, without first knowing what colonies are for? How do you get practical people to want to see beyond the ends of their noses and think about the origins and ends of their acts? Even more, how do you include the scientist in her science when what she least wants to know is herself? One who will govern others must ask such questions."

The remark about governing causes a little flash across the surface of Yori's mind as though the topic has something to do with him, but it's one of the dark remarks that only bear fruit, if at all, much later. When she seems disinclined to go on, he prompts, "People have been asking 'So what?' from the dawn of time."

"What's terrifying is that 'So what?' has no final answer. We want questions answered so we can turn them off. Silence them. But as this one has no off switch it's consigned to the dust heap or relegated to the dreamers. We were technicians and too busy to keep the real questions alive, but once we were down here isolated on the planet surface, all that changed. We crystalized into a community, and that multiplies experience. Together we were living into the new earth, learning its structures and its ways, beginning to belong to what could not otherwise be possessed. That brought the question of meaning back with new intensity. Which brings me finally to your father. He was a scientist, but he had lived with such questions all his life."

"Then I need to know what happened."

"Only incidentally *what* happened. Here's what you need to know now. If you take it to heart, you may find destiny— your destiny—in what comes next."

She doesn't rush on. Just sits with legs crossed under her, much more than a being at rest on her slab of rock in a dark cave. She seems to know that initiation is accomplished less by words than by ritual, spreading its warm glow like wine in the blood.

"Our group of twenty, you must know, had been corrupted. Subverted is the word. Mainly by your father. Akira and Claudio had spent years quietly infiltrating the technical circles with people who were more than technicians. Specialists, but specialists second. I was the first. Between childhood and that time, to *my* father's regret, the limits of my science were the limits of my world, or so I tried to believe. A part of a person pretending to be whole. Running away from the whole. It was your father who showed all of us the way back."

Of the many things Yori wants, what he wants most is detail about his father, how he died, why he had to die, but for all that he continues to wait.

"When Starship Command began 'developing' the planet, we balked. That was the beginning of our end. The particulars are unimportant, having to do with who the first colonists would be. We, the explorers, expected to be the core of that group, but Command wanted only technicians who would do what they were told. Especially, they wanted a quick and efficient settlement. No thought of the 'subjective' human dimension. We were busily planning something quite different, passively resisting their efficiencies mainly by temporizing. Eventually orders came and we refused. Then apparently it was decided that the easiest solution to blatant insubordination was an 'accident' in the life-support system. The solution that wouldn't expand the trouble and delay 'development.' So the bodies were left in the Chamber of Names. Mostly asphyxiated." Her voice wavers, and the cave swallows up her last remark.

"They killed my father!" Yori jumps up and begins pacing the floor in a quiet rage, searching for what is to be done where he can do nothing but run in circles and devour himself with resentment.

Paola says nothing. Just sits serenely disengaged. Then holds up a hand, palm out, until his attention returns. Soon enough he regains his composure, sits down again, and forces himself to attention. Listening to her silence, reading it, learning from the eyes that reach beyond the visible and see through him by not looking—through all this he begins to sense that she is the point where the rubble of his broken world might begin reassembling into new forms.

In time, she continues, "We three—Kwan Shi Wa, Edward Hamilton, and I—survived first by coincidence, then by intelligence and quick action. Presumably Command deduced that we had perished on our mission to the North or soon would, though they did leave the androids for insurance. No doubt we were declared dead and forgotten. Machines after all—and people who aspire to think like machines— have little use for memory."

The two, this teller of fortunes and her apprentice, sit on, one inhabiting her narrative, the other learning that narratives must *be* inhabited. Eventually, in a voice that hardly alters, she speaks as though following a thread of memory that leads into another world.

"I was a philistine and Claudio, my father, tried to keep me away from the conspiracy, but Akira, your father, believed in me and got me selected. It was easy. I was a botanist and a fertile female. At that point it was assumed that the landing party would be the first wave of colonists. So I was useful."

Yori restlessly follows his own thread. "My mother made inquiries, you know. What she eventually learned—the revisionist story—was that you encountered some exotic virus and all went mad."

"They may even have believed it. Unimaginative people, who like to forget that 'normality' is only a statistic, such people tend to assume that behavior with no precedent in their narrow experience must be pathological. The primary symptom is that we become highly impractical and unreliable, as though there were a chemical deficiency in the brain. Besides, Command had all the power. We had none. We were committing suicide. Proof enough to convince dull people that we were mad. That's how we came to be referred to contemptuously as 'The Immortals.' The accusation was that we thought we had some greater vision like the gods and were unconcerned with mortal things like the survival of the species." With that remark, Paola seems inclined to close the circle and end the story.

Yori, visibly struggling to assimilate so much history, gets up again and says apologetically, "I will have to wait for what happened next. My seminar meets this afternoon and I have to get back to the Academy." He gathers his few possessions and follows Paola up the usual way, through the dark toward the light. In the cavern where they met, he casts a last curious glance at the mysterious wall of names. Then, turning to leave, he pauses as though for some ritual benison.

She sees and smiles. "You may come here when you like. You have much to learn."

"That's all I have ever done." Then, as though daring her to decline another question, he adds, "What must I learn now?"

"You've been taught how to remember but not that memory is also forgetting. That's something your Academy doesn't know."

"How do I learn that?"

"First by unlearning, and my task is to teach you."

5

WEEKS PASS BEFORE YORI is free to return to the hills. He has projects and exams that keep him at the Academy. Present in body, at least, though his mind is hardly there. When not preoccupied with his father and what he has learned about the early history of the colony, he frets over his own lack of discipline.

Why can't he segregate his two lives, consign them to separate compartments and function well in both? In one he is on a fast track to success, almost certain to become a member of the Corps of Governors. In the other he's being shattered and recomposed, if at all, into an exile who barely recognizes his own name. The scission in his being, the trauma at the center that haunts his nights, is his father's murder. But in the quieter daylight hours when he's preparing for exams with what concentration he can muster, the whole "Paola event" remains at the edge of consciousness, coloring all his attitudes and seeking deeper root. Why can't he compartmentalize? Unless compartmentalizing—the expedient of file clerks—is a way of avoiding experience.

The day comes at last when he is free to leave again. This time he does not wander randomly about the hillsides or follow the direct route up the stream bed. Whatever his general state of mind, in small things he is thinking clearly.

Paola's situation has sounded an alarm about the risk she has taken in revealing herself. It's unlikely that anyone would follow him into these bleak hills and discover her, since no one but a slightly eccentric student with an odd taste for heat and rocks and solitude would venture into such a landscape.

No one, unless Lars should take it into his head out of pure mischief. Inspired by that suspicion, Yori chooses a diversionary path to conceal his destination from chance observers. Late in the afternoon as the boulders on the scorched slopes begin to cast cooler shadows, he finds a new path to the cave entrance. When he gets there, Paola is waiting.

"How did you know I would come?"

"I didn't *know*. All things considered, it was likely." To a disinterested observer, her quiet smile might be taken as evidence of happiness in having human company once more. After being marooned for years on a piece of rock that bears only the number of a year for a name, the prospect of being able to tell her story must bring relief if not joy. Not that she's much inclined to talk. In Yori's memory these visits seem to have been full of talk, intermittent questions answered in the long oracular utterances of a sibyl, but in fact the talk has been mostly an internal monologue.

As usual she senses his mood, and instead of proceeding deeper into the caves leads the way back out and to the shade of a red rock where they can sit looking out over the plateau without being exposed. The place is delineated by a great cantilevered formation of rock that shelters them from the late afternoon sun. Others provide sides rather like the arms of a desert cabana, and a fourth, a foot high across the front, conceals the interior from the plateau without interrupting the view.

As the sky darkens toward evening, the distant colony emits a soft glow that, from this elevation and this distance, resembles some alien biospecimen dropped on the desert floor and left to die: a multi-limbed mollusk perhaps, or the web of a giant spider, or the geometrical hive of a colony of bees. Under any of these aspects, it is shape without evidence of life. Just the glow and the distant, occasionally audible hum of a well-tuned machine in the silence of space.

However alien the view, being there under the great rock is like returning home after a troublesome journey. When the sun sets, Yori turns a contemplative gaze upward and nods toward a point of light in the sky, little more than one among millions in the cloudless expanse, and yet a reference point. It's the Galatea, hovering like a god watching over the little brown planet with an all-seeing eye. Or a tiny speck connected by an invisible line and swinging in orbit around the colony, unless the line should break and leave a dimensionless point in place of an imaginary ship, changing everything.

And what is Paola thinking? Her way of thinking remains mysterious to him, thinking by not thinking, by letting fixed ideas go and opening herself to whatever the moment gives. So they sit together and apart, watching the dot weave its slow way through the tapestry of the indifferent heavens, feeling the bond between planet and ship as a momentary gathering of earth and sky and person with person.

Eventually Paola gets up, takes his hand, and leads him under the hill. At the entrance a wave of cool air enfolds them, and as they trace the way down to her chamber, Yori marks the distance they have already crossed together with and without words. Omitting the prattle of curiosity has restored a certain peace of mind, assuring that whatever is said during this visit will have mattered.

Yet nothing is said as she collects materials for their meal and adds fuel to the small fire that provides what light there is in the Chamber of the Hearth. Although the process is too simple to pass for work, on some unmentioned principle, she involves him as usual. As they share the ritual of eating together, still not speaking, he begins to fathom another depth in her and a new patience in himself. Though she understands perfectly that he is filled to the brim with anxiety and resentment, she maintains the one-question rule to discourage his asking small things. Waiting for the question worth asking discourages self-absorption and makes room for easy questions to answer themselves.

After eating, they settle comfortably around the hearth. She turns a dark, still gaze on him. "What do we talk about tonight?"

"First I have something to say." It's not what's on his mind but a digression, and Paola watches him forcing his stormy consciousness to the point.

"I think that your isolation during these years must have been more difficult in not having access to Alexandros." Alexandros, for the ancient Egyptian library at Alexandria, is the ship's electronic museum containing the memory of man to which everyone in the colony has access.

He continues. "Having no one to talk with is one thing, but in books we also engage with others. That lack must have deepened your solitude."

Paola acknowledges nothing. Just watches him, seeing more than eyes can see. After some moments she says with an unusual glint of mischief in her eye, "Have you ever noticed that 'Alexandros' is not only the name of the library Caesar destroyed?"

Yori looks puzzled.

"It's also another name for Paris, whose lust for Helen of Troy resulted in the war and the destruction of the city. I wonder if a universal memory device has anything in common with Paris and lust."

That doesn't register, so he skips over it and continues. "My idea is to leave my communications devices with you. I can easily replace them."

She looks at him appreciatively. "It's a generous thought but not a good idea. What happens when the signals are traced? Someone logs on to Alexandros from the hills where no one can be? Then what? We haven't yet spoken of the paranoia of the colony. They would go berserk, as if some science-fiction monster threatened to invade the colony and eat their babies. The unknown is their evil god. All their resources are spent protecting against contingency."

"I've thought about the risk. For safety you would use the connection only when I'm here. There's no secret about my wanderings in the hills, so no danger. Meanwhile we could download a whole library of materials for the time I'm not here. Wouldn't you feel less alone? For you, a good book would be more sociable than a city full of people with small ideas and no questions."

Paola gives him an enigmatic smile that he can't fathom. "I see what you think. This must seem like deprivation, and it was hard at first, like being banished from the universe. But I wasn't completely alone until a couple of years ago. And since then, I've had my two books for solitary conversations, so I am still more 'with others' than not."

After a momentary pause, she adds, "Another time I'll tell you what I know of the fate of the other survivors."

But instead of moving on, another pause reveals her concern for her friends and the story yet to be told. "Eventually I came to see that I am no more an alien in the cosmos than Planet Ulro itself is, or was. I'm kin to these stars because I can think them. It's possible, if I'm willing to align myself properly, to celebrate the advent of each day. Sometimes to love more, one needs to have less. I came slowly to be grateful for being one of the minute points where the universe is aware of itself. I am kin to it all, the looking glass of the cosmos, and I am alone only by a perverse fantasy."

Yori, given to staring in incomprehension, finds no words to follow that. Certainly not a question. Indeed, today he never gets to the question.

But his plan is executed. They load his reading devices with materials of particular interest to her. Against his advice she chooses mundane things related to the conditions of concrete life rather than classic titles. It's the first time that her focus on the small things annoys him, but once annoyed, other annoyances are sure to follow. Primarily it is her rigid demand for order. He does not see the point of having so many rules for such a simple life—her Rule of the Hearth— and he understands nothing at all just yet about how such a rule might be a paradigm for life on larger scales.

As though divining his criticism of her preference for the ordinary, she only smiles again and says, "Thinking sets out from love of the world around us."

The next morning he wakes with a new idea. "I watched you making the bread," he says, as they sit at the hearth over the hot drink she calls coffee. "Tell me about making bread."

It's her ritual silent period at the beginning of the day when she never speaks. Once before when he thoughtlessly interrupted it, she raised her finger to her lips and said nothing. But this time she replies, "Our research missions included discovering what edible substances might be found or grown on the surface of the planet. We had grains and made a kind of porridge from them. Several times I succeeded in getting them to germinate but never found conditions where they would grow. When we began living in the caves, we cooked the porridge over the fire. It was hard and not very good, but it could be taken in our packs and eaten for several days.

"Later, we learned to let the dough ferment in the moist atmosphere of the cave. There were other experiments, like adding fresh grain and baking it on the hearthstone. By that time we were growing several varieties in the thin soil of the canyon. Next, we added various herbs to the dough. The limitation has always been that there is no way to bake bread in loaves."

Yori intrudes on her account reflectively. "I've been thinking about the bread, how even here bread binds us all together."

"Did you know that on the ship we had a total genetic record of the botanical phyla indigenous to Ulro? Specimens of plants important to humans were preserved for possible rejuvenation on a new planet. I studied advanced physics with your father and wanted to be a cosmologist like him, but when I was assigned to botany instead, I made my place as a researcher by developing several species of wine grapes from those records. Not enough to furnish the ship with wine, but I learned how. When I was selected for the landing party, all that had to be left behind."

"Maybe it has survived and will be made available to the colony."

"Perhaps. But the experiments with grapes won't do *us* much good. Even if we had the vines and succeeded in growing fruit of sufficient quality, it would take years of experimenting and a lot of technology to produce a good wine. Still, it would be satisfying to begin such a culture for our own pleasure and the benefit of future generations."

Yori nods as some other idea dawns on him that he keeps to himself. But a second more feasible idea has been germinating in his mind, to do with bread, and once he gets an idea in focus, he pursues it relentlessly until a solution turns up.

Paola watches with satisfaction his engagement in these homely topics, for if a bright young intellectual needs anything, it's to learn that thinking, too, is rooted in earth. For him to begin applying himself to the conditions of everyday life is a much larger step in education than might be imagined, for bread and wine are the very stuff of thinking.

"So what have you been thinking about bread?"

"About an oven. We could build an oven beside the hearthstone." He describes how the thing might be done, eloquently illustrating the plan with his hands. "We could put stones upright on three sides and one across the top. Then cover them with adobe that the heat would harden. A moveable stone in front would serve as a door. When the fire burns down, the bread could bake on a center stone, slightly raised and surrounded by coals."

"Why don't you set your other tasks aside today and play with the idea?"

He grins. "And what about the Rule of the Hearth? That would be breaking the rule."

"That's the point. The rule of the day is not a machine for dominating us. It's a flexible order that shapes and liberates. It expands and contracts like a lung, fitting the circumstances. The rule too is a daily venture in imagining even as we leave nothing undone."

And so, with faith in what is yet to be understood, he does as she says: searches out stones of appropriate proportions, hauls them in, brings a basket of soil for adobe, and begins constructing his oven next to the hearthstone. Rather than add the mud, he waits for Paola to use the oven once for bread. She does so that evening and borrows his enthusiasm for the oven to interest him in the bread itself. They let the flame die down, set the loaf on the bottom of the oven, and close the door. His improvement in a process she has long used yields satisfactory results, and the next day he adds the mud and dries it.

Thus progress making bread becomes the first landmark of progress in something less conspicuous. In time he will learn to grind the grain with a stone pestle, to make a dough, to set some aside for the next day, to add a variety of herbs, and so on. His pride is about more than cleverness or distinguishing himself in her eyes. In fact he barely notices when, instead of praising his ingenuity, her satisfaction derives from the ordinariness of possibility that has been lying there waiting for someone attentive enough to find it.

Two days pass without his getting around to the urgent business of his one question. A reason may be that his father's murder remains surcharged and too amorphous to formulate as a question, but there may be other less conscious reasons as well.

On the third evening, after they have finished eating, Paola smiles wryly. "Have all your questions now been answered?"

"Hardly." He laughs uneasily, shifting about on his stone seat. "What I want most to know may not be fair to ask you. It's what I can do to find out more about my father. There must have been investigations, reports, documents. A system with a fetish for efficiency keeps records on everything, even things that aren't worth recording. I want to see the official account."

"Almost certainly you can't. There would be records, of course, even records of suppressing the records. But all you'll succeed in doing is calling attention to yourself and becoming a suspicious person. You'll destroy any possibility of being useful in the future. So my counter-question is, what do you really want? What is your motive?"

Yori studies the problem for some moments before answering, "Curiosity at least. At most, revenge. If he . . . if they . . . were all killed for political reasons and you three were abandoned for dead, then someone should pay. Crime should be punished."

"That motive is shortsighted. Think again."

She waits for the bare contradiction to sink in, then asks, "What if the people on the ship really are the only surviving rational beings in the universe—that may be true, since we don't know what happened on Ulro—then why look for an individual to punish? Judgment is essential; punishment is not. Ultimately no one survives revenge against evil. It serves only to keep the evil alive, as feuds once did in families and tribes and nations. Having set the endless cycle of revenge in motion, you'd threaten the continuation of humanity. Wouldn't that be a crime greater than what was done to us?"

"But someone has to be responsible!"

"If you could locate blame and punish someone, what would that change except your feelings? Wouldn't you do better to absorb this evil, if that's what it is, let it go, and concentrate your energies on living well?"

"Then you do think it *is* an evil?"

"I have every reason to feel as you do." She makes a slow gesture around the cave as though putting fifteen years of her life in evidence. "And I have every reason to master those feelings. Our opponents, however shortsighted, are reasonable people. Remember I was one of them. They're not cruel people. They're devoted to stability and corporate interest. There's the trap. They want to protect against nasty surprises, and so they hate contingency. Survival and comfort are their supreme goods—their gods. Isn't that what the impulse to mastery is all about? What they don't understand is that that lack of courage is self-defeating."

"So what should I do?"

"Remember your father's ideals. Take your time, overcome your impulse, dispute the alternatives with yourself. Otherwise, you may betray the very things your father sacrificed himself for."

Yori doesn't want to take her point. Though he is schooled in the virtues of disinterested thinking, it is another thing to follow Paola's example in setting his desires aside and choosing to act rationally. So, divided against himself, he both sees and does not see how fleeting the pleasure of retaliation might prove to be.

"There is one thing you can do: Read *Starship Galatea* and get closer to your father. When you have done that, ask yourself what advice Akira Kashimoto would give you now."

For a long while that evening he doesn't open the book. Just sits with it in his hands like a sacred object that contains the key to life's mysteries, not opening it, perhaps, because he doesn't want to find what he knows will be there. Eventually, he does open it to the first page and begins. For the rest of that evening and all the next day, he reads. For hours he reads like a drowning man trying to stay afloat. At first the book offers nothing to explain his father's fate, but it gradually brings him closer in spirit to the man he most loves and respects.

He learns about the Elders' version of the history of the generational mission and how the spirit of the people mutated by living in a machine. Most of all he learns about the nascent conflict built into the mission itself like an Ulro virus passed on for generations. Prevented by Paola's warning against reading for curiosity, he skips the conversations of the Elders until the prohibition begins to ignite the very desire it forbids.

6

ON THE FATEFUL DAY when Yori is to give his seminar paper at the Academy, he emerges early from the caves into the light of a harsh yellow sun and begins the long descent to the colony. Leaving the high country feels like forsaking life, where the adventure of crooked paths and surprising relations opens at every turn on something new and where one whose feet are planted on earth can hardly resist reaching for the stars.

By contrast, the way down leads to a flat and empty world where a grumbling hive exists mainly for the comfort of drones. There the Academy shapes students into useful cogs in a mill that must be kept turning, for survival depends on it. Not the whole truth, perhaps, since the plain, too, is open to earth and stars, but no one there is foolish enough to reach for them.

In some other setting the discontents of a lone adolescent might be winked at, but in the tiny colony Yori's state of mind entails public risk. The reasons are complex. The generational starship operates under a quasi-military command structure and a hierarchical social order based on competence. When, after two and a half centuries in space the colony was planted on a not very hospitable planet, these organizational principles persisted. They made sense where the first concern was survival. Add to these considerations a few select students who are being trained as a next generation of rulers, and it begins to appear why an internecine quarrel between Yori and Lars Hanssen might become a danger. Especially when, seen in a certain light, both sides have their point and carry conviction. Add one more detail: Yori's "humanistic" attacks on the "life-support system" are beginning to gain traction among the more imaginative members of their elite group. So, when Lars responds with rhetorical violence to Yori's ideas, he is not simply being a bad-tempered reactionary. He, too, has reason.

As the students gather for class, there is an air of excitement in the seminar room different from the usual apathy. The promise that this session will be unusual is heightened when several outsiders turn up. They are recognizable as minor bureaucrats, bringing, of all things, electronic notepads. Where recording is as easy as the touch of a finger, the point of such an outmoded procedure can only be to intimidate. Nothing of the kind has happened before, so when the strangers offer no explanation for their presence, the tension in the air becomes palpable. Even the teacher appears stressed.

Yori is not inclined to be intimidated. He may not yet have a clear idea of himself as an outsider in the colony, but certainly he feels like an exception. Whether he admits as much or not, he senses that outside is the right place for thinking. Accordingly, the challenge offered by the strangers in class only strengthens his resolve.

He announces his title—"From Ulro to Where?"—and falters only briefly. No slouching in the chairs today among the seminarians sitting around the large oval table. No gazes wandering across the room or out the windows. As he begins, all backs are straight and all eyes are on his face. Here is what he says:

"I don't have time to review conditions on Ulro when the mission was launched in 2075 or to speculate on why it may have been planned in the first place. And there's no point in talking about life in space either. I want to speak to the present moment and a question always in the air but that we don't hear. The point is not to propose an answer to the question 'From Ulro to Where?' I only want to get my question heard and make it stick in the mind."

This unconventional opening causes some shuffling in chairs around the table and a worried look from the teacher. But they all know Yori too well to be surprised or uninterested.

He continues, "The forgotten question—you may think it is trivial—is this: What is the point of human life itself? What is the meaningful or 'good life' that all our other arrangements aim for? Today I will comment briefly on three over-large topics: (1) scientific rationality, (2) the psychology of certainty, and (3) the freedom to decide."

Lars Hanssen audibly slouches in his chair and groans for the benefit of all.

"First, let's put the question of scientific rationality in this form: What price do we pay when technology becomes destiny? Obviously the colony, like the starship, is a life-support system. Without it we would not have been born and would all soon die. For us, the Galatea is destiny. A Janus-faced destiny. One with two faces. Of course the same might have been said of the first tools. Destiny was written in the plow. Good destiny, bad destiny.

"One theory about Ulro—one suspicion, since evidence doesn't reach this far—is that either it finally succeeded in destroying itself or that life was reduced to primitivism by some natural or human disaster. If either of these is true, the Galatea may have saved human beings from extinction. In any event the ship is my mother and yours since it gave us birth. Good destiny. So I repeat: This is *not* an argument against either machines or science. It *is* about the courage to ask right questions in right places."

Two of the female students exchange meaningful smiles. Yori is the star of the class and much admired for his good looks, Olympian disposition, and sometimes-troubled face. That face has been known to elicit compassion in more than one maternal heart in the room, including Véronique Dumas'.

Meanwhile, Yori continues reading from his prepared text. Even as he speaks in a bright, clear voice, barely controlled passion is audible in the background and inspires more than a few puzzled glances around the table.

"My argument is about blithely accepting scientific rationality while blinding ourselves to its possible limits. Science investigates what things in nature are and how they work. Technology gives us control over the material conditions of our lives. The question is, what does this disposition to control leave out? How are we affected by the ambition for power? What if the demand for control ultimately displaces the human itself? Or already has? When such a question gets raised, it's usually regarded as unpleasant or obscure or irrelevant. But doesn't that even show a disposition to leave ourselves out of the reckoning?" Then with irony, "I know, the only practical thing worth discussing is how we get where we're going . . . which is where?"

He's not unaware of the audible stir in the room that such insistence causes, but where there's little or no will to think disquieting thoughts, one either abandons the cause or brooks the censure of others. What would one do if the life of a loved one were threatened? What more might one do if humanity seemed to be putting itself at risk?

Yori continues, "My second point is about *how* we have been altered by the demand for certainty. It's not just that we depend on machines that we don't individually understand. It's more than dependency. It's an altered frame of mind and a different way of living. We are shielded automatically from the desert heat by day and the cold by night thanks to programs in the life-support system. We walk into this room and it goes from dark to light without our doing anything. We sit down in our chair and Alexandros comes up on our monitors and puts all information at our fingertips. After class we go to the cafeteria to drink and eat.

"You get the idea. We are accustomed to an environment where everything has been calculated and arranged for us. But you and I don't understand more than a tiny fraction of it all. Someone else understands and oversees these miracles. We're habituated to the guarantees—or the presumption—of rational coherence and security. If we have a question, some specialist has the answer. Ask Alexandros. Ask the Governor."

By this stage in the argument Lars' impatience has reached critical intensity. It may be the scandal of the ideas, or it may be concern that Yori is exposing them all to ridicule and even risk—or it may be something more mysterious. Given the extent of his squirming and frowning, it may be all of these.

Perfectly aware of Lars' impatience, Yori presses resolutely ahead. "Now here's the point: Can calculation measure everything human? Can it even form a concept of what we have called 'human' for eons? What effect has technology had on our capacity for invention? Hasn't it encapsulated us in a state that is repetitive, conservative, and static? I'm suggesting that we have become uncomfortable with any region of life where positive knowledge or bits of information can't rescue us from chance and the threat of change, except when calculation can secure us from the threat of contingency. Give us security, and we gladly surrender imagination and freedom."

The uninvited guests busily scribble on their notepads, but Yori steels himself once more against all efforts to intimidate him.

"Third, what do we have to lose? In a word, the courage to decide. If I am comfortable, I feel little need to ask uncomfortable questions. Not illegal questions but impractical questions that might be critical of the status quo. One question in particular for which there is no final answer: How are we to live our lives and why? We say the question is self-evident or silly, and we avoid it. Why? Because in living under the regime of total rationality we can rest in the assumption that someone, some technocrat somewhere up the chain of command, has already programed that bit of information into the life-support system."

As the point sinks in, a chuckle ripples across the room in acknowledgment, though Lars, who may have a clearer sense of what's at stake in the argument than most, squirms again uncomfortably.

"Where our biological needs are supplied, the question of the life worth living wears away, and soon enough we forget to ask. But what if the point of living doesn't reduce to rational simplicity and a few bits of information? What if it must be decided and decided again at every turn? If we are born facing the unknown, all our other questions start here. Questions like, what is machinery for? How should life be organized? Why does knowing matter? Why invent ingenious systems to support life in space or to populate a barren planet? Because . . . but to go the way of 'because' we need courage . . . the courage to devise changing answers for changing situations. No final answer will fit the unfinished project of living."

The students in the room, the brightest the Galatea has to offer, most of them in the applied sciences, don't miss the challenge in Yori's questions. His point could hardly be made more clearly or responsibility assigned more precisely. Uneasy looks pass from face to face while the teacher, one elbow on the table and one hand to his brow, casts worried glances at the official visitors.

"Finally, I will just mention one further possibility. It is this: Maybe my question is idle and a waste of productive time. Maybe human freedom and the capacity to wonder are outdated. Maybe we are evolving beyond the need to ask disruptive questions without conclusive answers. What does it matter if, for all our prowess, we are adrift without purpose in an indifferent cosmos? Machines don't ask such questions, and aren't we aspiring to become efficient machines? Maybe it's only a primitive mind—or a deranged mind—that lets such issues come up. Nonetheless I ask, what life is worth living?"

A funereal silence holds the room in suspension until Lars shifts noisily in his seat again and breaks the spell. "I never understand, Yori, why you have contempt for common sense. Here, we are preparing to help manage the colony. Everything in our world—maybe even the survival of our species—depends on doing that well. Yet you spend your time finding fault with the way things are done. Why are you contemptuous of the practical good sense that keeps it all running and solves problems as they turn up? What's so wrong with being practical? We're talking about a system that lets you dream these subversive dreams like a parasite."

Yori responds vigorously but, not to inflame the situation unduly, tempers his rhetoric. "Practicality in its place. 'If it ain't broke, don't fix it.' Okay. But how will we know when it's broken? What makes the practical impractical is the closure of any system—the wasted motion that doesn't fit and must be excluded. In time we forget what's left out, even when it's us! Freedom *is* the outside of every system. Freedom doesn't want to throw a bolt into the machine. It only wants to step aside and look at things with a detached and appraising eye."

That detonates Lars' passion. "You're a subversive! You admit that the system is rational, but you prefer irrational fantasies about alternative systems. And you are courting social disruption. Know what?" He wags his finger in Yori's face. "If you were Governor, I'd have to fight you!"

7

THE EVENING OF YORI'S seminar, several of the students, including some who have begun to listen with interest to his ideas, meet in the commons. It's not unusual, but the atmosphere has completely changed. The mood is subdued, even exaggerated by self-conscious efforts to pretend all is well. Yori doesn't miss the fact of his exclusion as people avoid his gaze and leave a safe margin of space around him.

All, that is, but Lars and Véronique Dumas. Soon enough the debate continues, thanks to Lars, who can't let the scandal of Yori's presentation alone. Since he has no fresh arguments, he insists compulsively on rehashing stale ones. The particular bone in his throat this evening is the charge that technology is totalitarian, no doubt because he's too intelligent not to see—and to fear—the issue at the heart of the dispute.

Véronique and Sandra Mohr watch from the sidelines as the two males dance around each other like rams in mating season. Véronique is a botanist one year into her training for colonial duty but already second in command in what is anachronistically called the Agriculture Department. She is a svelte blonde who seems unaware of her seductive force, augmented by a habit of attention that never misses a word or a twitch of an eyebrow in a room.

Sandra, Lars' particular friend, is quite different. A talented musician but otherwise a rather plain young woman who attracts little attention at first meeting. She may not be as attractive as Véronique but is just as quick and more intuitive. However different, these two share equally in one thing: They know better than to enter the fray when two men of a certain age square off verbally. So they let the two go on, adding nothing new to what has already been said, then refuted and said again.

The next morning Yori sits alone in the commons over coffee, musing on the events of yesterday and on his beloved hills. How is it that people who share the homogenous experience even of a starship can respond so differently to this planet? It would be easy to say that some love it and others don't, but that would shed no light. To Lars the most interesting fact is that it's available, that they can stake a claim of ownership and put it to useful purposes. But when it's seen as a possession, doesn't the unique thing itself become clouded over until it's little more than an inventory of raw materials?

Others see it as it offers itself to be seen, even love it, but love it indifferently. Paola was forced to love it or die, and she has come to love it well. Véronique loves it too but loves it more generously. Her redesign of Government Square shows that she has looked out at the brown desiccated landscape and seen beauty there. He, Yori, loves it. First loved the brute reality of its corrugated surface thrusting up toward the sky, loved its rise and fall as he passed from the blazing sun on the ridges into the shady depressions on the back slopes of the hills, found joy even in stumbling on a rock and barking his knees or elbows on its jagged surface. And yet, he needed Paola and Véronique to show him how to see.

As he sits alone, not seeing the too-white artificial light, not feeling the perfectly adjusted temperature of the air on his skin, it dawns on him that he really began loving Planet 2314 when he began loving Paola. It's a shocking idea that pulls him up short. Then does he love her? But the idea is interrupted when Véronique enters and sits down with him.

She recognizes his mood as more tranquil than last night. He seems to have recovered from his alarming inclination to turn his back on the only world there is, a disposition that frightens her. Like all the members of their class, they have known each other since childhood rather like siblings. That may be why the romantic dalliance between them during their teen years always seemed more like inevitability than grand passion. Then they arrived in the colony, and he began to retreat into himself. By now, the self-sufficiency of that detachment and his solitary wanderings in the distant hills almost anger her. She would much prefer to have his company on their holiday trips back to the Galatea, but he always refuses. Most distressing is his growing discontent with the colony itself. However cogent his reasons, it borders on madness, and she wants nothing so much as to grab him by the shoulders and shake some sense into that handsome head.

As she sits down, he welcomes her with the remark, "A few days ago I was sitting in Government Square, studying your new design. I like it. What was your inspiration?"

"I was trying to relate the colony to its desert setting. Have you noticed how we turn inward and ignore the planet?

I don't think that's healthy. I was experimenting with ways of overcoming it."

"I see your idea. It's the first time anyone has tried that. I wonder why."

She nods and purses her lips as if musing. "I don't think we should shut ourselves in and ignore our surroundings. There's something paranoid in that."

"What do you mean, paranoid?"

"Well, take this bubble." She points at the ceiling of the room and toward the invisible dome beyond. "But not only that. The ground too. All the surfaces are paved as though we are afraid to touch the earth. You'd think the planet was contaminated and that space monsters were hovering just outside threatening us. Except for you, and to some extent me at work in outdoor nurseries, people almost never leave the enclosure, as though they might get polluted."

Yori is grateful for the arrival of this kindred spirit just when he's feeling like the one-eyed man in the valley of the blind. "I see what you mean. I was just sitting here thinking how you can't see this place—this earth—unless you're willing first to love it. Your design for the square shows you have discovered it."

Véronique continues, "We decide to land here after wandering about in space, but instead of being grateful, we think there's something second best about it. Like it's not up to our standard, so we curl up in our nest and ignore it. When you get outside and really look, you see its austere beauty. But we have to be *willing* to see it."

"You mean, I suppose, that we don't want to take the trouble. It's easier just to seize it for our own interests. If we write our names on it, it will be ours and we can do what we want with it."

She smiles and shakes her head energetically as they talk, her ponytail swinging briskly. "Some people in my department wanted to imitate the subtropical regions of Ulro in the Square, but I objected that it would have taxed the water supply and that rain forests don't belong here. I don't mean we need aesthetic integration, like making all the houses in a block match. I mean that when we're given something—like a planet to live on—we can't do just anything we like with it. We accept kinship and must treat it with respect."

These words help Yori see much more than what a unique thing she has done. Not just her job. She has brought a kind of global imagination to the practical matter of designing a public space. And isn't imagination another name for love? He adds, "Your Square is our first real bridge to the outside. Already it's become a natural gathering place. That's a good sign."

With a teasing grin, she adds, "If you think I can appreciate the 'austere beauty' of the outside, you could invite me to go with you on one of your explorations sometime."

He might reply that there are good reasons why he can't, but not wishing to rouse curiosity, he says instead, "I might do that . . . sometime." Then changing course, "Meanwhile, why not show me around your greenhouses? Teach me something about your research."

At this show of interest, her blue, still detectably French eyes beam with surprise and pleasure. He has never been much interested in her work, but part of his assignment just now is to observe the operations of the departments. His recent discontents have caused her anxiety. If he should decide to give up on the settlement and return to the starship, it would be worse for them both. She sees that they must—Yori especially must—tie his hopes to conditions that don't yet exist. Lars' temptation is to prefer the actual to the possible, but Yori's is to look the actual in the face and despair. If there is anything worse than Lars' deliberate blindness, wouldn't it be to become disillusioned with the only life there is?

Some days later she does as he asks and shows him her world, happy to see that he is not rejecting colony business despite the criticisms in the seminar paper. Together they make a tour of the various buildings where foodstuffs are grown, of the outside nurseries where adaptable plants are cultivated, of the receiving dock for materials ferried down from the Galatea, even the laboratory where she works on genetically altering plant material to suit it for local conditions. Through it all, expecting signs of impatience, she finds genuine interest.

Delighted as she is by Yori's unexpected attention, she is also puzzled. At one point when they are alone in the outside nurseries, she looks at him with irony and asks, "Why the sudden interest in botany? I've tried to bring you here before and you wouldn't come."

In his present state of mind, it isn't easy to put off the tone of official seriousness and respond playfully, but he tries. "Well, if I'm to become familiar with all aspects of the organization, where better to start than with food? Especially cereals for baking bread."

She smiles without believing, especially when, instead of the production and distribution that he needs to understand, he seems more curious about her research. Yet she is willing to show as much as he is willing to see and accept the attention as personal.

The thing that interests him on the tour is a silent comparison between his two favorite botanists and their gardens. In origin, Paola's garden belongs to survival, while Véronique's belongs to the colony mandate, but both women have given themselves beyond necessity and professional duty. He also sees that each might be helped by the other if there were a way to bring it about without betraying Paola. Her progress in adapting indigenous species has given her a significant advantage in a narrower path of research, but since the colony's food is imported from the ship, the nurseries have had time to develop a large and diverse agricultural plan. Both women have inherited generations of research based on the flora of Ulro, but Paula lost all of that at the time of the disaster so that now her operation is dwarfed by comparison. The comparison gives Yori the idea that if he could arrange to pass samples back and forth discreetly, both women would profit. For Paola, specimens from Ulro, like grains for bread, and for Véronique, types native to the planet. So he tucks the idea away in a corner for later consideration.

Véronique's next surprise comes from his interest in irrigation. He examines the system and even makes notes on how much water the nurseries use and what energy it takes to pump it from the deep wells. When this, too, puzzles her, he covers his tracks by asking whimsically, "What's even more important to the colony than food if not water?"

At the end of the tour they have coffee together in the canteen, and she drops a hint about Lars. "Do you know Lars' girlfriend Sandra very well?"

"Hardly at all. She's younger than the rest of us and has just arrived. Why?"

"She was alarmed by the fireworks between you two after your seminar. She isn't alone, of course, since you are becoming a rather dangerous topic. Well, a couple of days ago she made a remark that you need to hear. It was an innocent reference to an exchange between Lars and the Governor. She didn't say what they talked about, but here's what's important. The topic that brought the exchange to her mind was you. She drifted from you to that conversation. The point is that if Lars and the Governor were discussing you, it would have been around the time of your paper, and that may not be good news."

Yori makes no reply, but as he turns away to conceal uneasiness, she sees that he has taken her point.

This happy day together has distant consequences that may only be hinted at here. Véronique begins to get more of Yori's company than ever without knowing exactly why, as he begins passing information back and forth in a blind collaboration between two talented researchers. And not information only. Under the rubric "plants found on my wanderings," he supplies samples of Paola's work and silently passes bits of information on Véronique's work back to Paola.

This small subterfuge may be transparent on the level of conscious motives, but it might also be read as symptomatic of a quite different reality. Is Yori less than consciously trying to heal a division he feels widening within himself? Isn't that what his earlier desire to "compartmentalize" was about? In this first turbulent period of his life, he is being torn between the plateau and the hills, at once preparing to join the highest circles of colonial management and becoming increasingly suspicious of the whole enterprise. Consciously or not, he is becoming the battlefield where age-old ideals will struggle for ascendency even as he struggles to patch up his divided loyalties.

8

ONE EVENING, NOT LONG after his soon-to-be-noto-
rious seminar, Yori receives an invitation from the Governor
to call on him in his quarters. In a colony of a few thousand,
everyone knows everyone, but all are not equal or equally intimate. No word has ever passed between him and the Governor,
and so, given recent events, he feels uneasy, apprehensive even,
as he walks across the square from the Academy dormitory to
that other anachronism called Government House.

Well-lighted halls lead to an office at the end of the
building. He knocks and waits until the door opens on a
quietly lighted room that is less office than a technological
command center. Banks of screens stare from the walls like
the eyes of so many gods, except that here the Governor is
god and does the staring—into every nook and cranny of the
colony. There is even a live connection with the starship. This
one flickers off as Yori enters.

There are few traces of individual taste in the room,
and that gives the impression that the human occupant has
been shoved to one side to make room for the electronic
paraphernalia that constitute reality and authority. The old
man behind a large desk does not get up or extend a hand.
Without interrupting what he's doing or looking at Yori, he
says, "Please sit down."

Yori sits.

The Governor is tall and erect, with white hair, neatly trimmed. An imposing figure even sitting. The badges of authority on his jacket mark this as an official meeting. So perhaps does the absence of the personal tone. For a few moments he continues studying one of the screens, makes a note on an electronic pad, then looks up with a touch of nonchalance. Taken all together the scene leaves Yori with the impression that however his performance in class may have been reported, his existence barely interests this man.

Eventually he says, "I knew your father." Four words. Full stop. Then, leaving the impression that Yori is a discredit to his father's memory, he adds, "I've been watching your progress from a distance." Another interruption. "I know something of your frustrations."

Instead of opening the topic of his misbehavior and promptly banishing him in disgrace to the mother ship, instead of delivering a sharp reprimand and a warning, the Governor asks about his rambles in the hills.

Then, irrelevantly, "Your father and I didn't always agree, but he was a man of great intelligence and impeccable character. You have his mind, and I think you will be like him in other ways. That was not overlooked when you were selected for the elite. There are always too few people of that quality. We can't spare any."

Were it not for what Yori has recently learned about his father, he might take these remarks as settling several questions about his summons, but in light of Paola's account, they only deepen the mystery.

When, instead of going on, the Governor is distracted by something on one of the monitors, Yori uses the time to study the man's face. It is not as old as first appears, unless it might be called prematurely old. What is not evident at first, perhaps because of the way the equipment in the room pushes him aside, is the man's commanding presence. The narrow face, chiseled features, small intense eyes, long nose, thin line of mouth—not quite aristocratic in bearing. Descendant perhaps of leisure and excellence but compromised by the strain and the discontent of serving norms, reduced to the anxious spirit of a busy man in a race for empty success.

In the lines of the face one can trace the burden of a static life where lust for authority has been neutered by the status quo. In different circumstances, such a face might be weathered by conflict and the spirit seasoned by strategic gambols and brave acts. But more of this life has been spent studying computer screens than putting itself in the line of fire and marshaling forces for high purposes. The flesh still gives off the barest scent of ancient passion, as though intervening generations of bureaucrats and functionaries have not quite succeeded in breeding out the last traces of appetite. Yet fear of imbalance and disruption overrules desire in this man. Alert but tense, always watching and listening for the prohibited slippage in the system, always guilty when anything is allowed to happen. Freedom precluded; adventure forbidden.

Something Yori does not observe is his own authority. Even in one so young, the habit of thinking more than he says and having more to say than he thinks reveals a depth that the man across the desk will not have missed.

"May I ask a question?" His own voice startles him as much as it does the Governor. He sees the muscles around the old man's eyes flex for an instant. "I would like to learn about the circumstances of my father's death. There must be official reports on file somewhere that identify the cause."

The Governor passes over a faux pas that might have been taken as insubordination and pauses, without bothering to conceal that he has to decide how to respond and compose his response carefully. The reply, when it comes, is moderate if a touch more formal. "I understand your interest, but that was years ago. I seem to remember that your mother raised the issue forcefully at the time and learned very little. Probably there was little to report because little was known."

Yori persists. "But there were twenty and all died. The colony had to start over. There would have been an investigation and there would be records of that . . . unless it was hushed up for some reason."

By now the Governor has apparently decided how to take the challenge. "You were a child when it happened." Genuine or not, he produces a kindly paternal smile. "Has this been festering in your mind all these years or has something happened to renew your interest?" He levels a scrutinizing gaze on Yori as though searching for a catalyst.

Then, taking his time, "I tell you what. I will make some discreet inquiries through appropriate channels. If I dig up anything useful, I'll report it to you. Until then I suggest you lay the issue aside. We don't want to stir up a tempest without good reason."

The Governor lets his eye pass again across the screens behind Yori's back, then he takes a different path. "Now, tell me about your rambles in the hills. You probably know the land better than the geologists do." He laughs comfortably, without awkwardness, but a narrowing of his gaze hints at more than idle curiosity or a friendly chat.

Yori holds the gaze as he considers how the Governor has let his question slip away. "I doubt that," he answers, referring to the geologists. "There isn't much to see unless you like rocks and deserts. I enjoy the solitude, having my feet on solid ground, even in the heat. At night I camp under the stars or in the crevice of a rock and listen to the universe. Comfortable as we are here, I can think better in open spaces."

He sees his words accepted with a degree of reservation that shows in the intensity of the old man's eyes. Then the eyes drop the subject.

The Governor goes on in a voice neither cordial nor unfriendly. It's the voice of a man who hasn't the leisure or the desire for the personal. A speculative voice from an indistinct middle distance between duty and boredom. "I asked you here because I want to know you better . . . and those long thoughts you think alone under the stars."

There he stops as though considering how to put whatever it is he wants to say. "You know that one day these quarters"—he waves one arm casually across the room—"will be occupied by someone of your rank." Then, as close as he will come to the expected reprimand, "If you stay on the track you're on, it could be you."

Immediately he passes on to things that Yori knows are for his ears only. There is no request for confidence or oath of secrecy. The older man would probably think it insulting to them both to mention such a thing. Besides, if Yori lacks the capacity or the judgment for discretion, the one with more experience will have learned whatever he wants to know from that too. Still, it signals a minimal level of confidence.

"I suspect you have sat up there on one of your hills at night following the Galatea with those keen eyes, thinking that a starship can't keep orbiting a planet indefinitely, like a nanny. The time will come, and before long, when Command will have to decide what to do next. Something always has to be done next. If we stand still, we die. That's why you get out of the colony when you can. Things tend to move in a circle here. I can see that for you that would count as standing still." The wily eyes, out of focus but attentive, wait for a response but find none.

Yori also waits for whatever other speculations about his odd behavior might be hovering out of sight behind that shrewd face. To keep Paola at a distance from consciousness lest the old man sense a mystery, he asks, "Has the decision been made already? About the ship leaving?"

In the confusion of his late ideas, the question strikes him with a sense of loss, the unexpected loss of the only world he has ever known. Of course it must happen, and it will show up first in people growing weary of spinning around in orbit for years without any prospect of change, as though they were slaves to the shrinking needs of the colony below. They will become impatient to move on even if it's on—perhaps for more generations—to that other monotony of searching for habitable planets. It will be seen as the chance, at least, for something to happen. Without knowing it, the colony also wants the starship to leave because, dramatic or not, it will make room for the unexpected here.

In response to his question the Governor answers, "No, the departure hasn't been decided. The question hasn't come up, though it must have crossed the mind of a person here or there.

Nothing decided unless we understand that great decisions are made before they reach consciousness. Starship Command hasn't yet acknowledged that the question is unavoidable and that it has only one answer."

He studies Yori's face for a few moments before resuming. "I'm sure you've noticed that the shuttles between the ship and the colony are less frequent. Except for final decisions about personnel, we are now self-sustaining and don't need them. For the people remaining with the ship, it will mean sailing off once more with no destination in view. That's not a particularly attractive prospect. Earlier generations lived like that, and few would care to repeat it. But then, not everyone would want to feel permanently stranded on this piece of rock."

Yori may not take in the full import of the point about the decision, but he feels the point about the future like lead. His intelligence rushes forward, unfolding one implication after another, taking full account of the immensity of the loss to everyone affected. To live without the watchful eye in the heavens will be like losing his home, like becoming a man without a country, as people used to say. Even the colony will eventually find that its psychic authority has come unstuck, and loyalties will begin to slip into new places.

The Governor's eyes don't move, presumably having not seen the storm he has unleashed inside the son of his late colleague. It's not even clear that he admits to himself how deeply invested he is in this mere boy, though he is able to evade that thought. "Up there on your hill you have realized all this, haven't you?"

Yori meets the question with another. "Why not expand the colony and accommodate everyone here?"

The Governor smiles. "Because once you've made a discovery or built a machine, your invention or your discovery predestines its own use. When Ulro split the atom, using it was unavoidable. Or the steam engine. Or the plow. We little suspect how destiny is written in our acts. Far beyond our calculations." His emphasis on that term, and an involuntary pause as his gaze briefly crosses Yori's, tells another story: The Governor has read a transcript of his seminar.

"This little world will have to be reinvented or die. Life support alone won't support life. And yet . . ."

He stops to debate some point with himself. "And yet life is more precarious in a space colony than our well-oiled machine might suggest. Security requires a high level of uniformity among the people. That's why the basic discipline is military. Even on a starship, uniform as the life is, there's more room for diversity. Many on the Galatea would not fit here. Conventionality may be boring, but there's life in it."

Again he stops as though coming to a point that needs deciding. He decides: "A governor, you know, must have the courage for your long hill-top thoughts. He must see things as they are. More important, he must see where they're tending. But, he must not brood on them. Sooner or later they have to be shared with others who are qualified in mind and spirit."

Another dramatic pause, punctuated by the deep sigh of a man who's growing weary of life, gives Yori time to wonder if the Governor is fishing for him to make some reference to the ideas in his seminar paper, but if so it's to no avail. He keeps the peace.

The Governor gets up from his chair and extends a hand in a signal that the interview is over. "I'm an old man now," he adds. "I need the spark of a brash young voice. I want you to begin writing down what you think about every aspect of life in the colony. Those pages will remain your private journal, but they will also be your talking points. From now until further notice you are to come here at regular intervals for a good talk. I'll send for you, but you mustn't neglect your nocturnal rambles. You'll tell me what you're thinking, and I may have a thing or two to say to you that will be useful later."

9

THE GOVERNOR'S BLESSING HELPS Yori cope with the double life of colony and cave. In one place he continues working his way bottom to top through the practical operations of the settlement, preparing for a junior position on the Board of Governors. During each stay he suffers the uncanny feeling of being divided and set at a distance from himself. In the other life, he can't say what exactly he's learning except that it's less learning than initiation into a different mode of being. The adventure of forcing his mind to go to strange places comes with an exhilarating sense of being on the edge of discovery without knowing what there might be to discover.

Under Paola's Rule he has to conform to unfamiliar ways, not obedience to alien norms but thinking about how the day may best be used. "Learning to dwell is not easy," she says. "It means discovering forgotten kinships. It's learning to *live-into* the place we are by becoming what we do."

Yori sees well enough what dwelling with things is not: It is not possession. That lesson comes easily enough since there was never much on a starship to possess. However, nearly everything was a tool, whereas in the hills the idea is not about use. Generations ago technology had overcome the primal curse of labor, but the overcoming had also destroyed the closeness of things. Nurturing the plants with his hands in the soil and working for his food restore the plants and the earth to themselves. Bringing in brush for the fire is ritual respect for the primal place of wood in baking bread and giving light, and hauling it restores a self that he has never known. Planting and harvesting alongside Paola—"helping the earth say beans"—belongs to a strangely gratifying order. "It is to live," she likes to say, "like the gods."

She gives him time to learn that there is no interval between the *content* of the day and the *form* of the day. What there is no time for is the self-indulgence of not *wanting* to do what needs to be done. Tending the garden, keeping the plant beds damp, bringing the daily water from the spring—all these raise practicality from unconscious and habitual to conscious and willed.

It would be a wrong turn to describe a typical day. To consider days as belonging to a type misses the uniqueness of each. Yet every morning they take "coffee" to a bower in the garden that is little more than a rocky cove in the canyon wall. It's not coffee, of course, but a mutation of the coffee bean that, like the wine grapes, had never been cultivated in the hothouses of the Galatea. Not historically exact perhaps, but, as they've never tasted the real thing, they can't know the difference. The point is that what happens every morning belongs to an essential ritual that, taken as a whole, "attunes" them to the tasks of the day.

One morning during this period of meditation as Yori tries to empty his mind of thought, he bursts into speech. "I have an idea!" Then, repenting the infraction of the Rule, he says, "Sorry. I know this is the quiet time."

"No." She answers. "You have just discovered how emptying the mind disconnects us from habit and opens space for invention."

"Like sleep."

"Except in sleep we dream. Dreams break consciousness into fragments and let us start over, but emptying the mind brushes even the fragments away and makes us receptive." With a backward gesture of one hand, she waves all this aside. "What's your idea?"

"Why don't we build an irrigation system for the garden? It would reduce the labor and we could expand the growing area. If I didn't bring provisions from the colony, there would hardly be enough food for two."

Paola looks at him inquisitively without replying, and he continues. "When we walk from here to fetch water, it's all uphill. The water level in the cave is several feet higher than the canyon floor. We could design a simple channel in the stone like an aqueduct. Then devise a mechanism for hoisting the water a little above the rim of the pool and into the channel. Gravity would do the rest."

"How would we raise the water?"

"By hand at first. As we raise it and haul it now. We might build a hand-operated water wheel if we could find materials, but that would be difficult without the right tools. It would be easier to rig up a small solar-powered pump if I could get the parts. I'll look around when I go back."

So he does. Scavenges for used parts slated for recycling and brings them, a few at a time. Meanwhile over several visits he uses what primitive tools he can devise to clear a course for the stream. The work of dividing and extending the channel to the plants will be long and arduous, but the immediate result in work saved is that Paola begins modestly expanding her experiments and the food supply.

Increasing intimacy between them produces something more. Yori begins to see her differently as she goes about her work in the rustic shift with a cord for a belt or sits with the dignity of a Buddha conversing in that seductive voice. It's erotic. He's accustomed to the close-fitting uniforms of the girls in the colony. Véronique Dumas, for example. With her he has had occasional physical encounters of the awkward, embarrassed kind that are wary of the terrors in the blood. Now when he watches the motion of Paola's ubiquitous shifts, he wants her, but wants her differently. Not like waking in the night from feverish dreams and seething loves that exceed all objects. Not ravenous. Not even thinking of desire. Wanting only to exist with her without barriers, looking together into the heart of things. Flesh too, but not the surging of physical passion. He no more thinks of her as an object of gratification than he thinks of the air he breathes or the light that gives him sight. Besides, being young, he's quite sure that his interest goes unnoticed.

One night, quite unexpectedly, she stands up from the hearth, interrupting his discreet observations. Facing him with the warmest glow in her eyes he has yet seen, she approaches, takes both his hands in hers, and delivers an astonishing non sequitur: "I have told you that there is a kind of learning beyond the truth of *things*. It belongs to a love you have yet to learn but to which you already belong."

He waits, attentive, wanting more. She stands still directly in front of him gazing into his eyes as though searching for who he really is. Apparently satisfied with what she finds there, she takes a step closer and lays a hand on each side of his face. Drawing him forward, bringing his lips to hers, she holds him in a long embrace. "Paola's kiss," as it would forever be remembered— eroticism of flesh beyond objects or sensations, beyond even the encounter of individuals.

She leads him to the table of rock that serves as her bed. Though there is no prohibition between two possessed by a love so much larger than themselves, they don't make love. Not at first, for neither is asking to be loved. Eros infusing all things from boundless space to the moment between the beatings of the heart. Where there might be passion—or might come to be—there is no fever or frenzy. In place of hunger, a nurturing encounter in this most unlikely of places and under the most implausible of conditions.

It will take time for the one who still does his thinking with ideas to learn how to think about this night. In the morning he speaks with simple intensity, "I think I'm in love with you. If you will let me, I would rather live here with you."

According to the mysteries of the older woman with the younger man, she studies his innocence, looking ahead toward an unforeseeable destiny, looking for how she, older by fifteen years, might shape him by teaching him first how to love her. If he has the imagination, he will learn in loving her to love all she loves, to live in and from and beyond her life. And he will learn to love her image of him as the one he may become.

Finally she responds to his declaration with detachment. "You must not use that word. Not yet. Love is something larger than you know. It is for that larger love that you must be prepared. It's why you're here."

As though not hearing, he insists, "I do. I love you. Maybe I don't know what the word means, but I love you."

Again she holds his gaze. "Love has many names."

Heedless of her words, he goes on searching for his words. "I don't know how to think about this great thing that has happened."

"Here's how I will understand it," she says. "One day I was visited by a young god. His kiss ignited in me love for all things. No matter what happens hereafter, that kiss will have fallen as a light across my life. It will be a permanent standard in a changing world. If it happens again or a thousand times, it will always be for the first time." Then, seeing how little of all that he is prepared to hear, she concludes, "'Yori' means trust. Trust me."

10

A DAY AFTER THE ENIGMATIC exchange on the topic of love, Yori has to leave again. This time he does not head directly down and across the dry crust of the plateau. He lingers. Even in the heat of the day he lingers. After such an extraordinary night, he is more alien from the colony than ever, and so at some distance from the caves he finds a shady spot where he can delay a little longer.

He may not know how to think about love or what to make of Paola's forbidding the word, but he knows he is loved, and the fact gives his world a luminous point. Under that influence and in her presence, he can even face the colony and a troubled future with gratitude for things as they are. But when, as now, she's out of sight, courage begins to wane. As he dawdles on the hilltop looking across that flat, empty plain, the proportions of reality shift and the distant colony appears one-dimensional and banal.

He loiters, reliving a prior evening at their favorite hilltop observation post looking out over the primeval lake. At the time she had roused from her meditations and pronounced as a firm command: "Stand up!"

He had recovered from the surprise and stood facing outward toward the distant colony.

"Now without removing your feet from the ground, jump!"

He bent his legs and sprang up.

"Again!"

He jumped.

"Again!" A moment later she said, "Do you feel the ground under your feet? Focus on it. Think about it. That's not a passing sensation. Feel what you have never felt before. Take it to heart; brood over it; turn it into experience. In the colony people may have the sensation but they miss the meaning and learn nothing. It takes work to turn sensation into understanding."

He felt like a clown and resented it. "Yes? So?"

Taking no notice of his resistance, she commanded again, "Don't rush. Take your time. You aren't feeling the earth yet. Rock back and forth on your feet. Think of the impenetrable ground. Stamp a foot on it. Take it in. Give yourself to the stress between the pull downward and the thrust upward. Find your place between."

He tried again and she added, "That's not the sensation of an outer object. It reaches into your soul. We call this 'ground' because we have the capacity to be grounded. This surface isn't just a platform to stand on. It's a dimension of us as the sky is. We're made of them. It's why you love this place."

At such moments he could never tell whether she was very wise or stark mad, but, remembered now, he sees that if it's madness, it's an acutely sane madness. Often, he doesn't understand a word like "ground" until much later, yet he feels the lure of the words like the force of gravity. But now, without her beside him, the sky is going empty, and he is growing dull. So getting dully up, he begins the long descent to the colony.

In the trek across the hot flatland between hills and settlement, alienation grows. He uses the time to shrink himself to the Lilliputian proportions of a colonist. The chasm opening between himself and his friends is one source of anxiety, but the deeper one is the destitution of a colony itself that is intended to give humanity another chance. The colony is divided between lethargic bored people for whom time has stopped and tense shrewd people for whom time is the enemy. The best, living minimally like drones without hope, have lost the spirit to care, while the worst, the young Atlases bearing the world on their shoulders, move industriously in circles. For the first there is nothing to hope because the second, the cautious clever ones, diligently prevent change in the order of things. And so, in his between-times, crossing the plain of the ordinary, Yori's dilemma gains only this much clarity: There must be a third way. Otherwise, one of the two will inherit the new earth, and humanity, if it survives, will face a destitute future.

As he passes through the narrow lanes trying to recover his colonial identity, the stone paths hold him above the earth while the transparent arcades above depress his sprits. Paola may have opened his eyes to the placelessness of a starship and of a container camp on a planet without a name, and she may have given him a *place*, but the price is that at each return he feels less capable of being where he is and belonging where he belongs. Gazing at the stultifying life around him, he suffers the conviction that he's getting something terribly wrong, though he can't think what.

It's well after dark when he reaches the dormitory on Government Square. In the commons area his sudden arrival casts a pall over the conversation of Véronique, Lars, and Lars' friend Sandra. Embarrassed silence suggests they may have been discussing him.

Lars, the quickest perhaps if not the subtlest in the company, greets him. "Well, if it isn't our peregrine roommate! Returned from the desolate hills." The bright tone of irony shows that Lars really is glad to see him, perhaps even worries a bit when he's away. "One of these days you're going to disappear, and we'll forget all about you. We never know whether you'll reappear or not."

Though Lars' banter is a transparent effort to conceal anxiety, Sandra tries to soften the effect. "Did you have a good weekend, Yori?"

"Not bad. Mainly doing research on Alexandros."

Véronique is the one who, seeing most clearly, feels most acutely the changes in Yori. Her worry is that at every return from the wilderness he is more changed than the time before. But she has been in love with him all her life, so she hides all that, forces a smile, and nudges gently: "You've taken up geology and need the desert for your work?"

He returns the smile but makes no reply. Sandra is close to Véronique and suspects even more than she knows about her feelings for Yori. Probably in defense of her friend, she persists, "But what do you really do out there?"

In place of the annoyance he has felt with them on recent returns to the colony, this time he sees the three with a compassionate eye. Well might Véronique see him changed. It's true that he returns a different person after each visit to the caves, and this time he has a quite different aura. The person he was a few days ago has fallen in love, and love has begun to make him more receptive to everything around him. It's this new person who answers Sandra amiably, "I find a place in the shade to read and think. I love the quiet, the big sky, being alone with the universe. This time I was trying to learn about the first landing party."

Lars, always itching for the sensation of a fraternal brawl, strikes again. "So you wander around the Hills of Elrond"—the scoffing reference is a garbled allusion to the idyllic home of the Elves in an old book he once read—"you ramble around worrying about a past that's over and done with while the rest of us toil away on the future. If you would sit still long enough, we could get you an honorary position as academic dreamer-in-residence."

Instead of responding to the challenge, Yori sees his two oldest friends—and Sandra whom he knows less well—looking at him with uncertain faces. Lars may find evidence in it of deviancy, but Véronique? Recognizing their mystification, and sorry to cause distress, Yori tries clumsily to restore the conversation to wherever it was when he entered. "So what were you discussing when I interrupted?"

Before Lars can answer, Véronique proceeds bravely. "We were catching up on each other's projects. We've been so busy we haven't had time for a good gossip." And she begins describing a new venture at "the labs," as she calls the Agriculture Department.

"We've just opened space in the nurseries for public gardening. Do you remember that the Elders did this in the starship nurseries at the bottom of the ship? It wasn't necessary for food. It was intended to give purpose to people who were bored. They were happy to plant, to watch things grow, and to take their little baskets of fruit or vegetables back to their rooms. Now we're trying the same thing. We supply the plants. You wouldn't believe how many people come out to get their hands in the dirt."

It's a brave effort on her part, but to him this speech sounds like a provincial defending her neighborhood against outside criticism. The effect is even more pronounced when Sandra picks up the theme by describing new developments in the arts that might be informative if he had been absent for more than a weekend. Sandra may not think of motives at all; Lars may think he's exposing his motives for all to see; Véronique may try to make her motives disappear; but it's all defense. The music of their words is the chatter of birds whose nest is threatened, all three responding to an obscure need to defend the colony. In Yori it stirs both compassion and guilt. He has become a threat to more than comfortable friendship, and they sense in him some vague danger to their general well-being.

Perhaps to steer the conversation as far as possible from contention between the two males, Sandra takes her cue from Véronique. She describes how the colony is benefiting from the renaissance of musical instruments on the ship more than a century ago, building as well as playing them. Her remarks are loaded with consequences and overdetermined by the anxiety in the air.

"The surprising thing," she continues, "is how much interest there is in learning to play. It's understandable among the children, but the adults also. Isn't it wonderful when older people want to take part?" She means the whole range of subjects in the Academy. "There's a waiting list for elementary instruction. The best of the children are even turning teacher. Now there's a movement to establish a choir." Her eyes beam with an excitement that momentarily overtakes any other sensation.

Her surge of enthusiasm is enough for the moment to distract Yori. Sandra is different from the others. She's younger and plainer but when she picks up the cello her plain features disappear, and the force of her inspiration passes to others in an irresistible current. Her education also sets her apart. She didn't follow the standard curriculum of liberal studies. It's part of the genius of the Galatea system that the especially talented—and the especially untalented—receive unique training. The result is that her background is both narrower and richer than theirs. Though primarily a performer, she combines the artist's immunity to convention with a bright temperament and motherly disposition that make her a popular teacher.

Several years before Lars was assigned to the colonial branch of the starship academy, he and Sandra had been close. Since it wasn't his family that drew him back to the ship for holidays, it was probably she. At least during those periods their bond became more serious so that recently, when the colonial school curriculum expanded into music, Lars encouraged her to apply for a new teaching post. Now, after only a few months, she has ignited enthusiasm by giving recitals and public performances in Government Square.

Lars beams with pride in Sandra's accomplishments and, under the cloak of celebrating progress, repeats his political creed: "You see, the welfare colony that you regard as totalitarian is a pretty exciting place to be. Things are gradually evolving in directions even you might approve. We also have the go-ahead for the new building project. Now that a higher birth rate is sustainable, everything needs expanding. All this shows how wrongheaded you are about the place."

Véronique listens as though from a distance, hanging fire, the silent person in the room with the most to say. When something puzzles her, she has a way of looking not *at* others but a little *past* them as though she sees better by the indirect gaze. Certainly she's the one who tracks Yori's changes. When they visited the labs and nurseries together a few weeks earlier, he had been almost his old self, but since then he has become quieter and moodier. His old sociable self has retreated behind a mask of politeness. During the week he keeps more and more to himself with his head buried in his reading. Then today he walks straight in from the hills like a different person. Without being able to attach any idea to the conviction, she's sure that something has changed.

Eventually Sandra and Lars leave. For fear Yori might also leave, she suggests they go outside. It's a lovely evening under the dome of the Square. Evenings are always lovely there. They amble across the open space without speaking, and she guides him through all the loitering people into a quiet street beyond. Finally, she says, "I can see that something has happened. Do you want to talk about it?"

In that moment something unthought dawns on him that brings a pang of deeper guilt: Véronique is in love with him. Not at all the youthful infatuation he has felt for her. Hers is a deeper love, and he can see it because he has experienced it for the first time with Paola. He stops in his tracks and faces her. It is a moment of unbounded compassion on one side and sad recognition on the other. He holds out a hand, the hand of a lifelong friend. She stares at it as at an object, then, sadly appreciating the kindness, decides to accept it.

Together, hand in hand, they walk on without daring to give words to what has passed between, both perhaps searching for a topic to fill the silence. Eventually he asks, "Have you ever wondered what really happened to the first landing party all those years ago?"

She replies mainly from gratitude for his having rescued them from the awkward moment. "We know, don't we? Weren't they killed by a virus or something? You're still thinking about your father?"

And so they plunge ahead with perhaps unequal zeal for the topic as he adds, "I didn't want to mention it in front of the others, but this weekend I searched the records on Alexandros. All I found was a suspicious absence of information. It's almost casual, as though the topic was not important enough to spend time on."

"The crew must have had good reasons," she answers. "Maybe if the whole truth had been told, there would have been resistance to further exploration. We're insiders now and we know things aren't done arbitrarily." She and Yori have been as close for several years as the very young can well be, and yet this is the first time she has heard him mention his father's death. Has he lived with the mystery for most of his life and kept it that close? If so, what brings it to the surface just now? It occurs to her that Yori might have become more paranoid than the colony. "Are you thinking that Starship Command had a hand in it?"

"I don't know what to think. But something in their indifference is not quite right. If the act was deliberate and could be treated so cavalierly, then Command didn't think they owed anyone an explanation. That's even more troubling. Either I'm crazy or the case of the landing party is more complicated than we know."

They walk on, Yori looking straight ahead, the very image of his father's now legendary formality. Véronique sees him with a new and subdued detachment: in a serious mood, the authority of his straight figure; the piercing yet relaxed intelligence of the eyes; even the narrow face with the sharp chin—traits that cause him and his ideas to be talked about by more than Lars Hanssen. Without opening his mouth he can be persuasive, and that, under present conditions in the colony, may make him more dangerous to himself than to others.

Eventually he drops her hand as though forgetting and continues. "I don't have any evidence that anyone is—or was—guilty of anything. I can see the same possibilities anyone else can see for what happened. And yet . . ." But what more can he say without mentioning a source? There is a third person in the conversation who must remain unheard.

Without further comment the random walk continues for some time, passing up and down the empty lanes, aware of nothing around them, engrossed by different topics until, by some devious route, they find themselves back at a nearly deserted Government Square.

By a gentle hand on his arm, she compels him to stop. "I mentioned before that your ideas may be causing comment, and not only from Lars. The colony is a fragile system, you know. Civil unrest would force repression . . . just for survival. No one can let it come to that. Whether there is any basis for your suspicions or not, I'm worried for you."

He answers indignantly. "I am not a revolutionary, you know!"

She lowers her eyes as though searching the ground instead of avoiding his eye. "I know that. But in a pinch who will bother to distinguish between words and deeds? What do you think will happen if you are seen attacking public security? The enemy of the colony would also be the enemy of the starship. Remember Hans Rückert's seminar. Reading about Socrates? He was at risk in his little city-state, but you could be in much greater danger here. He could have accepted banishment, but in space there would be no difference between that and a death sentence. I know your intentions are good, but your timing may not be. And something else Rückert used to say: 'The meaning of an idea includes the effect it has in the world.' I think there's good advice in that, and you should take it."

Later, as he lies awake in the night with the low ceiling adding to the weight on his spirits, the altered relation to Véronique and the generosity of her advice nearly defeat him. Her idea that under threat, violence may have been necessary to sustain the colonial system and could be again—all that sparks a new idea about power. It is this: It requires creative power to establish any system (as his father was trying to do), conservative power to sustain it (as the Governor would be obliged to do), and a power to change it (as he would like to do). At the sticking point, power means violence . . . as does love! So violence all around, is it? How is one ever to cut though that knot?

He has been on the move all day, but now, too restless to lie still, he gets up and goes out yet again. He wanders for hours through the colony reviewing his situation. Véronique is right about him but for the wrong reasons. He *has* changed. Love aside—is there any way to set love aside?—he's troubled about the fate of his father but not much about his own situation. In fact at this moment he would like nothing better than to go live in the caves with Paola if she would allow it.

Sometime in the early hours of morning he returns to Government Square, where he is startled again by its new design. Véronique bears on his anxieties in several ways, but here it's her genius that occupies him. The conditions that make the colony forbidding are largely overcome in this little square. There may even be a solution to the problem of violence in her design if he could only grasp it. She hasn't staged a revolution or tried to reform things from the ground up. She has simply responded to the job before her as well as she could. In deftly arranging rocks and succulents into a park that people love, she has bypassed ideas and arguments. It occurs to him dimly that if there were a third way other than status quo or revolution, it be might something like this.

11

A FEW DAYS LATER YORI receives a summons from the Governor. Their exchanges are irregular but routine, depending, he surmises, more on the older man's mood than on his schedule. When he enters, Governor Nasser is not sitting at the desk as before but comfortably disposed in one of two chairs arranged for conversation. Yori has noticed them before but never been invited to sit there, evidence that their earlier talks, though friendly enough, remained formal. Given Véronique's deductions about Lars and the Governor, he watches for any hint that his criticisms have reached the official ear.

"Come in and be comfortable. I think I'll have a brandy. At least what we have learned to call brandy. You have one too." And he gets up to fetch glasses.

It crosses Yori's mind that there might be an ulterior motive for offering alcohol, but he rejects the idea as paranoid. And yet something in the tone of the remark sounds false, as though the relaxing of formality might actually mean the opposite. Is there something vaguely staged about the scene, or has the older man lost the touch for dealing with others as equals? Not distance elided but distance covertly insisted on? "If so," Yori reflects as the Governor returns with the brandy glasses, "then the conversation will not begin with whatever he wants to talk about."

He accepts the proffered glass and resumes his seat. What he wonders at that moment is whether the subject of his father will be mentioned. If not, since it will not have been forgotten and both will know as much, then the omission will have been deliberate. So much knowledge floating around a room without either person claiming possession adds layers to a standoff in which each knows the other will not blink. What Yori may not see at the moment is that it also deepens an unacknowledged bond between them.

"Tonight, I would like to trade ideas with you on a topic I've been thinking a lot about. By now we have expanded the neighborhoods in the colony, stabilized production facilities, enriched the education system, and secured all essential services. I'm sure you would agree that's a good record for an experiment new in human history."

There is more than one assertion in that speech. Yori chooses and supplies a minimal acknowledgment. "I've been hearing about the public gardens, the music program, and a new building project. You must be proud."

So begins the dance. The Governor lets the moment pass and goes on. "Yes. Yes. All is well." He chuckles gruffly. "Better, I'd say, than being on that tin can in space for the rest of our lives, huh?" Then his expression changes. "But we are a restless species. What I've been thinking is that too much routine is not healthy. Trouble of all sorts sets in. People need aims. The colony is going to need a new challenge, especially when the starship leaves."

When he waits rather than going on with whatever he has been thinking, Yori answers politely, fitting himself to the rhythm of the exchange. "I think I see what you mean. As long as there are buildings to build and systems to design, life has shape and purpose."

Apparently that satisfies the Governor for the moment. "You're a historian. You know that in the age of the nation states on Ulro when people got restless, leaders could use external threats to unify the populace, or technological challenges like going to their moon to breathe new spirit into them. But we have no enemies unless little green men from the Andromeda Galaxy decide to invade, and new technological challenges are pretty much routine."

He chuckles and sips from his glass, then resumes with a vigor that seems more beginning than continuation. "Here are two ideas I'd like to try out on you. The first is expanding the colony. Not inside, but outside. One or maybe two satellite stations at a distance might serve for research. Then after a time if it seemed feasible, they could become permanent. That would mean expanding and diversifying all our systems. Of course we'd need more administrators." He eyes Yori shrewdly. "That might appeal to you. To administer a satellite colony." The last are statements, but he gives them an unnecessary interrogative inflection.

"Both ideas are new to me." The irrelevant remark provides another boundary marker in the effort to find the amorphous point of the conversation. Is the idea that he, being a restless spirit, might be shunted off into the wilderness? It arrests him only for a moment on the edge of a more dangerous response.

"I do see what you're aiming at. Boredom often follows on the heels of routine. We're capable of more than repetition."

The Governor appears to muse on the last remark as though wondering how far down this road Yori has already traveled. Having set him on the track of the idea, he might let him run to see where he goes. But Yori doesn't take the bait. Just waits until his host chooses to resume.

"I like that. You've got a good head on your shoulders. Governing is sometimes a matter of inventing goals for the public good. When people get too comfortable, they get lazy and atrophy sets in." He stops again, leaving another opening, but it, too, is declined.

"My second idea is to introduce private property. It's an idea that we lost sight of during the Galatea years. Understand-ably. But now we have room enough again. It would mean competition among people. On Ulro it ultimately led to the global city. I know the theory that considerations of property set the forces in motion that ultimately made the Galatea mission necessary. You may even agree with that view." For a third time he pauses, and for a third time Yori chooses not to respond.

"On the small scale of our eventual planetary village, competition in ownership might provide the incentives that keep people vigorous and innovative. Of course, property and expansion might go hand in hand. Two antidotes to lethargy."

The fact that the Governor himself mentions no argu-ments against these ideas is a warning to proceed carefully. What exactly is he, Yori, being asked? To salute? To volunteer the critique himself? Is this a test? Perhaps he's being invited to expose his 'subversive ideas'? Instead he tries to turn the tables. "Since you haven't begun either of these, you must have doubts. What do you see as the downsides of each?"

"That's what I brought you here to help me think through." This time the laugh is not reassuring.

It's as close as Yori will get to verifying that his ideas have reached the Governor's ears and that this is a game to draw him out—or draw him in! And why not? Where security and social harmony are the chief concern, aren't all means fair? In that moment another possibility turns up.

The Governor could be tempting him to put truth above interest, to see where his heart is, whether he will put his own welfare at risk for a higher cause. In an ambiguous world where the game of means and ends is a gamble at best, his instinct is to trust the higher motive. It brings an old formula to mind: The life of calculation is unworthy of a free man. Under that inspiration, he plunges ahead into the dark with one reservation—he takes care to let the Governor see that he is counting the consequences of not counting the consequences.

"Is there a risk that the solutions might just postpone the problem and even magnify it? Teaching people to put their individual interests above collective well-being could lead to a repetition of Ulro's fate, couldn't it?"

The older man takes time to mull this over, looking away toward a door that opens on a small private garden, actually a tiny wasteland that offers no evidence of human care. When at last he decides to speak, the subject appears to have changed. At least the tenor is obscure.

"I know this is all very theoretical, but a ruler—a leader if you prefer—doesn't have the luxury of being merely practical. In the long run it doesn't help to rush in with quick fixes just because it's possible. He spends most of his time apparently doing nothing but inventing alternatives and testing the atmospherics."

Again the subject swerves and he skips several connections. "You're imagining a principle of organization different than we have. I've heard something about your view that technology is totalitarian. But it's not true, you know. If it serves people's interests, it can't be despotic. Even the old naval discipline of the starship was balanced by other forces. Here we sit, ready to invent new directions and respond to people's changing requirements. We spend our time serving the general interest. That's hardly totalitarian. In time you'll appreciate the difference."

Another chuckle makes Yori begin keeping tabs on the chuckles as further boundary markers in this wandering conversation, trying still to find a center in the field of reference. That belongs to his cautious side, but in the same moment he does the opposite. Having gone so far as to hint at criticisms, he goes further without quite deciding to do so. "I wonder if benevolent motives may be inconsistent with freedom?"

The fact that the Governor makes no visible response to the question shows it has hit the mark. In this room no response is more dramatic than a raised eyebrow. "I don't know what you mean. You'll have to say more."

"I mean," Yori continues, "if you care for me, does that make me a strong citizen?"

"It is true that someone has to be above self-interest. Not out of high-mindedness. It's not a moral point. Out of disinterest. That's key."

Yori searches for an inoffensive but true response. "Isn't that a dangerous place to be? Not beyond interest. But above the system that supports the others. Or do you mean that everyone should be above the system, according to his talents and training? I suppose we're not trying to make everyone his own shoemaker."

"You mean that producers must be masters of their production; professionals, masters of what they profess; and governors, masters of what they govern."

Yori responds with a broad smile. "I think this is getting over my head. Mastery is too big a word for me."

At that the Governor gives a hearty laugh and stands up. Whatever he has been fishing for, he gives every appearance of being happy with the results as he shakes Yori's hand and sees him out.

And Yori? He goes away without the slightest idea whether he has contributed to a real conversation or signed his own death warrant. And yet he goes away happy for not having let his own interest cause him to say things he doesn't think. What doesn't cross his mind, however, is that he may also have revealed himself as a man with potential.

12

YORI GOES THROUGH THE motions of his duties living for the day when he can return to the hills. When that day finally comes, he's filled with anxiety about Paola. Does she really love him as he loves her? He is the only person she knows. Maybe she "made love" with him out of loneliness or generosity or desperation. He almost dreads the moment of meeting. What will she do or say? Such questions fill his thoughts during the long trek across the desert to the hill.

When he arrives, she's waiting in the dimly lit cave with the inexplicable wall markings where they first met, "in the hollow of time"! Every time they pass that way, he wants to ask about the names, who etched them, and why. Each time the rule of one question interferes, but he no longer resists. The apt question needs time to germinate, and for that, one must wait. Meanwhile, many things are more urgent than this wall. And yet Paola is waiting for him as though the time has come.

She sits in silence as before in the deep shadows opposite the inscriptions and does not speak. Until his eyes adjust he doesn't see her, but having become sensitive to the unseen in his surroundings, he feels her presence. For some moments he strains to make out the marks on the wall, then, without turning, asks, "Why have the names been etched into the wall?"

"This is the burial place of the Immortals."

Another incomprehensible remark. He knows that when words are real, they don't start or stop at face value. They belong to a broad tapestry, visible and invisible. He crosses the chamber and sits beside her. She lights a torch and together they face hundreds of names extending beyond the light in all directions. He climbs down again, and she passes the torch to him. Walking back and forth before the wall, examining the rows at close range, he picks out a few names he knows best from the history of Planet Ulro. But what he can't make out is why the explorers would have taken the trouble. To stave off boredom on long, cold nights?

Rather than comparing, searching for themes, and multiplying empty questions, he studies what is given, looking for a key in one name only: Thucydides. What is a name anyway? The very absurdity of finding this name as an artifact, light-years beyond any imaginable field of reference, is jarring. It causes wonder about names themselves. Considered from here, the name refers less to an individual somewhere down the corridors of history than to something harder to grasp. Because Paola does not stop the question by providing answers that satisfy his curiosity, he holds the enigma in mind, studies it, gains experience, even begins to question questioning itself and the one who can ask questions. "Thucydides" belongs to multiple neighborhoods—Planet Ulro, ancient Greece, the Peloponnesian War, the dawn of historiography, and infinitely more—but the name is also an archeological fossil that may inspire worlds yet to come. Not a dead man from a distant planet preserved in a sign, but an eternal thought waiting for one who might be able to receive it.

"I never knew that names were such mysterious things!"

Paola pulls her legs up under her on the rock and answers. "Names can't just be made up. Think about giving a name to P2314. It needs one. We've lived here for a quarter of a century and still we use this arbitrary date in lieu of a name. But try thinking up a real name for it and you fail. It can't be arbitrary. If it ever gets one, the name will be *given*, not assigned. Its *own* name—its *proper* name will be a discovery of what belongs to the planet. Imagine calling your colony—it also has none— 'new town.' It's absurd. You can hear it's not a name, though in another time and place the same word might be."

Yori wistfully brings her back to his point. "This random collection of names stares at us like elements from a dead world. They almost cry out for us to make something new of them."

Looking again at the wall, he reads more names having little connection with Thucydides: Confucius, Buddha, Leonardo, Shakespeare, Bach—random juxtapositions, discontinuous and unrelated like breaks in time inviting new constructions.

She interrupts his thoughts. "Some things *are* eternal. On an underground rock in orbit around an unnamed star, 'Thucydides' makes many things thinkable."

But Yori has dropped the thread. "Who did all this work?"

Climbing off her rock, she joins him in front of the wall and begins another story involving his father. "Shortly after our landing we lived in a camp on this edge of the plateau and often used this cave for sleeping. I explored the caves, found the pool and the canyon, and set up my research there. The wall was a pastime, a sort of game, recording the names of our heroes and telling stories to explain our choices. As the wall filled, we rolled boulders into place so we could reach higher. The mystery is why it was so important to us and so satisfying. We didn't ask about the meaning. Meanings are often traces, unintended consequences."

She appears to study the wall for a moment before continuing. "Think of the social history recorded in the graffiti on the walls of Ulro cities. The difference is that instead of carving our own names so the wall would say 'Akira was here,' we celebrated the ideals of our history by naming the heroes. We didn't know—well, your father probably did—but the rest of us didn't recognize each one as a declaration of allegiance. But it was. An oath of loyalty to each of these barely connected artifacts. Yet it's the breaks, the spaces between, that count. They are the sites for creation. Carving these names, we blindly set in motion a transformation more human than all our measurements and calculations. We began weaving an accidental tapestry that was waiting for your equally accidental visit to this underworld."

Yori says nothing in response, giving the obscure words time to come to rest and take root in his mind.

After a while, after "whiling" for the time it takes to read his thoughts, Paola resumes in her oracular mode. "I am the guardian of the dead and you are like Odysseus or Aeneas, come to the underworld to consult their spirits. Their bones aren't brought from Ulro like relics to medieval churches. But the timeless thought of the honored name—ancestor, leader, discoverer, creator—transcends the changes of time. Each word invites us to enter '*the thought of the thought of the thought of the name.*' What echoes in the name isn't a thing or a person or an act that can be known and explained. Real or imaginary hardly matters. What matters is the nameless figure in the name. Being nameless, it is outside ordinary time."

"In the hollow!" Yori exclaims in a moment of insight that will vanish as soon as it arrives.

"Yes. These figures are not living and they are not dead. They cross past, present, and future. They are immortal."

"Is this why you were all called 'The Immortals'? Sneered at for being impractical enough to etch eternity into a rock?"

The incongruity strikes her as laughable. "Command probably never knew about our little game. Only the leisured mind *has* the time. They were interested in planting food-stuffs, but they wouldn't have noticed that we had planted something far more useful. A starship has no time for what is unrelated to its purposes. These marks, if they were noticed at all, would be stored in Alexandros where they already are and go unnoticed as forgettable bits of past reality. Whatever is exemplary in them has already decayed into 'information' and the oblivion of 'psychological impressions.' But, once created, the exemplary doesn't cease. The idea may wander like a space traveler through wormholes into unimaginable dimensions and affect new systems, or it may retreat underground and await rebirth in some unrecognizable guise."

"Why do you speak so mystically when you're only talking about memory? Our imaginations are fed by the past. We build with materials from history. Why make it mysterious?"

This time Paola sighs and shows a bit of impatience. "You overrate knowledge. Consciousness. When the past inspires us, it comes like the echoes of unfamiliar footsteps in the night. It comes as mood, tone, taste—before there's a clear idea. To speak of the Immortals is to describe things more clearly than what history calls causes and effects."

Though Yori doesn't understand a word, he has a pertinent question. "Can the Immortals teach us how to turn a life-support system into a city?"

"Ah! See?" She responds, happy that he has caught something. "Your question is inspired by echoes of unremembered sources, unremembered antecedents. When a man lying in his tub in Sicily had a eureka moment, a chink in the human cavern was opened by a new idea. When a man in Judea fell off his horse and saw a great light, the human capacity for rebirth was discovered. When a man in Pisa dropped a rock from a tower, humanity gained a new habitat. If there ever is a livable city on this planet, it will be thanks to a fresh assembly of the eternal pieces of an unknown puzzle. The pieces may find a home where people have the courage to live beyond what they can even hope. And it will come by gift, not blueprint."

This conversation cuts Yori adrift among feelings for which he has no corresponding ideas. On this threshold of the unknown, drawn by love without an object, Paola takes him into her bed. Like the first time, they share something wider than the present and the personal. In the embrace of love he again becomes responsive to all things known and to the boundless beyond the known. Afterward, awake beside her on their outgrowth of rock, enjoying the afterglow that may be love itself, he is drawn beyond life in the caves and the growth of the plants and the organization of a colony and exploration of the stars.

The next day they don't speak of the obscurities or the glories of the night before. As they go about the usual order of the day, Yori feels like a blinded man who has emerged into a too-bright light rather than one stumbling into subterranean dark. In the evening they go out and sit in the observation post, enjoying the stillness made audible by the distant bee-hum of the colony. Then he tells her about his talk with the Governor and adds, "The more I hear, the more I wonder how we will ever get from a colony to a city."

A brief smile crosses Paola's face at the return of the question—his question. "You don't. There is no golden string to follow. If you know where you're going, you only get somewhere else. All you can do is care for the little things in front of you."

To help get the idea clearly before his mind, Yori elaborates, "What I mean is, when we have lived for generations under a command system, how do we even create the desire for a messy world of invention where people with different interests decide together how to act? Where do we find the courage?"

"What makes the question pressing just now?"

"The Galatea—did you know?—will be leaving soon." He pauses. Each time the idea arises he feels dislocated again. "That will be a wrenching experience. It won't be felt suddenly, but it will slowly dawn on people that the king is dead and there will be no more kings."

"With what consequences?"

"Who knows? You remember the Colloquies from a hundred years ago about the social effects of wandering in space without a destination to hope for. Something similar may happen now. Constraints will loosen and, as long as we don't lack for food or shelter or comfort, we might just linger on this planet like the dead with no vision of anything worth doing."

Paola's reply, if it is relevant at all, must be connected by some verbal rhizome underground. "One who wonders aloud about inexistent things and unimaginable possibilities will make enemies. Your father was like that. He was a scientist, but he knew things science can't know. He led the landing party because he knew how to live with the enemy. Like bamboo in the wind, he knew how to bend without breaking. There is no guarantee of success. All you can do is go with the enemy's line of force until he defeats himself. But the wise man knows that in winning nothing is concluded."

13

ONE EVENING SEVERAL WEEKS later Yori is invited to the Governor's office. He receives no greeting nor is he asked to take a seat. He is left standing in a suffocating silence facing the man behind the desk like the first time he was here. In the oppressive atmosphere he is as anxious as a naughty child awaiting its fate.

"I've asked you here to give you a choice. As much as I enjoy our talks, I cannot allow you to disrupt the harmony of the Academy or risk unsettling the colony. I don't intend to be harsh, but I will do my duty. You must either return permanently to the Galatea, which means leaving when it leaves, or accept voluntary banishment to your beloved hills." However solemn, the alternative coming from him sounds almost tongue in cheek, as though no sane person would choose a death sentence.

"If you chose the latter"—he elaborates the option as though to preserve an illusion of choice—"you could retain access to Alexandros, and you might request provisions as needed and collect them periodically at the northern gate. But you could not enter the colony or have any contact with people inside. I don't have to underscore the fact that under the first option you would almost certainly live out the rest of your life in space or, under the second, that if you survived, you would live the solitary life of a man without home or companion. You have until tomorrow morning to decide."

This speech invites no response, and Yori offers none. After a few moments of studying a monitor on his desk, Governor Nasser adds, "That's all. There's nothing to discuss. Please send me your decision by morning. In either case you will have three days to gather what you need and leave. There's a shuttle currently at the dock. That's when it returns to the ship."

In a last glance at the old man's face, Yori finds no trace of regret, though in a few conversations they have become almost friends. Yet some impressions from that moment will stay with him. There is something strange, something forced in the Governor's manner, some mystery in the sudden and peremptory sentence.

The first among many questions that flash simultaneously across his mind is, has he found out about Paola? Have I somehow led him to her? With what consequences for her? Or—this one feels closer to the old man's tone—does he not trust himself to discuss the issue? What could he have learned from their last interview that might have led to this? Is he acting under orders from Starship Command? Perhaps Command is sensitive to a thing so small as the ideas of a single student, but that would be a tacit confession to having been massively in the wrong somehow. And why make such a point about the sentence being for life? By now the two know each other too well for the Governor to imagine that he would look banishment in the face and not respond seriously. What other explanations are there?

Without speaking a word, Yori turns around and walks out.

He spends most of the night gathering his belongings, checking the electronics that will henceforth be his lifeline. Then he sends the following message: "With gratitude for our conversations and for your friendship, I accept the second alternative. Yori Kashimoto."

There is one other message to write. Addressed to Véronique: "As you will have heard by now, I have been banished from the colony. I can't say how sorry I am to be leaving you, but you must not fret on my account. I know very well how to survive in the wilderness. Please, for your own welfare and for your position in the colony, do not try to get in touch with me. Love, Yori

He folds the paper and leaves it on his desk.

This time Paola is not expecting him. She is not in the Chamber of the Hearth and she is not in the gardens. Hot from his determined walk across the plain, loaded with his belongings and the numbing weight of his situation, he waits by the cistern where she will stop for water on her way in.

Until a few months ago, his present composure would not have been possible. No shock or regret, no sense of fate or of a burden lifted in being free of the colony. In this first effort to think it through in an orderly manner he doesn't analyze or weigh his options. In what Paola calls "emptying the mind," he simply feels his way slowly into his new situation. And it is in that state that, arriving unseen, she finds him.

For a few moments she observes from a distance as he stares blankly into the water. The fact that he does not feel her presence provides a measure of his absorption in whatever has happened to bring him here now. The face is too blank, too unconscious for serene detachment. Blank as from a severe blow. His life will have been turned upside down yet again, though she makes no effort to imagine how. Her own face passes in that moment from shadow to brightness, happy to have him there even bringing great trouble with him.

He looks up, surprised, and responds as though he might be intruding. "Hello. I hope this isn't inconvenient." It's not his voice but a distanced, spiritless voice imitating Yori Kashimoto.

She contradicts the suggestion with a shake of her head, and his news erupts in a single phrase: "I've been banished."

He gets up and begins pacing calmly yet compulsively up and down the path that leads to the garden. Without encouragement, he recounts the final interview with the Governor then adds as an afterthought, "Don't think that in declining to return to the ship I mean to impose myself on you. It's just that even banned from the colony, I know my destiny lies there rather than on the Galatea. I've learned that much at least from you."

Though he has not mentioned the reasons for his expulsion, Paola shows no curiosity and asks no questions. Nor are questions expected. Instead she continues to observe until she has understood his state of mind. Then in an assertion of the stubborn and salutary reality, she moves from her place and begins drawing water. Passing the jar to him, she leads the way toward the Chamber of the Hearth.

One who believes that what a person in distress most needs is sympathy will miss the point here. Yori has already learned better. There will be no inducements to wallow in sentiment, draining—and savoring—the emotional content of his misery to the last drop. Even in the emptiness that is certain to follow, he knows without having to think that Paola will go about her work until he finds his center again. So now he follows her, talking all the way, a man compelled nonetheless to express his sense of abandonment.

"I can see that the Governor had little choice. The last thing he can tolerate at the moment when the Galatea leaves is disruption by a gadfly undermining confidence in the colony. There will be enough for people to adapt to without internal dissension. Still, dissension may be timely as people discover that things are about to change anyway."

He pauses, but not long enough for the answer he knows he will not get. "It's hard to come back into the hills where I have been so happy, knowing I can never return. You know this better than anyone—the moment when your future is annulled, and your life is over."

And so it goes throughout the afternoon while Paola goes about her duties, refusing to let his distress disrupt the Rule of Life. Eventually he passes from the numbness of his earlier composure to a quite different state of mind. Pacing again, up and down the cave, rehashing what has happened and how nothing remains but an empty future in which nothing will ever be worth doing again, digging himself deeper into the new hole in his life. Finally, as the light begins to fade in the crevice of the rock high above the hearth, Paola leads him out through the Chamber of Names to their perch above the plain.

Ritual silence brings calm after the long afternoon monologue. Even in his distress it is one of the relaxed moments that defines their indefinable bond. Not unity or a bid for unity. The relation *is* the distance between them, communing across the limitless interval of age, gender, experience, language even, and destiny. So they sit quietly in the dying light on the shore of an infinite ocean of sky, closer than ever to the threshold of the unknown, one filled with gratitude for all that is given, the other flirting with despair over all that has been taken away. And yet the same: his emptiness and her fullness.

Eventually Yori speaks and not about himself this time. "You've never told me what happened to Shi Wa and Edward or where they are." He means Kwan Shi Wa and Edward Hamilton, the others who escaped the wrath of Starship Command. No practical reason for the inquiry. Just that his choice to live outside the colony rather than return to the Galatea forms a bond with these people he has never seen, as though together they now make a quartet of outlaws.

"Shi Wa and Edward disappeared about a year before I first spotted you in the hills. Maybe that's why I followed your wanderings. You were the only human being I ever saw. For a long time, I didn't risk attracting your attention because I was afraid you wouldn't return." She appeared to be revolving some idea in mind before continuing the topic of her friends.

"In our division of labors my part was to develop the garden and theirs was to explore for new plant species. Their hikes went north beyond the hills, away from the colony, each time venturing a little farther. Eventually the distances kept them away for days, even weeks, but they always returned with specimens and stories about exotic plants in rough terrain many miles away. Then they just didn't return. I couldn't leave to search for them since I had to maintain life here. I had no idea where to look. Besides they were in love. When they left on the last trip, Shi Wa was pregnant, and they might have decided against raising a child in the shadow of a colony full of enemies. Or it might have been an accident or illness. They could have starved. It's all speculation. Otherwise, I know nothing. But it's hard to imagine a happy end to their story. We either learn to accept contingency or we move into a fantasy world of our own devising and lose touch with reality as given."

"Then it's also possible," Yori now speculates, "that Shi Wa had her baby and they're living out there somewhere." She nods and he adds, "Isn't it amazing to think that somewhere in that wilderness there may be a human family? Seeds of another colony? Someday another city—if we ever become capable of political life."

And so, in conveniently forgetting that he no longer belongs to a political "we," he may have stumbled onto a possibility that no one can see until the time is ripe. In being exiled from the colony, being "excepted" for not fitting the template of properly belonging, he now occupies a unique place. From one perspective his situation marks the defining line between the colony's inside and its outside. Paradoxically in being excluded he is the most included, because exclusion now becomes the central preoccupation of his life. Even more than Paola and her friends, who from the point of view of the colony don't exist.

She doesn't respond to his fantasy of a second colony. Instead, she smiles at the instinctive optimism by naming a choice rather than a mood. "You can look out from the observation deck of a starship into the depths of space and see nothing, or you can see potentiality everywhere. The one may be as true as the other, but it matters infinitely what you choose to see and what not to see."

"I suppose you mean that just now I am seeing the future as empty and life as pointless. Until you, my life was comfortable and well-ordered. But it was repetitive and empty. Isn't 'pure possibility' just another name for emptiness?"

At that, she gives a rare smile of satisfaction that he misses. "You can say 'No,' or you can say 'Yes,' or you can decline to say either. That's the heart of being human. Freedom at the nub. Which you say *will have made* all the difference."

Presently they return to the cave and share their meal. Then as casually as possible Yori remarks, "I guess tomorrow I'll move on too . . . if I can stay tonight. Maybe sometime I'll come across the others and be able to bring you news."

"You will not move on tomorrow because there is nowhere to move. Shi Wa and Edward were hardened to this life and knew how to survive. I've been out there. You'd starve or go mad."

"Then would you mind if I live here . . . in another cave?"

She indulges him, "If you want a space of your own, it can easily be arranged"—she gestures in the direction of the garden and then toward the Chamber of Names. "That's only a detail. Meanwhile, I'm glad you have come to stay."

14

FROM THIS DAY FORTH Yori and Paola live together in the Cave of the Hearth under "the Hills of Elrond," as Lars had once christened them. The next morning, the first morning of a new life, she announces, "Now we will go for the silent time." Nothing strange in the announcement except the formality of including him in the activity. She walks away toward the gardens and the little resting place in the canyon wall. Yori follows but with no eagerness in his step.

When they are settled in the shade of the towering cliffs, she makes a point of showing him how to fold his legs, to straighten his back and rest his hands in his lap, palms down. This is new. Not commands. Explanations, of how ordinary things are done. Externally he responds as usual to her requests, knowing that none are arbitrary, postponing questions. But inside are the first stirrings of resistance. Not of her exactly, unless she is the available target for frustrations that he is determined not to show. It's just that here, on the first morning of a new economy, things accepted before and passed over as exotic now strike him as pointless nuisances and leave him touchy and sore. Then the festering begins.

To a guest, going and coming at comfortable intervals, her rule of life had been interesting, especially these "exercises in unknowing." When of old she began each day with quiet contemplation, sitting in the lotus position with hands folded, eyes open but focused on nothing; when before each meal she observed another quiet moment in the same posture, or again by the cistern or across the hearth before the evening conversation—all these had been curious exceptions to real life. The only requirement was that she not be interrupted. Now it is life itself and that sets everything in new light. Where living without an agenda, doing whatever needed doing, added spice to a holiday from the Academy, time now stretches out before him with no aim in sight but the daily round of the Rule. Now he may discover that he has always been a creature of ends and means—or not.

Objectively considered, as though there were no people involved, the new life is easy. Two to do the work of one. Sharing provides time for Paola's botanical experiments and the additional advantage that they are not always in the same space. Still restlessness grows. Increasingly Yori feels claustrophobic, confined day in, day out to the underground existence of a mole. No one to talk to but Paola. No one to argue with but Paola. No one to avoid but Paola. The same schedule for the same domestic chores except when he devises "improvements" that can occupy him for days. But usually he helps tend the garden and reads randomly on Alexandros— history, fiction, science, political theory—desperately reading without direction.

Sometimes, with or without Paola, he takes long walks in the hills. Evenings, she likes him to read aloud, poetry mainly, and that becomes a new ritual. A source of inner conflict is that he loves her and wants to be with her even when she becomes an obstacle in the empty path of his desire. The meandering stream of well-ordered but aimless activities begins to break up on the rocks of frustration.

The only activity with a purpose is reading *Starship Galatea*, and or two reasons. Because "The Book" seems like an inheritance from his father and because some parts foreshadow his present condition, especially the ones about people on the starship when they felt they were living in a vacuum, going nowhere at warp speed.

The pressure of everyday life where there are no pressures soon prompts a showdown. The rule again. One day when he doesn't respond quickly to her hint that his reading device and the copy of The Book be put away before they go to the garden, she gives an instruction and he explodes. "Is it in your way? I don't see that it's hurting anything."

"You're judging by utility as though you were a machine." The quiet reply is disinterested where he wants passion. Calmly, she adds, "A free being develops outline and character by living to a rule," then moves on to tend the mushrooms on the opposite wall.

He stops in his tracks, gives the stone hearth in the middle of the room a firm kick, and replies angrily, "If that's the way you want to live, well fine, but I don't care to be a slave. I'll just pack my things and move on."

"Move on where?" she asks indifferently, without interrupting the seamless motion of her work.

"Well," he stammers, "I'll move into another cave far enough away that my slovenly habits won't offend you!"

She stops and turns slowly around. "Please sit down." She returns to the hearth and assumes a posture that honors the words to be spoken, waiting until he yields to her example.

"Now. You are free to leave when you wish and go where you like. You understand the risks. But some things you don't understand yet. If you choose to move into another cave, you must know that it won't be like your own room in a large house. If we live together at all, we live by a sensible order that you help devise. But the order is not about your opinions or mine. It's about what needs doing and the provisional stability that human beings need to live up to their measure. If you want to work when you feel like it and not when you don't, keep silent when you like and speak when you want, you may go your own way. But it's inside or outside. Either live the rule or there's no place for you here." And she walks away in the direction of the cistern.

Within five minutes he has followed. "I'm a grown man," he cries. "Why shouldn't I be free to do what I like?"

"That is disorderly feeling without a message. Like an animal cry. It doesn't begin a conversation or invite participation. Life is too precious to spend in random outbursts. If there's a real question in there somewhere, we can discuss it, but only after you've given it shape. Now I'm going to dig tubers. You sit here and face your decision. If you're leaving—even to move into another cave—do it tonight. But remember: What you decide here is decided for good. Life begins here. If you're leaving, leave tonight." She gets up and goes to the garden.

Yori remains beside the cistern, idly dangling his fingers in the water as though to cool his passion. He understands perfectly that he's being irrational, but it isn't easy even at his age and under his present stress to change the habits of a lifetime. Especially not easy in the intimate region of life where no practical consequences seem to follow from leaving his clothes on the floor or a book open on a table or a plate unwashed until morning. And he knows that the quarrel is not with Paola but with himself. How many times has he argued with Lars that material utility is different from care for the soul? Attention to the little things, to order in the house, these *are* care for the soul where soul is not a *thing* but the *being-related*.

Yet there is a real question here that he would like to ask. Paola uses the word freedom in an odd way he can't get clear. He mutters to himself, "I'll ask that after dinner." Then gets up and goes to the garden where, without a word, he begins watering the beans a few rows from where, without noticing him, she digs her precious potatoes.

So ends their first and last disagreement, in which more than Yori can imagine is put at risk and decided well. When the garden work is done, he hauls water and wood for the hearth, spends an hour reading The Book, and helps prepare their meal. But this is only a hiatus in the passions generated by his new condition. It takes time for a man, separated from life as he has known it, to learn tranquility. What he can't see in the middle of his trials is that he is not the person he was before meeting her, living with her, loving her. Tonight, however, no more is said on the subject and no self-conscious glances pass, not at least on Paola's side. If there are a few on his, she doesn't choose to notice.

By the next morning Yori is a bit less enclosed in himself and a bit more open to the world. During the ritual silence in the bower, he surveys the variety of growing things and reflects on his developing bond with the plants and the land. Without breaking the silence, he names it the New Earth. Before meeting Paola he was the only person in the colony to spend time exploring their environment with more than scientific interest. Still, he had *looked at* the landscape as classes of things, which was not the same thing as *seeing*.

She, too, had had to make this transition from *looking-at* to *seeing-as*. The botanist recognized what others passed over but still within the horizon of what was useful for research. Once survival depended on knowing the plants, she had to observe more closely, but even then, with an eye to the food supply. Having found the roots and berries and fruits and seeds that were edible, she might have stopped there, but she didn't stop. By seeing beyond the useful she went on to discover uniqueness everywhere.

The three-foot Joshua Tree for example. It was the only one she had, but she loved that tree. She caused Yori to see in its form the prophet with arms lifted to the sky, made him attend to the rounded crown and the rosettes of needle-shaped leaves at the ends of erect branches. She made him look closely at its egg-shaped flowers in creamy yellow and green and examine the large green and brown fruit, the capsules containing flat seeds that she collected to scatter at select spots in the hills. It was her idea that the planet, like the tree, needed nurturing as a baby is nurtured, and that if it were, this might eventually blossom into a green and fruitful land.

The point was to see the Joshua Tree as Paola saw it—as an instance of *seeing* itself, of attending to it as she did, letting it soak in until seeing became love.

Her friend Edward Hamilton had originally prepared for exploring the planet by studying the prehistoric populations of the great Ulro deserts, especially plants useful in human diets. After surviving the purge by Starship Command, the three friends had largely lived on that knowledge.

Shortly after Yori built his primitive irrigation system, Paola had begun to teach that lore to him. She had discovered a scrubby tree on the north side of the hills rather like the Pinyon pine native to the deserts of Ulro's western hemisphere. It didn't look like much but, using the lure of utility, she taught him how to harvest the cones and extract the nuts. They were edible raw or roasted and could be ground into meal for soup or into flour for bread.

Another desert plant, similar to the Agave family, had long roots for searching out subterranean water among the rocks. She had learned to bake its roots in a crude, dish-shaped hollow by adding hot rocks to the surface until Yori's oven improved the process. The result was a sweet and hearty substance that could be used in a variety of ways. Yori's favorite was as seasoning in the soup she made from the pine nut meal.

Thus under the benign influence of the Rule he began to be fascinated with how plants adapted to the extreme heat and aridity by sending down roots that reach deep into the fissures of the rocky planet. One especially delighted him. In the daytime it went dormant and the branches were covered with a waxy scale, but at night the scale blossomed with tiny leaves that Paola had found edible and worth the trouble of nocturnal harvesting. He became interested in the native plants she had domesticated in the garden as she had the native mushrooms in the cave. None of the plants had names, of course, so she borrowed the Ulro names closest to them: the Joshua Tree, the Saguaro, and the Creosote Bush. She learned that soaking the leaves of the Creosote Bush in water provided an effective antiseptic.

In learning to see the uniqueness of a plant, a rock, the cool spring that fed the underground cistern, the seismic shift that had made room for a canyon garden in the middle of a hill—these opened the way for seeing much more. As Yori concentrated on what was in front of him, the barrenness of the barren earth gradually morphed into the beautiful. Just when—or was it because?—banishment made him impatient with Paola's "arbitrary rules," he began to find what it meant to belong as he had never belonged anywhere, had never had a real *place* for belonging. After being placeless in starship and colony, he and Paola had stumbled separately into the Hills of Elrond, "come to earth," and begun to live-into the place that had been assigned to them by pure contingency.

15

"I'M GOING AWAY FOR a while."

Paola had never mentioned going farther than their occasional hikes in the hills. "You can care for things here. I'm going to search for traces of Edward and Shi Wa."

The suddenness of the idea and the decisive way she puts it leaves Yori to understand that it is mainly about him. She's giving him space to get his bearings in a topsy-turvy life. Being there day by day as he struggles with hopelessness makes sympathy tempting, but the nurturing heart-to-heart talk is the last thing he needs. Though he may feel it as further deprivation, at some level he knows it's not pity he needs, that "pity divides the soul." He needs to decide, and the unbending reality of his situation will bring him to a point of decision sooner if maternal care does not fix attention on his distress. He must find his way to loving the hand that fate has dealt him, and the sooner the better.

"But where will you go?" he protests. "You once told me there is nowhere to go from here. You could starve in that wilderness."

"You forget. I've been there before. Many times. I know the land for some miles north, and I know how to survive in the wild. If I don't find my friends, I may find some trace of their fate, and that will be a comfort."

"Will you come back?"

"My work is here." Unnecessary to add that *he* is her work and what his life comes to will also be what hers will have come to. And so, without further comment, without advice or instructions, she makes her simple preparations and leaves the following morning before he wakes.

His first sensation on waking is the resounding emptiness of the cave. The void is palpable. He can feel it on his skin and in the hollow of his chest as it returns a silent echo of the emptiness of his life. Having learned to set the self aside enough to let his senses saturate the surrounding space, he can feel the presence or absence of another. And the vacuum grows. The missing dark voice that melds with these stones leaves them cold and bare and menacing. The joyful beam of light from the opening at the top of the vault appears only in eerie shadows fluttering on the walls. As these and other facets of Paola's absence come over him with a stab of physical pain, he wants nothing so much as to get out of the cave and into the light.

He eats no breakfast. He does not go to the bower for the morning silence. He does not plan his day so that it will have been well-spent. From the moment he bypasses ritual meditation in the bower, the day begins to unravel. Restlessly moving from one place to another, from the Chamber of the Hearth to the cistern to the gardens and back again, he decides to avoid the underground altogether by going on a hike.

The intensity of morning light along the edges of the plain is punctuated only by patches of sickly yellow weeds that accentuate his emptiness. Trudging along in the crushing heat, going nowhere in particular, brings on the vertigo of negative freedom, *freedom from*. For a restless while, he loiters in their favorite places, even tries to escape the blankness before him by reading. That pretense also fails. Finding no consolation for the interminable hours of solitude, he repeats the distractions over again and returns just at sunset to the rock bower at the edge of the plateau, their place of peace that Paola has recently begun calling their "temple."

When he asked why, she made another of the oracular remarks that lately annoyed him as nonsense. "Because," she said, "it binds earth to the sky and us to both. I don't know how it happens, but when we consider ideals and possibilities—even the names on our wall—they seem oriented vertically, toward the sky."

Well, let her call this abandoned spot by whatever name she likes, there is no peace here today. The great red disc hanging in the sky is the mouth of a furnace whose flaming beams paint the brown earth red before fading eventually into the dull rusty-grey of evening. When finally he returns to the Chamber of the Hearth, he encourages himself with the idea that there is freedom in Paola's absence. Doesn't he deserve a vacation from the tyranny of the Rule? Until her return he will do exactly what he likes when he likes.

And so time drags immeasurably through day after livelong day of a week where nothing is decided and nothing is done. There is only the nothing and growing dissatisfaction with himself and with the inescapable earth. He can have the cool, empty darkness underground or the scalding empty brightness of the hills, but he has lost his *place* and its various locations. He drifts into the pattern of spending the night hours in the cool outside air and the days in the cave sleeping.

The Chamber of the Hearth becomes more cluttered than might be thought possible—so large the space, so few the possessions. There are no clean utensils for eating, no fresh water in the urn, and no brush for the fire. He neglects the garden so that the delicate young plants begin to wither. He neglects to harvest what's ready to eat and within days runs short of food. For the first time in his life he neglects to keep himself and his clothes clean. Sometimes at night he sits in a state of feverish distraction, staring at the stupefying glitter of stars, and harangues the universe for the Governor's injustice and for Paola's abandoning him. It's one of those points at which a perfectly sane person may prefer to escape a tormented consciousness by sinking into madness until he dies a painless death by eating and drinking nothing.

And yet, sometimes when a disease is at its worst, the cure is nearest. One afternoon in the second week, he awakes hungry and in a different mood, as though the bare vitality of youth has pulled him back from the brink. He gets up and takes a torch to light his way through the tunnel to the garden in search of food. Back in the cave he works for hours restoring domestic order to a troubled mind. By torchlight he bathes at the cistern and cleans all his clothes. Into the little channel they call their aqueduct he restores the stream of water by which the garden lives, and when the first beam of sunlight falls on the hearthstone, he takes up The Book and retires to the garden bower. Instead of reading, he assumes the lotus position, carefully folds his hands, and lets all the cares of a troubled mind flow away up the canyon and beyond into uncharted wilderness.

The restoration of the Rule brings a clarity with results hard to put into few words. The sense of limitlessness, passed through like a dark night of un-relation, opens the idea of what must have led Paola to the Rule of the Hearth in the first place. Not particular rules since there are none, except the ones projected by his resentment. Rule is governance itself. What saved Paola's days and years from anarchy but necessity and the salutary rituals of the day? Wouldn't she, confined to solitude, sooner or later have gone mad? What but the pure forms of the days provided her life and world rather than chaos and madness? Without form, not even the form of chaos, only the void.

From this moment of clarity the silent periods of bringing himself into tune with the contingency of things amount to much more than a planning session for tasks to be performed. Each day expands before him as a gift, and each act arises as a decision freely made. From then on he eats his morning meal at the hearthstone, observes the silence in the arbor, waters the plants and gathers the brush, with the growing satisfaction of being responsive *to* and responsible *for* the day.

Thereafter he devotes some days to hiking more deeply into the hills, venturing farther north than ever before into the peaks where he can scan the distance, hoping for a glimpse of Paola returning. In late afternoon he takes her copy of the *Iliad* to the hilltop overlooking the plateau and spends the last hour of light reliving the Trojan War.

Recently the two of them have been reading it aloud together and gotten as far as the twelfth book. In school he had read it only as the story of the warring Achaeans and Trojans, but during Paola's solitary years Homer and *Starship Galatea* were her only companions so she had soaked in both. But why, he wonders, would she have chosen the *Iliad* to bring down to the planet in the first place? Later, the solitary years were nihilism incarnate: abandoned, marooned without hope, living under a death sentence. She must have felt kinship with those Greeks, but she could not have foreseen all that.

Anyway, her *Iliad* was not his *Iliad*. When they spoke of it, she seemed to be talking about a book he had never read. All about the dull Olympian gods who cannot die but pass their time making sport of mortals except when they are bribed with the smell of burning flesh and wine poured on the ground. The superstition of it is just enough to arouse curiosity. How can she care more about the imaginary beings than about the mortals? Now he tries to read it in her perverse way, always asking how an intelligent person, who doesn't believe that gods exist, can take these dead gods seriously.

Each afternoon as he resumes the reading he begins to feel, distantly, that the tale coincides with his own situation: cast up from the ocean sea of cosmic space onto a barren rock, confronting a blank future without a battle brotherhood for solace. And yet isn't he, too, facing the unknown, tempted by whispers from inaccessible dimensions? Gods or not, faced with complete uncertainty, he begins to welcome the idea that to a receptive spirit the heavens may not be blank and alien to hope. The empty heavens are filled with contingencies that matter to him. And so he goes on reading avidly but reading differently.

As often as not he sits on into the evening trying to hear what in her strangely impersonal way Paola might say about the part he has just read. What she had actually said once when challenged was that the epic had saved her! At the time they were sitting here in her "temple," his lookout. The cap of dark hair turned slowly toward him as, from beneath the heavy black brows, the eyes glowed from within as they often did when she was about to say something important. At first all she said was, "If we don't respond to what the names of these in-existent gods invoke, we will lose our way and not know ourselves."

Then she had taken the book from his hand and opened it to a single passage. It was where Helen of Troy blames Aphrodite for stealing her from Menelaus and dragging her off to Troy to marry Paris. She read the lines then asked, "Who is Aphrodite?"

Now in her absence he gets a first glimpse of what he had missed at the time. At the time all he could think to say was, "Aphrodite is the goddess of love. She stole the most beautiful woman in the world from Menelaus, king of Sparta, and gave her to Paris as a bribe for him to judge her, Aphrodite, fairer than Hera or Athena. The Trojan War is about getting her back."

Paola repeated, "Who is Aphrodite?"

"A personification of erotic love."

She said nothing.

Feeling ignorant and exposed, he tried again. "The gods are anthropomorphic. So when the Greeks are mystified by the power of sexual attraction, they project a human image and make it responsible. Just as Zeus and Poseidon and Hades are ways of explaining the sky and sea and earth in a prescientific world. Aphrodite is such a figure of psychic forces."

Paola mused for a few moments. "That's all very quaint and scientific. And completely anachronistic. You're tripped up—as logic usually is—by the question of existence." She went on to explain how knowledge, beginning to end, is concerned with what exists. "But search your experience closely, and you will find that you can't consistently believe that the 'real' is limited to what exists. I don't mean mystical experiences or hidden realities, but dimensions of ourselves that we cut off because, since we don't see them or feel them, we pass them by and don't give them names."

In a speech of greater length and greater passion than any he could remember, she led him to consider that aspiration has no limit, that desire is insatiable, that imagination is infinite. "All the great adventures and discoveries and works of art show that we are open to the infinite. For them, enough is never enough. Nothing less that the inconceivable and unpossessable *all* will satisfy."

To Yori's ear she spoke like one inspired by the dead gods, but that, he knew, was also superstition.

"The *all* isn't a *thing*. It doesn't exist. It more-than-exists. We may say it's the surplus that in-exists and, recognize it or not, it matters absolutely to us in every moment."

Now, alone, Yori remembers that he hadn't understood a word of this, though he was capable of one remark that fit. "You mean, I suppose, the name Aphrodite is not a sign for the sensations of love or for the instinct to breed."

"True." She answered. "Aphrodite is a place-holder for the large field of erotic relations—creative and destructive—that affect us. Also the name relates the erotic to other fields that bear the names of other gods. So when we hold to the names, we maintain relations with these shifting fields of experience. And that makes our world intelligible."

"So"—he had tried to take it a step further—"then doesn't Aphrodite exist in my mind?"

"No. The gods don't exist anywhere. Yet they come toward us as figures or images of the boundless. They give themselves and we receive them, if we will, in proportion to our capacity."

He had made every effort at the time not to quibble about anthropomorphism and the status of the imaginary. Just to be tolerant toward her strange understanding or her delusion. At that juncture all he could think to ask was, "How did the *Iliad* save you?"

"All that was left to me was a hostile and forbidden colony, an empty landscape, and the void beyond. Homer gave me images and names that let me live with gratitude and hope. You'll learn that gratitude doesn't ask about the existence of what it receives. It accepts what is given—so much water or so much wine as the urn will hold."

This conversation, remembered in Paola's absence, brings him closer to her and makes him more receptive to her ideas than if she had been sitting beside him. And so on subsequent evenings he spends still longer hours in their temple surveying all things from the perspective of a tiny space station.

In the third week he sits in the cool air listening for a while to the faint pulsating hum of the slumbering cell of life sprawled on the desert floor in the distance. After contemplating his banishment in a new and more charitable mood, he looks up and scans the heavens with no idea in mind. Looks once. Then scans more carefully and catches his breath. It's gone! The familiar dot of light in its orbit—it has vanished!

He jumps to his feet so quickly that he raps his head sharply enough against the rock above to daze him, yet barely notices. In the moment before reflection, panic seizes him. How can the erasure of one barely existent point in the panoply of the heavens empty the universe and strike being itself with nothingness? The effect may be imagined like this: One casually looks up for a peaceful evening star and finds a gaping black hole where the sun and the stars have been swallowed up, leaving only this lone rock behind.

"So it has happened!" he cries aloud, recovering his balance. The absence and the sense of further abandonment don't pass quickly. It forces a different state of mind. It's one thing to be banished by a sovereign authority as he and Paola are, excluded yet belonging, belonging more intensely for being excluded. Quite another to be deserted as the colonists too will come to feel deserted by the mother ship. Few down in the colonial bubble will have realized that the departure was imminent, and fewer still will have known exactly when it was to happen. Those who did know, being occupied with public business, will have been too busy to dwell on the loss.

In the wake of his own crisis, the departure of the Galatea is like the end of a novel. It invites him to contemplate the horizon of human possibilities, remembrance and anticipation:

archeology and teleology contracted into a present moment of vision. So here I sit on a lone hillside gazing "down the vast edges drear And naked shingles of the world," mourning an indifferent cosmos to which I don't belong and the death of a humanity to which I can't return.

PART II
THE CITY

The listener who listens in the snow
And, nothing himself, beholds
Nothing that is not there and the nothing that is.

—Wallace Stevens, "The Snow Man"

16

TIME PASSED, IF TIME can pass. A decade in all. As measured by the chronological conventions of Ulro still used on the starship and in the colony. Ten years since Yori Kashimoto's banishment, but in the hills of the new earth time runs differently. For Yori and Paola it is more like a wormhole than an arrow shot from a bow. Imagine entering one of those old aquifers under the hills, wandering around for an immeasurable period, then emerging at any random point on the planet surface to find that the surface and underground occupied different dimensions. Life in the hills of the new earth shows human times as just so discontinuous. Is it only psychology when Yori, now twenty-seven, sits on a hill looking across the plain at that colony while sharing closer proximity to Achilles at Troy or to the absent Paola or the long-departed starship? Is the time of creation different from the linear time of causes?

Since like all fictions this one sinks or swims on an understanding of truth, let's start again at the same point: A decade earlier Paola had gone north without finding her friends Edward Hamilton and Kwan Shi Wa. What she had found here and there were the signs they had always used to mark their paths, but the distances had been too great to follow the path to its end. A decade later, she announces that she's going to try again. This time, Yori being fully initiated to life in the caves, she is gone longer. He has no way of knowing where she is or when, if ever, she may return.

She does return and finds him working in the garden. By way of salutation, as though after an absence of only an hour, she says, "I will tell you about the trip later. First you must come with me. You'll be surprised." And she leads the way upward through the caves to the Cavern of Names.

His eyes fall first on an old man sitting on the same stone table where he had first seen her. It's the Governor! His appearance there is nearly as mysterious as hers had once been. Thus the expansive moment includes Yori's first meeting with her and his last meeting with the Governor. Wasn't each just a moment ago? Obviously this meeting is by plan, arranged between the guardian of the law and the outlaw, presumed dead for more than twenty-five years and long forgotten.

Instead of trying to account for the situation before him—why the Governor should turn up here, what secret communications have passed between the two, why Paola has kept him in the dark, why he should be the central figure in the mystery—he simply waits for one or the other to speak. There is time enough for wonder all round as he watches the Governor taking his measure to see who has replaced the boy he once banished, as Paola watches who knows what?

The old man whom he had expected never to see again, sitting erect on the rock openly studying him, appears shrunken and worn by the years. In the dim light the features are indistinct except for white stringy hair that falls around a time-ridden face. Were it not for the resonance of the hard walls, the raspy voice when he speaks would be swallowed up by the cavern. Paola's voice is always proportional to its space and conveys the luxurious expanse of the unique event. Not so the Governor's. In voice and manner he is out of tune with the place. Even perched on a subterranean rock he is busy. His object seems to be to answer all questions in one minute less than no time at all: more information about Akira's death; the discovery that there were survivors and his contact with Paola; what he had learned from her about Yori; and why the secrecy.

The short of it is that some months ago he had sent Véronique Dumas on a covert mission to track Yori down in the hills. That led to the discovery of Paola and, according to subsequent instructions, to the first contact between the two women. Eventually Paola had been invited to meet him at the colony and, mystery on top of mystery, the two had gone north together by land rover to find Shi Wa and Edward. The Governor had made peace between the three renegades and the colony, but the primary purpose had always been to find Yori. This meeting is the result.

The Governor speaks as he moves, like a man who is making his last arrangements and has no time for delicate feelings or personal concerns. "You may never have known me by name. My name is Talib Nasser . . ."

"Aw," Yori muttered involuntarily.

". . . First mate of Starship Galatea. But all that can wait. The point is, I am dying and I must appoint a successor. That means choosing the right person where there is nothing to measure by." The old man stops to catch his breath and sits still for a moment, wheezing.

"A ruler," he continues, "must be able to hear the mute summons of an unknown destiny when it raps at the door. The right person will be willing to wait at this and all other doors. But waiting takes more courage than rushing in to make the world shape up."

Again he pauses. The frail body, nearly concealed in the deep shadows of the cave, seems to tremble under the necessity of delivering a last message or a plea. "The ruler must know how to wait until the practical choice confronts him—even if it never does—without regard to anything but the terrible inventive moment. What's done then is done for eternity."

Governor Nasser stops as though the passion of the speech has exhausted him. Neither of the others speaks, and Yori hardly moves. He's astonished as much by the figure in front of him as by the words. It may be the exertion of his journey north, but nothing seems to remain of the man he had known ten years earlier. The imposing presence, the detached intelligence, the subtle exchanges of conversation—all gone. This man seems to be no more than a messenger of destiny who doesn't ask—or even look—for a response. Not daring to respond to such a figure of desperation, Yori waits for a signal of what's to happen next.

When the Governor has grown calm, he gestures for Paola to help him off the rock and lingers a moment as though uncertain of a decision forced on him by age and illness. The now stooped body turns toward Yori. "I'm saying things that you won't understand now. Never mind that." A trembling hand waves the matter aside. "I'm leaving the words in this chamber. They will teach you."

He drops his head for a moment and doesn't move. Then looks up and adds as though it's a practical detail, "I intend to appoint you Governor. You are to return to the colony the day after tomorrow and take up residence in Government House. You will have one week to look about you. Then you will begin shadowing me in all I do until I think you're ready or until I die."

Yori is stunned by incomprehension. And Paola? Well, Paola is Paola, and the two accompany him across the chamber toward the little shaft of daylight. Halfway across, he stops before the wall of names and passes his eyes over the dim surface. Then, turning slowly to face Yori, he speaks again as though from years of premeditation. "I hope you have learned the lesson of time and eternity. A city will need a ruler who acts for something greater than a few people whimpering about their interests and their comforts. It's not about them and it's not about you or me." He gestures irrelevantly toward the wall of names. "Study this wall. It will show you how history works. I'm told it's your father's legacy." Then he turns his back and hobbles out of the cave, leaving Yori and Paola standing before the wall hearing the echo of his inscrutable pronouncements.

Thus it happened that in the most consequential interview of his life Yori did not speak a word and understood less. Since neither Paola nor he is inclined to dilute such moments with inquisitive chatter, nothing more is said. Like two monastics passing along their ancient cloister close to the wall in silence, they return to the Chamber of the Hearth and make their meal as if their world hadn't just changed forever. As they eat together Yori tries to adjust himself to the advent of an unknown vocation for which he has been blindly preparing for years. Even now it lies open before him as little more than an empty figure. When the meal is over, the two settle down with the fire between and begin filling in gaps that will keep them talking late into the night, for all the next day, and until his departure for the colony on the third day.

He begins it all with the remark, "So you are restored to human company and to citizenship, whatever that can mean in the absence of a city. How long have you known?"

Her reply is long and thoughtful. "Restoration is a subject that can wait. You need to hear about that in detail. I have known for several weeks. It was essential that you know nothing about what was going on. The real issue all along has been the welfare of the colony, not us. It will have surprised you to learn that Véronique Dumas was the emissary in everything. It was she who told me the results of the Governor's inquiry into the death of your father.

"Apparently Claudio, *my* father, received a cryptic signal from Akira at the last moment—his last act—making the situation clear. In case you still have doubts about his taking your question seriously, know that the Governor calls it 'the execution.' There is some evidence that members of the Council of Elders on the ship may have suspected foul play at the time, but it's unclear whether Claudio told them about the message. My guess is that he did not because our fathers had always believed that the future of humanity was at stake in their acts, and that left no room for settling scores. From the beginning the purpose that inspired the mission was to redeem the follies of Ulro."

She gives Yori a curious, searching look. "Interesting that the Governor trusted all this to Véronique. They are two people I look forward to knowing better. She's an extraordinary woman. He appears to have surrounded himself with such trustworthy people. We—Véronique and I—have become friends." She paused again for punctuation. "I wonder if you know that she's still in love with you."

To this he makes no response. What can he say? Not something disingenuous like, "It has been a decade since we met and may both have changed beyond recognition." Disingenuous because Paola would know that love—even one-sided love—is eternal, that however great the change, they would recognize each other as being almost the one remembered.

If Yori had had a ready answer, what might Paola have thought? That she had lost him and her work was done? Isn't that after all what, on her side, these events came to? Not that it would have banished her love. That would always remain undiminished.

Whatever her reflections at that moment, she continues with what is, for her, an oddly rambling account that might, to a person more disinterested, betray feelings she doesn't intend to reveal. "Governor Nasser asked to see me only after all that preparation, but I was not told why or why you were not to know. I met him for the first time at the beginning of the trip north. He had me picked up in one of their overland vehicles and taken to the colony. A long discussion began with a formal apology for the past, but the real subject was you. He wanted to know everything. Véronique had prepared the way by telling him about me, but being limited by her commission, she had asked very little about you.

"You can see how it was: The Governor had to know whether he could trust me in order to learn what he wanted to know about you. In fact he wanted—and over several days of conversation he got—an exhaustive account of your development from our first meeting to the present. Then he went with me to look for Shi Wa and Edward. One of the landing craft left behind by the Galatea had spotted traces in the mountains some two hundred miles due north. We found them easily enough, and they received the same apology. Then they were invited to return to the colony as his guests whenever they chose."

Yori interrupts, "I can't figure him out . . . Nasser. He did call himself Nasser?"

She shakes her head.

"That name ought to mean something, but I can't think what." He considers the mystery for another moment before continuing. "The last time he saw me I was a troublesome boy whom he had to send away for the welfare of the colony. He didn't want to. I saw that much. Something I didn't see at the time was his uneasiness that I might choose to return to the ship. He did what he had to do. Now this. I wonder if he's got it right. Is this a good thing?"

"That's not yours to decide. He knows the colony must go somewhere he can't take it even if he lives. He has always known—you told him the first time you met—that it had to become a city. As colonial governor he has ensured security, public order, the material welfare of the people. But he knows that the colony has become moribund, that its spirit is in decline. What he said about the ruler standing at the threshold, indifferent to good or evil, ready to act without

156

calculating the consequences—he knows those are things he can't do, but he saw the capacity in you long ago. He has become a good man with the instincts of an old-fashioned moralist who wants to do good. That's his limitation."

Yori finds one implication amusing. "So I'm chosen because a ruler must be a monster!"

"Must be *willing* to be. Or willing to *appear* to be. You were a bit of a monster in school. Just the right sort with your questions about technology and freedom and what the whole venture had been for."

"I had only begun to see that an academy should be a place where people search further than they can see. With the Galatea leaving, it was the wrong moment. All I wanted in those days was to know how to turn the life-support system into a city. On that I have made no progress."

"But you see the task differently. You will have to make people uncomfortably free when they prefer to be comfortably secure. One can't govern and be a moralist or a sentimentalist. It's not about being loved or respected. In time you'll either learn that or you'll fail. If you fail, all fail. But you know all that."

Yori considers those remarks for some time then changes the subject. "What did he mean about the wall, the names? Why would he call it my inheritance?"

"I don't know how much he meant, but we both know what he *should* have meant. It has to do with the function of names that was once mysterious to both of us. Above all others a governor must learn the lesson of the eternal names." She stops as though not intending to enter on a complicated topic so late in the night.

"Well?" He says with a smile, no longer with the eager ignorance of old. "Aren't you going to tell me what I above all others must never forget?"

"Not tonight. You have honored the names on Akira's wall for years and you won't forget. The ruler must live in the company of the Eternals."

17

So THE NAME YORI Kashimoto was restored to the register of citizens in the small colony on planet 2314, though who exactly it was who had returned from exile remained to be seen, by himself as much as by others. There was no public announcement, and few noticed. To the few who did, it was as surprising as his banishment had been. The Governor wanted his return to be as inconspicuous as possible, and the only public statement, distributed the day before his arrival, was on a quite different subject. It was about "new historical information" on the "unfortunate accident" that had resulted in the death of the first landing party.

In any event, twenty-five years on and a decade after the departure of the starship, the news made little stir among people who habitually thought only of the present. The interesting feature of the report was an account of the three survivors: Paola Rucai, Kwan Shi Wa, and Edward Hamilton. Their discovery, their history, and their return to the colony overshadowed the detail about former academy student Yori Kashimoto.

When Yori arrives, he is shown to an apartment in the Guest Quarters just behind Government House, once used by official visitors from the Galatea. He recognizes everything in the small, commodious space that his senses have forgotten. Forgotten the unchanging light against smooth, monochromatic industrial walls, the unnecessary artifices of form-fitted chairs and soft beds to which he would much prefer a rock, and the bare table on spindly legs where he finds a formal invitation to call on the Governor at 15:00 hours.

The hour arrives, and he is received without ceremony. By a silent gesture he is invited to take a seat in the small area on the side of the room not dominated by banks of electronic monitors. The Governor lingers a moment to finish something on the desk and gives Yori time to study the face as he remembers having done on his first summons here. The face behind the desk is crosshatched now by age, by the spent passions of youthful ambition, by anxiety, disappointment, and physical pain. No marks of joy.

The figure is recognizable as the man he had once known but not as the one in the Chamber of Names who might have been the high priest of some mystery cult. At that time he had been weak and ill, worn by the long journey north, and that raises a further question: Why had he undertaken the task in person when he might have sent others to establish contact with Shi Wa and Edward, even had them brought to the colony? Now he appears stronger—though compared to a decade earlier, reduced in character. The chief bureaucrat of a small outpost on the frontier of nowhere.

Holding himself nearly erect but moving with shuffling feet, he brings a paper from the desk. "First, here is your schedule. I'm giving a small party in your honor tonight. A chance for you to see your old friends and classmates and one or two others. Remember you are only a guest. You have no plans. We want to rouse no curiosity." This speech conveys the sense that they are only expediting a duty as efficiently as may be.

Without punctuation, he continues, "As your month unfolds, we will decide how to manage further information. Behind the appearance of nothing happening, events will move quickly. In the first week your only official appointment will be the routine meeting of the Council. That's familiar territory since you used to attend as a student observer. This time you will be there as my guest for old time's sake. I may or may not announce that I am taking advantage of your presence as an outside-insider to provide a fresh perspective on general conditions. That will go as the wind blows, all more or less as it used to be when you were a troublesome student." He manages a somber grin. "The object is to open doors and forestall curiosity."

Then comes the point: "What you will really do at the meeting is take the temperature of the group. As for the survey of conditions, I don't think you'll find much to report. The colony is a well-oiled machine. But we will meet regularly to discuss your observations. Meanwhile, this first week you are to do nothing. Look around, set your nose to the wind, listen to the pitch of voices in the public spaces, pick up the tone of the place. I don't have to tell you how much more important that is than the facts of routine operations."

This exchange in which no response is expected or offered remains at the level of the relevant facts and is even more curt than the hurried speech in the cave. Given the reason for his restoration, Yori hardly knows what to make of it all. Cautiously he risks a question about the public response to the Galatea's departure years ago and the effects since.

The Governor throws him a glance as though the question for some reason troubles him. He answers as briefly as possible, too briefly by half. "It doesn't seem to have mattered much. Nobody mentions it now. Anyway, all people really ever saw were the shuttles going back and forth. Once they stopped running, the starship began slipping from memory. Out of sight, out of mind."

Yori risks no further remark and is dismissed until the evening. Back in his quarters, he is free to speculate on this strange interview. Maybe the Governor is seriously ill and running a race against the clock? Perhaps he resents having to surrender his position, a bit jealous of the hungry generation closing on him from behind? But these speculations, leading nowhere, are quickly abandoned.

The reception takes place in a nondescript room designed—if there was any design—for multi-purposes. It has no character at all. The walls, floor, and ceiling—in a color too neutral to have color—are intended to look as little like themselves as possible. Turned upside down the space would appear unchanged. Which, no doubt, was the point. The furnishings, like the room, accommodate equally everything or nothing. Lightweight and portable, artificial—if the word still means anything—stackable, presumably disposable. The monotony is relieved only by two bare windows, opening onto an unexceptional pathway along the outer wall of Government House.

The reception is a bit like a class reunion among people whom Yori scarcely knows and who don't know him at all. To understand the shock to his senses as he enters and faces this blur of people, one must compare it to how he has lived. Until a couple of day ago he had seen only one other person in years. Now he walks into a narrow room filled with bodies that, even standing still, seem in aimless motion and all talking at once. In his world bodily movement is for integrated domestic activities and hikes in wide open spaces under the dome of the heavens. For him conversation is speech limited to what is worth saying about things that matter, but in this din of voices "conversation" is reduced to simultaneous monologues in which the point is to add decibels without stopping to hear. Under the oppressively low ceiling there may be room for squandering idle words but no space left over for the meaning of words. The prodigal son returns to find that banishment was freedom and restoration is a life sentence to a prison that he will also be expected to manage.

As soon as the Governor finishes his short speech, Lars Hanssen, taller and sturdier in build, flings his arms around Yori with the enthusiasm of boyhood friendship long interrupted. Leaning aggressively forward he takes his arm and ushers him from person to person as though showing him off and gaining some vague distinction by his eager authority.

One person Yori is especially happy to see is his old teacher, now middle-aged, wider in girth and balding on top. The man's slightly discontented face causes Yori to realize that he, the teacher, is the only person in the room who is not a colony administrator. Not another person from the Academy! In contrast to the brief, directionless exchanges with others, this man shows some curiosity about life in the wilderness, how he survived, what he did with all those years. This is the person in the colony who had understood the cast of Yori's mind in his student days, hence the one—Véronique perhaps excepted—who might now be most interested to know who he has become. Yet even his questions are purely factual. There are none about what he has thought, how his ideas may have changed, what he has learned about the wilderness itself.

Most people present are by now department heads and members of the Corps of Governors. The only classmates missing are two or three who had chosen to return to the Galatea. The Governor greets each person and, after chatting briefly, disappears, and the gathering settles into a mood that corresponds to its environment.

The only real topic of interest is colony business. Not at all unfriendly toward Yori but largely indifferent to his adventures or the reasons for his return. And that might be thought odd, given his wider experience of their planetary environment. But the situation is not uncomfortable for him even marooned as a spectator or an eavesdropper. At least it saves the effort of talking when he has so much to conceal. So he spends the time observing the patterns of interest, the tone of relationships, and the lack of concern with everything except bureaucratic chores.

Under the Governor's charge to "pick up the tone of the place," he is attentive to the disposition of the administrators, who remain as intelligent and energetic as they ever were. But the youthful enthusiasm of their student days has settled into the nearsightedness of practice. The old spirit of inquiry has subsided, and he wonders what that might eventually entail for political life.

He remembers the day when most of them first arrived at the colony together. Then the mood was completely different. They, especially he and Lars, could barely contain their excitement. For a week they rushed up and down exploring every building on every path, poking their heads into every dark corner with a sense of adventure that left them dizzy with expectation.

Now the spirit is neutral, colorless. Understandable perhaps, but the old quickness has also vanished along with the play of imagination. Unless it is he who is going slowly blind, a stultifying literalism has settled in as past and future drop away and life shrinks to pure presence. Once these same people, meeting an outcast who had lived ten years in their unknown land, would have been filled with curiosity. But now? If he were Marco Polo returned from the East, would there be any questions? Not tonight.

Somewhere along the way one person does ask why he is the Governor's guest. He stares for a moment at the idea before replying with a smile, "I don't really know. I guess since he banished me, it was up to him to reinstate me. It's very kind of him." Increasingly as the evening passes, he feels that a decade of living in an incubator has caused a diminution of perception. Unless he has gained one eye too many?

However, tonight there is an advantage. Accustomed as he is to silence and the ascetic rule, if Yori were bombarded with insistent questions, it would be hard to adjust and fit the unimaginable to the ordinary. Initiation into a new life and a new identity takes years.

Meanwhile his thoughts drift off to a more pleasant and more urgent question: Where is the face Paola had prepared him to meet? Where is Véronique? On entering he had scanned the group looking for her and felt a pang of disappointment. By an act of will he set the idea aside, though having once let himself think of her, she remains more present in her absence than the others in the room. So when he suddenly sees her slip in unobtrusively, he feels a thrill. In fact she had been delayed in her department office, though one who didn't know better might be forgiven for suspecting that it was to give him time to miss her. Their eyes meet across the room and her face opens in a broad smile. As she advances toward him, he realizes that hers is the first welcoming face he has encountered since leaving the caves.

What could he have been thinking when he speculated that they might not know one another? The same sensitive face and searching blue eyes, the same blond hair pulled back in a ponytail above her shoulders. The teenage animation may have calmed a bit, but the passion still hovers just out of sight behind a quieter face and a more thoughtful manner.

She approaches, they chat briefly, then as inconspicuously as two who have been together every day for years, they blend into the group. Before long and as though she had arrived at the end of the evening by design, the breeze subsides in the sails of the party and people begin to drift away.

18

WHEN THE GOVERNOR'S GUESTS have cleared the reception room, Véronique and Lars are left alone with Yori. Almost immediately Lars' friend Sandra Mohr arrives. Not being a member of the administrative elite, she had not been included in the invitation, but Lars, impatient to know all, had arranged for the four to have a good talk together.

Sandra had been in the colony only a short time when Yori was banished so they were only slightly acquainted, but now they all settle comfortably together by pulling chairs up to a table where they begin the slow process of stitching their lives back together.

It turns out that Lars has been more observant than may have appeared. And Véronique? Given her secret relations with the Governor and Paola, who can tell what she may be seeing? Exactly how they've been reading Yori's situation is even less clear, but their impressions precipitate a quiet drama that will play through the remainder of the evening without resolution.

Lars sits in a chair spreading his body out, legs apart, commandeering the space of the room, and when he speaks, the tone is little short of interrogation. "I see how little you're volunteering about how you lived out there in the wilderness. What have you learned in all these years?"

Yori chooses his tone and his limits carefully. "I learned to work. To be self-sustaining. I learned how to grow food, how to build a primitive irrigation system, how to cook. Most of all how to see the glory of this planet." He ends enigmatically, "It teaches you to care."

Sandra interrupts, "I like that. Tell us more. What was a typical day like?"

Lars intervenes sardonically, "Yes. 'Glory of the planet.' That's good to hear. That's more rationalizing in one breath than I remember having heard before."

It's not provocation but there is anxiety enough in it to make more than one person wonder if he feels some threat to himself in the return of the wanderer.

As Lars appears to hear only the empty shell of words spoken, Yori wonders if it's deliberate or if the habit of attending to what words actually say has atrophied. Even the habits of concentration? Examining Lars closely, he half suspects that his old friend, though mellowed and matured by responsibility, may be looking for ways to resurrect their earlier differences. He is now second in command in the Department of Technical Services and newly appointed as a member of the Corps of Governors. Yet as the sharper physical lines of youth have grown rounder, Lars hasn't acquired the aspect of a man who is satisfied with his achievements or even intent on his prospects.

In fact a slow study of his face reveals something troubling. In place of the old energy that could turn defiant in a moment, he seems diminished in spirit, seasoned more by fatigue than by wisdom. The old belligerence may have died away, but the intensity is also gone and, with it, the sharp attention he used to give to things. When words pass him by unnoticed, it's as if they aren't worth the effort. As though in finding his place he has lost interest in the process or, worse, in leaving wonder behind, he has forgotten how to question. Yet some nameless anxiety seems still to be nibbling.

Lars rallies and gives another push. "Then you have outgrown your preference for abstractions over realities?" Still a bit of the diplomat, touching lightly on the old sore spots as though testing to see who Yori has become or at least what the present situation might mean for himself.

Yori settles for the simplest response. "Abstractions perhaps. Not complexity I hope."

The context for this response is approximately this: When conversation still meant living together and "keeping company," people knew how to listen for more than their own echo. Then there was "conversation" beyond words in shared explorations of a shared world. Two of these four are such people still. It's why he, having absorbed Paola's "Zen consciousness," can read the crosscurrents in this little quartet through Véronique's nerve ends as though she listens from a fifth dimension in the room. He watches her watching Lars circle him without being seen to move and watching him evade the hunt. And he sees her attention to Sandra's efforts to draw him out on his experience in the wilds, for Sandra also has those nurturing, maternal depths. But he doesn't need Véronique's mediation to detect Sandra's finger on Lars' pulse, monitoring his anxiety as the two of them spar.

Yet most of all Véronique. She is now Chief of Biological Research, highly trusted by the Governor, and a member of the Council. But there's much more. Even now, chatting informally with friends, there is something extraordinary behind what others may see as her faraway distracted look. Is it of her own doing or has she begun to pick up from Paola the "spherical" sensitivity to everything in her vicinity?

Either way, knowing whatever she may know about him from Paola and from the Governor, the changes in him do not surprise her, and her simple being-there enlivens the monotonous dead room, suffusing it with spirit and light. It is clear why the Governor would have trusted this woman with a confidential plan to investigate his possible successor.

The whole situation opens a range of secrets between them that are the more provocative in being intended by no one. Neither has any idea what the other actually knows. Yori's current knowledge of her is limited to two things: that she met Paola on several occasions under the Governor's instructions and that, according to Paola, she is still in love. Otherwise, he has no more idea what she may know about him than she has of what he knows about her. With so much ignorance to go around, he protects himself by putting all memory of their past out of mind even as he finds it hard not to look for the traces of love.

Sandra remains inquisitive about his primitive life. "I wish you would back up and tell about all those things you did for yourself. You mentioned digging in the earth for food and cooking for yourself and living in a cave. You must have spent much of the day underground out of the heat. It sounds dreadful."

He replies, "It wasn't so bad. Not at all a random life. The time was shaped by a deliberate ordering of every day."

At this point an involuntarily arched eyebrow shows him that he has made a mistake and let Véronique see more than he intended. The mistake was nothing more than the past tense—as though all *that* life is now over and done. It has shown her something she hadn't known before, that he may not be a guest after all, but back to stay. He can't know exactly what she has understood, but for whatever reason the fresh glow in her eye looks very much like imagination enlivened by new possibilities.

At least something of the sort lingers in the air between these two who listen to *"nothing that is not there and the nothing that is."* When an involuntary look passes between them as though they understand each other, he stares at the idea long enough to wonder if she may have grasped the Governor's whole plan. As there is no going back, he accepts the point and lays it aside, except for one thing. Whatever she has just learned, it obviously pleases her in ways that have little to do with the colony.

When Yori says no more about life in the hills, Lars asks, in a friendlier mode, "Did the primitive life help you get over your technophobia? Remember how we used to argue about all that? You seemed to think that civilization went into decline with the invention of the wheel."

The remark is light and seems to harbor no ulterior motive, but Yori, having taken the measure of the divergent experience, feels no obligation to connect with it or to imitate the banter. Instead he asks with startling abruptness, "What was it like when the Galatea left?"

Lars replies, "There was no fanfare. Once people found out about it, it was talked about for a few days. Then it all died down and was forgotten. Not like the rising of the P2314 for the hungry eyes on the Galatea."

He drifts into reminiscence and the edge vanishes from his voice. "Remember how your father got the two of us up early in the morning to go to the observation deck and watch the planet grow as we descended? It was the most exciting thing that had ever happened. The recent departure was nothing like that. The ship was just there one evening and gone the next. Véronique was already on the Council. She may have known more."

Véronique lays aside her reserve and adds with some animation, "It's true. A few of us may have had a fleeting sense of being marooned, but we were too busy to dwell on it."

Lars laughs. "It never sank in. It isn't as though people had been watching it day by day. The sky hasn't changed its hues."

By now the topic has run its course and Véronique is ready with another. "We may have one bit of news for you. Did you know that before the ship left select people were allowed to choose to live in the colony or live on the ship? When there wasn't a rush that would overwhelm the systems, everyone was allowed to choose. In fact few decided to move either way."

Yori doesn't answer but the startled expression on his face says enough.

She continues, "Several of our classmates decided to go with the ship, but here's the interesting part. Some members of the Council of Elders—some of the older ones—elected to move down here, where the Governor found a place for them to continue their way of life. They don't have the same influence they had on the ship, over the schools for example, but I think their being here may interest you."

Yori makes no reply. He's too busy wondering why the Governor has not mentioned such an important point. And why invite them to come but give them no authority? Then another idea dawns on him: Whoever those members are, if they have been at the Governor's elbow for years, they could have influenced the change of heart that led to his own reinstatement. And they may have—would have—known his father! That thought leads to a question. "How many Elders chose to come?"

"Five," Lars answers rather too quickly. "Not enough to be seriously disruptive."

"Of the ship, you mean?"

"Of the colony."

Sensing disagreement, Véronique recurs to the prior subject. "Does it surprise you that the departure was an event only in retrospect?"

Yori smiles at her. "I may have known more than you. I was always searching the sky from the hills, dreading it a little more every time. Then one night the dot of light simply wasn't there."

What he does not say but pauses long enough to think is, "The ship was home as the colony never was. It felt like my father had died all over again and was farther away than ever. Never so bereft. Not even being banished. Unless the full blow of banishment fell only at that moment."

Lars interrupts his thought. "How could you have expected what no one knew was going to happen until almost the end?"

His answer is almost offhand. "The decision had to be made sometime. Only one choice made sense." Again for an instant Véronique's eye crosses Yori's with something like complicity. He continues. "I'm afraid I made all of you uncomfortable in those days, having to live with a 'subversive,' as you used to say."

Then, turning back to Sandra, he changes direction again. "I'd like to hear about what's happened to your program in music education. When I left, you were expanding the curriculum in the schools and—do I remember correctly?—you had people of all ages waiting in line for lessons. There was even interest in a choir. I've thought of it often and wondered."

Sandra's eyes drop and go a bit vague. The lips draw in and the forehead puckers into a frown. She speaks with rigid clarity, "Disappointing! It has all been disappointing."

"In what way? You were so good at it. When you first arrived, people crowded into Government Square to hear you play."

Her eyes come back to him. "I don't know what to say. Maybe I wasn't as good as I thought. A flash in the pan. Anyway, there's nothing to do but keep slogging away."

In some way Yori wouldn't be able to account for even if he tried, Sandra's experience bears on his own prospects. He is uncharacteristically insistent. "What's happened? I'm sure you're not responsible for the problem. Please say more if you're willing."

"I don't understand it. The enthusiasm at first was very encouraging. It's true that in the beginning everyone wanted to be a part of the new arts program. Maybe it was the novelty. But when the hard work came, the enthusiasm faded. We still get a good turnout for concerts and recitals, but we have too few musicians accomplished enough, and if performances aren't really mature, you lose your audience."

Véronique, who respects Sandra and tries to keep up her spirits, sees that she is finding comfort in Yori's interest. It's visible in her face. She also sees Yori hanging on Sandra's every word, taking it all in. In fact, it's the first thing he has heard all evening that has really touched him.

To encourage the topic, she adds, "It's not Sandra's fault at all. She is a good teacher, a good mentor, and a hard worker. The problem is the will to work. People seem to think art is about their pleasures when it's really about expanding our vision through discipline and hard work. Students have become practical and unimaginative. They want to know the results before they invest the effort."

Yori asks, "What's been done? What's been tried?"

"It's a downward spiral," Sandra returns in a tone of deep discouragement. "They have to be born to it, grow up with it. If they don't have music in their ears, they don't see the point of the sacrifice. Without being inspired by the glory of great music, they don't have the energy or quickness or sense of adventure that it takes. And those don't come without hearing good performances."

She pauses and sighs deeply. "I'm not giving up, but I now see what a long time it takes to establish a musical culture."

Something in the situation has cleared for Véronique. It's in her eyes, and Yori sees it there as she pushes the description a bit further. "There's something else," she says. "On the Galatea we boarded at school from an early age. The Elders planned it deliberately to expand on the influence of parents.

Without living in an environment of excitement and discovery, where everyone is working hard and enjoying it—without that model, they remain oriented toward future rewards and see the process as labor."

The point registers and Yori takes it to heart. But he sees other things, among them, something essential he must do. He sees that Véronique has seen it too and seen more. In fact, it's her grasp of some unforeseeable prospect awaiting them all that rouses in him the first intimation that he is exactly where he belongs.

19

DURING THIS FIRST NIGHT back in the colony Yori lies awake in the dark rehearsing the encounter with his old friends. The reception felt like a sealed room where Véronique was the only window open to the world outside. The comparison between her and Lars is astonishing. Both children of the Galatea, similarly trained in the sciences, working side by side in the same environment for years—yet completely different. The one vividly aware and open to wonder; the other bound on a wheel of repetition, dimmed down to the practical status quo.

This reflection brings him back to Sandra's dilemma and the conviction that, if he should become governor, he might take education as his personal portfolio. Surely governing is less about housekeeping than about helping citizens find their shape.

He reviews these topics restlessly on a bed designed for comfort until, frustrated, he moves to the hard floor. There he lies open-eyed, listening to the monotonous hum of the machine. That low murmur may be consoling to the colonists, but for him it's the old unrelenting hum of the starship obstructing the silence of the heavens.

The next morning, according to the Governor's instructions, he begins a random tour of the colony, wandering through arcades and remote corners of quiet neighborhoods. He pays little attention to the people on this first day because the state of the colony reveals itself to him first through things. In a decade little has changed. Oh, there are material changes: The physical plant has grown, the neighborhoods and connecting arcades have been extended, the industrial base expanded. All this owing to the change in birthrate. On the starship, where population growth could not be allowed, births were held to replacement levels. But once the colony was securely established, it had begun encouraging more children and that had led to all the rest. Given the complexity of the material changes the technical well-being of the settlement is obvious.

And yet the closer Yori looks, the stronger the disquieting sense of nothing having changed. The houses always were machine-fabricated boxes and all these years later they remain in perfect condition, unscarred by growth or decay. There are no marks of experience on the surface of the walls or in the pavement of the walks outside. It's a pristine scene without life, like a movie set or a museum, though one feature in particular attracts his attention: There are no thresholds! An extraordinary if not a trivial observation, since the only things remotely like thresholds are located at the vestigial airlocks on the perimeter of the colony. He has no experience of sills at doorways, neither here nor on the starship. And the caves surely don't have them. So why should the lack of something he has never seen strike him as singular in these houses?

Or, perhaps that's the point. What was his first descent from the Chamber of Names to the Chamber of the Hearth if not a long transition from outside to inside? A threshold experience of preparation and passage more dramatic than his transfer from the Galatea to the colony. A threshold is an enduring signature of passage between worlds. Here, if there were such a thing, it would be from public space to the private shelter where one always returns. But in these colonial boxes there is no mark of distinction because these aren't dwelling places. They are anonymous containers for storing workers when they're not in use and have been turned off. Where there is no distinction of life, no tread of generations coming home, there are no boundaries to mark.

If Yori is depressed and alarmed by this view of the colony without thresholds, it's because he has lived differently, where different locations and regions of experience are integrated into a living world. But it's also because he may soon become responsible for the failures as well as the successes of galactic colonization.

However, from another view, conditions could not be better. So long as development of a barren planet is the only aim, all that matters is the relevant technical requirements and careful planning. So all that's needed is to ensure that systems keep up with expansion—food and water supply, health care, education, the usual infrastructural parameters. That future could hardly be brighter.

Still, there are no thresholds!

During this first day's walk through the passageways under the glass-roofed arcades—the name borrowed from nineteenth-century Paris seems vaguely ironic—his image of the interior begins to meld with the exterior as it has often appeared from his observation post across the plain. In this double orientation, he seems to be passing through the transparent veins and arteries of the sprawling earth-bound organism that, viewed from the hills, might be a crustaceous alien. After a quarter century, the enclosure remains a protective shell, valued the more for there being nothing to protect against except the extremes of temperature.

Yori's preoccupation on his rambles is with something quite different from the trappings of material success. All he sees spread out around him is accompanied by echoes of distant voices and a single question: Has the two-and-a-half-century odyssey of the Galatea been worth it? The early flush of adventure passed, essential building projects completed, comfort assured, what is the condition of the human spirit now? How are the people themselves faring? If the starship was really a projection of Planet Ulro, and if the colony has been created in the image of the ship, then how close to the tree has the fruit actually fallen? The question brings him back to the departure of the ship as the one real event during his absence and the single turning point since the first landing.

He turns his attention next to the people passing up and down the walkways engaged in their daily pursuits. Again he's startled by blank faces looking neither to the right nor the left, passing one another by without salutation, intent on whatever individual aims they have in view. Do they even have aims? Person after person he passes looks artificial. Not a mask exactly. A mask isn't a mask unless it conceals something. That's its truth. But these faces are panes of opaque glass like a television screen concealing nothing. He doesn't for a moment think there is nothing there, but the appearance makes him wonder how their little world looks to them, what they care about or hope for, who they love, or what "to love" even means to neutrals passing up and down the walkways.

For closer observation he finds a seat with a view of the people in a market square and settles down to observe. In the market as in the neighborhoods nothing is objectively different. The well-maintained buildings, neatly groomed walks, and garden beds teeming with greenery remain much as they ever were. What differs from the past is the spirit of the place. It's as though the colony has been abandoned without the people leaving.

The plaza around him is not like Véronique's, but it expresses the vitality of expanding prosperity: well-designed, nicely planted with interesting specimens, and well-cared-for. But the public mood is disconnected. As though people move about on tiptoe for fear of waking the sleepers.

At the end of the day, Yori sits again in the square in front of the Academy studying his impressions. The Governor had predicted that he'd find little to report from his rambles, and it's true that he *will* report little. How is it that the man who sees how much more *tone* reveals than operational details—how does such a man not see that the energy and sense of expectation have escaped like air from a leaking balloon?

An old story comes to mind. A fairy tale his father used to tell him about the cicadas and the ants. Not the fable as it was once told, but the same story adjusting itself to the present situation.

Once upon a time the cicadas had been men who lived busy lives, filled with ambition and hope. They built cities and distinguished themselves by acquiring things. Distracted by the pendulum of desire and gratification, they didn't notice the law of diminishing returns, that desire gratified leaves emptiness behind. And so it was that as each ambition died of fulfillment, they remembered to get up in the morning and live the day moving from lack to lack without noticing that what was lacking was soul itself. Eventually, they so lost touch with themselves that they died without noticing. Then, by a kind of justice, they were reborn as cicadas who do nothing but sit in trees making clicking sounds amplified by their own emptiness.

Just as Yori is thinking of the cicadas, the children begin pouring out the door of the school and passing through the square toward home. The bright faces and energetic voices recall him from his somber thoughts, and it occurs to him for the first time that this generation is native to the planet. Their eyes are unclouded by the idea that they are condemned to live on a piece of nameless rock. For them it's the New Earth. No wonder they are eager to join in Véronique's "field trips" to the nurseries outside the walls or listen to Sandra's music with open hearts.

So at the end of a disheartening day he is reinvigorated by eager faces and bright eyes that confirm his resolve to cultivate the young. And on that vision of promise he returns to Government House.

At the end of the week the Governor summons him again. His host opens their talk in as cheerful a tone as a worn and aging man can manage. "Now that you've had some time to look about before your official duties begin, it's time for us to exchange notes. You can tell me your first impressions, and I will report on what I've been up to meanwhile."

Sensitive to the fact that in founding the colony and overseeing its development the Governor has accomplished what no one else could, Yori wishes to let no shadow fall across that record. For other reasons, too, he is disinclined to speak freely. He does not want to offer newly formed and possibly mistaken impressions of the populace as firm judgments. That might create opposition before there's anything to oppose. So he chooses to comment on the idea of boredom.

"My primary impression is that the people are bored."

The Governor seems in the best of spirits. His mode of laughter is a kind of dry chuckle, and that's how he responds to the idea of boredom. "I told you long ago that we needed to invent things to keep people engaged."

As Yori only smiles, the Governor continues. "And where the people are bored, do you think that's the governor's problem?"

The question, taken seriously, of course, gives Yori much to think about, and he takes his time. To speak truly at this juncture is complicated. What, without appearing to criticize the status quo, without letting speculations be taken as plans, above all without giving the impression that he has some particular future in mind for the colony—what can he say?

What after those few thoughtful moments he does say is this: "You're going a little fast for me."

There's a long pause before the Governor replies, "One has to start somewhere."

These are deep waters, and Yori plies his oars carefully. "A wise man once told me, 'We don't invent solutions; we wait attentively for them to arise. The ruler must know how to wait.'"

A trace of a smile crosses the Governor's face at hearing his own words quoted back to him verbatim. "And what do we do meanwhile?"

"Until we see what to do, we can only back up and start over to see if we've got the analysis right."

"You mean review the facts."

"The *meaning* of the facts at least. Where the facts tend." He retreats into his formal reserve and waits for a response that does not come. Eventually he adds, "I can't say how people *ought* to live when I'm not clear what—or who—people are."

What Governor Nasser might once have said with contempt, he now says with a trace of sadness: "I think the philosophers never agree on such things."

"No," Yori replies with a faint smile. "Perhaps unique situations don't conform to general principles. And yet the more closely we observe, the better our judgement of the singular case may be."

"And who has the time and the will for the slow thinking you're proposing? Ordinary people have time for dissatisfaction without the disposition to understand it. And the Governor is too busy. How is he to find the time?"

"I don't have the experience to answer that question." He drops his eyes to his hands folded in his lap. But after a moment's reflection he risks an answer: "If a governor can free himself of bureaucratic management, wouldn't slow thinking be what he does as he waits for the 'soft tap on the door'?"

Yori smiles pleasantly at his host. "I am told that it takes more courage to wait than rush in and shape the world up."

To that there is no reply. They just sit together for a long while enjoying the first moment they have shared when the two minds are in complete accord.

20

KWAN SHI WA AND Edward Hamilton arrived at the colony with their two children shortly before Yori was named Governor Designate. In fact Governor Nasser coordinated the two events. The idea was consistent with his long-standing view that the chief executive should be as inconspicuous as possible so long as it didn't compromise open governance. By drawing public attention to the visitors who would be joined by Paola Rucai as official guests, he could divert attention from Yori's introduction to the Corps of Governors as his successor. And so it happened that the three survivors and Yori—the four "outlaws"—were guests in Government House.

The public story about Edward and Shi Wa was this: that he had trained as a biologist and joined the original landing party where Shi Wa was medical officer; that long after, on a research trip north, Edward had fallen and broken a leg; that the two had never returned but had found temporary shelter in a cave in the mountains; and finally that, while he was recovering, a first child was born who later died.

Yori paid attention to what was not reported: that subsequently they established a life similar to the one they had shared with Paola after the liquidation of the landing party; that she was abandoned to total solitude a few miles and worlds away from the colony on the equatorial plane of P2314 until

Governor Nasser suddenly turned up in a land rover, took her north to find them, and restored them to a colony they didn't know existed. Now, restored to their own kind, they were guests of the same power that once had tried to destroy them.

At the weekly Council meeting the Governor opens with this introduction: "Today we welcome our guests Edward Hamilton and Kwan Shi Wa." What he doesn't mention—and it's enough to make the unusual character of the session clear to all—is that Paola and the five transplanted Elders have also been invited to this meeting. He mentions Shi Wa and Edward's training as useful to the colony, then addresses them:

"It is my pleasure to invite you and your children to take up residence in the colony whenever you are ready. Living quarters await you. People with your skills are especially valuable here."

Edward, now in early middle age, is a burly, weathered man of almost peasant aspect owing in part to the difficulties of life in the wild. Not a winning personality at first meeting. Behind a veiled, suspicious manner lurks a hard glance and, when provoked, a sharp tongue. No doubt they—he, Shi Wa, and even Paola—all have ample reason for suspicion in the colony, but his gruff reserve does nothing to encourage easy trust among strangers. However, when he begins speaking in a loud, assured voice, the conviction behind his words mitigates his rough appearance.

"Thank you for that kindness, Governor. Since you made the trip north with Paola Rucai and cleared up the history of our misfortunes, we have discussed the possibility of returning if the offer was made. I will describe our reasons for declining."

That causes a stir in his audience. Those who lived in the colonial cocoon were not in the best position to understand why anyone might decline an invitation into the best of possible worlds.

Edward continues, "We have a good of life in the north. We live comfortably in a cave with ample water and food. To you it might not seem like much, but we love the land and love being self-sufficient. It's the only place our children have ever lived, and they wouldn't want to leave it behind. There are deprivations, of course, especially for them, and it's mainly because of them that we want to make a counterproposal."

So little are members accustomed to anything out of the ordinary at these meetings that his words are startling. The Governor recovers quickly and replies, "You are as free as any other citizen to propose what you like."

"Thank you. Shi Wa has agreed to give you a brief outline of what we have in mind. Afterward we will elaborate more fully on any points you wish."

Once upon an Ulro time Shi Wa might have been mistaken for a country woman come to town in her plain, homespun clothes. Except that the features retained from her Chinese heritage—slight build, quiet disposition, modest, sensitive—don't match her appearance. At her first words, addressed to more people than she has seen in a quarter century, the timidity of the back-country woman vanishes into an attractive and spirited intelligence. Her energy is so persuasive, so contagious even, that the members are half-seduced by the proposal before she describes it.

Here in four points is what she says: "We take the following facts as given. First, in the future the colony will inevitably expand across the planet. Second, our experience in a distant part where the climate and the opportunities are quite different may serve expansion when it comes. Third, your researchers know a great deal about the terrestrial features of the planet, but we know the earth intimately. That might prove an advantage not to be underrated. The colony will want to assure that development is not random and that expansion does not lead to an adversarial culture. Fourth, our children need a more diverse education than we can provide, especially since we are both scientists. You see already what we have in mind. We are asking you to consider a satellite village in our region as advantageous to us all."

To Yori the force of Shi Wa's presence and the effect of her speech on the Council is amusing. The sleepy routine of the session sustains a shock from which it will not quickly recover. The members may not recognize their own appetite for something—anything out of the ordinary—but they are thrown unexpectedly face to face with an audacious dream that, once described, appears perfectly rational. The first effect is a kind of stunned silence as when someone offers an utterly simple explanation of an age-old mystery. As members begin to wake from apathy, they exchange almost embarrassed glances, and the room breaks into a cacophony of private remarks. The Governor lets it run until the noise dies down. Then he invites comments and questions.

Lars Hanssen, always ready to recommend himself to his elders, volunteers first. "I think this is a promising idea. It raises all kinds of interesting practical questions."

His voice is pitched somewhere between swelling Rotarian goodwill and imperious resolve. "I have been saying for some time that the colony needs practical aims like expansion or competition for private property to rouse it from lethargy. Both would bring new vitality. This project would be a first step toward a planetary expansion that would give zest to life for years to come. I say we should agree and take the first steps as soon as is feasible."

Yori, sitting at an angle across the conference table from Véronique, watches the play of intelligence across her handsome face as she listens to Lars turning a visionary's dream into engineering calculations. How, he wonders again, can two people, she and Lars, be so different when their experience is so similar? How can she be so different from everyone in the colony? Her acuteness of perception and sound judgment might derive from her intimacy with the earth, from planting and nourishing growing things, but that came late after her character was set. Does her clear gaze owe more to the recent friendship with Paola? Not for the first time he detects between the two women a resemblance in tone and, in those blue blue eyes, the true bent of Paola's mind. Both have a way of looking away from the person or the subject they are contemplating, as if the eye got in the way of seeing and the ear silenced the word behind the words spoken.

Others follow Lars, most pointing to one or another hypothetical advantage or difficulty in Shi Wa's proposal, but the tenor of the exchange is positive. Yori recalls the Governor's point about political realities often being decided before they are recognized. And so the discussion is allowed to run until the animation begins to wane. Then the Governor sends another shock wave through the room.

"There is one other item of business today. You have all been discreet about my age and my becoming detrimental to the colony. I thank you for that. However, the time has come for me to step aside." He pauses and looks down at the table in front of him as though the announcement costs him more than he might have expected. "I have decided to appoint Yori Kashimoto to succeed me as Governor."

In two short sentences Nasser breaks the history of the fledgling colony in half and opens a new time. The blow is staggering. A threat of immediate annihilation would hardly have been more convulsive to people whose principle of life is status quo. "This may surprise some of you," he continues, "but I have investigated the matter exhaustively and I am confident that it is the best course for the future. Today's discussion provides an unexpected means of transition."

Again he stops as though to calm himself and catch his breath while no one else in the room thinks to breathe. Then in the tone of authority absolute, he says, "I am assigning Yori to lead an investigation into the proposed expansion and to consult with us along the way. It is to be understood from this moment that Yori will become Governor at any time I'm unable to fulfill my duties. I will not ask you to give your nominal consent on the spot. That can wait, though it may not be long."

There had already been more drama in this session than had occurred in years. Shi Wa and Edward had amazed them, but that is all forgotten. The Council is left speechless. More than speechless—or even less, like an animal unexpectedly roused from hibernation. Where Nasser might have adjourned the session immediately, he chooses to discourage factional reactions by letting a collective response take shape in his presence. Within a few silent moments some unconscious verdict seems to be reached. Shock ebbs before recognition that they all had missed something obvious. Here and there around the table an eye flickers with interest. Not approval exactly—approval takes time and decision—but surprise. A long-dormant energy wakes beneath the wave of silence and slowly swells into a tide of approval. Some unrecognized barrier collapses before unimagined possibilities.

Yori is as surprised as anyone, since the Governor had proposed that he be integrated into official life gradually and inconspicuously. Then suddenly, publicly, he had done the exact opposite. That, rather than the reality of his appointment, is what leaves him almost breathless. But he has time and the presence of mind to observe two quite different responses outside himself. Lars' mouth drops open, he turns positively white, and slumps unselfconsciously into his seat. By contrast, Véronique slowly lowers her eyes to the table. Had not a stray lock of hair fallen across her brow that required the quick brush of a hand, a secret smile might have been detected passing across her face.

The Governor takes no notice of any of this and concludes, "So, in the absence of other pressing business, this session of the Council stands adjourned." And before anyone seems aware, he is simply gone from the room.

Later, as he and Yori have a drink in the Governor's quarters, the old man says with a chuckle, "I had intended to settle with you how the appointment would be announced, but destiny intervened. It's all about being able to wait for the moment of action and recognizing it when it comes. I'd say that today, after years of living in a desert, we have seen two such moments."

There being nothing more to say on the subject, Yori passes to the proposed settlement. "You think the idea is a good one?"

"The mission from the beginning was to populate other planets. Now that we're here, it's as inevitable as the Galatea's departure that the planet will be developed one way or another."

"So we face the unexpected contingency and try to shape it?" He pauses for breath.

"That's the idea. Otherwise when development comes, it will bring a chaos of diverse settlements. In some places educational standards will be rudimentary and living conditions at subsistence levels. Governance will evolve in rival forms that could lead to insecurity and even war."

After another of the diplomatic Japanese pauses that by now the Governor even expects, Yori asks, "Is it uniformity we want then rather than difference? Don't differences enrich the imagination?"

"Yes, there are dangers and temptations on every side, always. But you would hardly want to leave people marooned at near-animal levels of existence. And, like it or not, we always act for posterity."

Yori seems puzzled. "When you first mentioned expansion to me ten years ago, the reason was to re-energize a colony that was becoming lethargic."

The Governor gives him an amused glance but makes no comment on a conversation that he undoubtedly remembers very well. "It will generate energy and energy is needed now, even more than it was then. I think your objection at the time was that expansion would treat the symptoms rather than the disease, but now it will buy you time to study the disease."

However serious, there is a respect in which this conversation is another game of chess, and the Governor's craftiness perhaps beyond Yori's age and experience.

"So your view is that we play the hand chance deals. Cooperate with contingency. Oppose nothing."

He nods. "Empower opposition, and expansion will come by blind ambition and incoherent spurts with unexpected consequences. If you act always for human well-being in the present, cooperating with circumstances moment by moment, you may enjoy some happy results. But chance creates the situation"—he looks hard into Yori's eyes, as though testing—"including your father's sacrifice! Ask that guru of yours which is better: to play the hand you are dealt or to try to invent a new game out of nothing."

Then the solemn gaze dissolves into the only relaxed, almost mischievous grin Yori has ever seen on that timeworn face. And it is as close as the old man will come to recommending that he keep Paola within reach.

That evening Yori meets Shi Wa and Edward in Paola's rooms where, by a single roll of the dice, the four outsiders are suddenly the ultimate insiders. Little is said about Yori's appointment. He and Paola have been expecting it, and to the others it is no more unusual than everything else in the colony. So the topic of conversation gravitates naturally to the idea of a new settlement.

However, Yori and Edward don't warm to each other. It's easy to see why. The brawny older man seasoned by hard experience might easily mistake the monk-like aura in such a young and inexperienced stranger as a pose, and yet he must now accept him as higher in authority. For his part Yori doesn't much like Edward's air of distrust, his way of not meeting his eye, and even looking beyond him as though he weren't there.

Paola sees and sees that Shi Wa sees. What in retrospection both will have seen is two men, more akin than they know, making silent adjustments for the sake of a common cause. Yori will come to trust Edward because he's Paola's old friend and the protégé of his father, and for the same reasons Edward, who may have expected to deal with grey-haired officials, will adjust to relying on an untried novice. But for now, even in the intimacy of this little circle, they don't find it easy to talk to each other, and the conversation has the willed quality of high stakes and diverted eyes.

Yori quietly concentrates on the people before him. He needs to understand their idea through and through, not the plan only. Plans are not political; people are. And these three know what no one else but he and the Governor know, that the colony is on the threshold of the first truly political experiment in its short history. Their ready responses show that the three others have been through it all before and are in essential agreement. At times their questions and answers sound rehearsed, and that raises for Yori the intriguing idea that Paola may be the moving hand behind the whole thing.

The most important lesson he learns is that even as he is assigned to explore the possibility of expansion, the thing has been decided already, not by "outlaws" but by a confluence of circumstances. The real question is how?

As Shi Wa and Edward discuss the idea with increasing attention to practical detail, Yori observes the scene through a historical lens. It's another threshold moment. The age-old conflict between the crew and the Elders on the starship has been dormant in the colonial technocracy until now. Only he, in the brash voice of his student days, ever questioned the "biopolitical" ideal of security and comfort, whereas Shi Wa, Edward, and Paola, scientists all, the ones "turned" by his father, have longer memories for which they have paid every day of their lives.

As the others happily talk among themselves, Yori wonders if they appreciate how much more than their settlement is at stake. They stand on the cusp of a transition the Elders once dreamed of: from machine to polity, from colony to city. But it won't be easy. Once the novelty of something happening has worn off, opposition will come. It will come in some quarters from the dead weight of conservative habit. In others from ambition for power, individual or corporate. Then there will be dark days and unpredictable circumstances. Together they will need the wisdom of disinterest, or the mission will fail. So he thinks as the others talk, but he is careful to keep such thoughts to himself.

When the review of all that has been foreseen comes to an end, Edward gives Yori a sharp, apprehensive glance and asks, "Now Yori, how do you propose to go about this thing?"

Yori lowers his eyes as he often does when there's more to say than he's willing to venture. "How should I know? Except for this very helpful description, the whole idea is completely new to me . . . but for one thing."

"What is the one thing?" Edward's lip curls and he knits his brow.

"A source of danger. During my trouble-making student years, the Governor used to invite me in to talk about the welfare of the colony. One night he mentioned two ideas for regenerating the public spirit. Then this afternoon both those ideas recurred in Lars Hanssen's speech in exactly the same form!"

Edward's small eyes widen in recognition of unsuspected subtlety. "You think there's a connection."

"No way to know. But yes. In those days things said in my small circle had a way of turning up again in the Governor's conversation. Phrases I had used in a seminar paper returned as echoes in our evening chats."

"And you thought you were being set up."

"Sometimes. Who knows? True or not, I decided that I couldn't let it bother me. One night the Governor floated both ideas, expansion and private property. And he pressed me to describe their weaknesses."

Shi Wa asks, "And you said?"

"Little. But I wondered if expansion might just cover over the problem of lethargy and if competition for wealth might risk repeating the fate of Ulro. Something like that." Yori laughs at a connection he hasn't thought of before. "Maybe that's why it was the last conversation before I was expelled."

"Doesn't look that way now, does it?" That's Paola's first contribution to the conversation. Her object has been to be quiet and let them all find their way to common ground as quickly as possible.

But Edward is itching to begin developing a concrete plan. "Who do you think will be most helpful in getting the plan approved and getting us underway?"

Sticking to his point, Yori says, "My guess is that opposition will come first from Lars."

"But today he was the first to support the idea." Edward's response suggests how little one learns about political experience living in a wilderness.

And once more Shi Wa shows herself more perceptive than her husband. "Maybe he saw the inevitability and rushed to slant it his own way. What he actually supported was expansion and individualism. Not quite what we have in mind."

"Shi Wa is right," Yori replies, mainly to Edward. "Lars is bright and talented. He is so dangerous that we should bring him in at once and keep him close. Since we cannot pass him over, he should be made chief technical advisor to the project."

Edward stares. "I don't see why! Can't the Governor do what he thinks best?"

Yori recognizes one thing that Edward has yet to see, but for the moment, at least, the two of them have laid their personal differences aside and are on the same side.

Paola sees as much and offers a further precaution, "Why not include Véronique? She understands Lars. They could divide the technical responsibility between them: building and engineering to one, food and water to the other."

By the end of a long evening the four have devised a tentative plan. The early slant of the project will be toward food production, water, and housing. Paola will go north with Edward and Shi Wa for the critical planning phase, leaving their children behind in school. Yori will make a brief trip to get acquainted with the site, then Lars and Véronique will travel north together to make more specialized surveys. Véronique's skill along with the support of the three "outlaws" should assure an orderly plan. Meanwhile Yori will handle aspects of infrastructure from the colony, beginning with expanding the communications system and setting up the selection process for the first settlers.

Thus within twelve hours of the first mention of a settlement, the guiding mission and its custodians are established.

21

THE NEXT DAY THE Governor summons Yori. So far he has revealed little about his observations of the colony. When pushed, he has understated his impressions: "If some of the luster of adventure has faded, it's no more than was to be expected." When required to say more, he has mentioned details as though they were temporary.

But today the Governor has bigger game in sight. He wants to discuss the broader issues of the settlement, specifically how Yori wishes to proceed. That, at least, is what he implies, though he may also want to see Yori's mind at work on these problems. It's his chance—perhaps his last—to judge his instinct, subtlety, foresight, caution, steadiness of purpose. So instead of offering advice on how to get things underway, he simply asks, "How do you propose to go about your settlement?"

Paola has taught him to attend to the small things, and he notices how much the shifting little words in a sentence can reveal. It's the pronoun in the Governor's remark that clarifies the situation at once: The project is his responsibility, and Governor Nasser intends to be a sounding board rather than an active participant.

Yori answers, "You foresaw some time ago how valuable Paola, Shi Wa, and Edward might be to the colony, so you won't be surprised if they already have a fairly clear conception of how we might proceed. I heard as much in a conversation last night. I think you might find their views as heartening as I do."

"So what do they think?"

"The first principle is the quality of life, the settlers themselves. That should come first. Planning a village and building a house is part of the cultivation or education in the good life. So they want settlers to take collective responsibility for themselves by building their own lives literally from the ground up. This is not surprising because it's what the three have been forced to do, and they've learned from it."

The Governor studies the idea for a moment before replying. "When Paola went north with me and we saw how the other two lived, she remarked that they didn't live toward some future condition. The quality of their life, she said, was in the activity of the day that lay before them. That's not an idea that's easy to grasp, but it simplifies the question of what we should get up and do at any moment."

When Yori does not reply, he adds, "Am I to understand that you agree with this philosophy?"

Yori nods his agreement, adding only, "Subject to your approval and to the unfolding of events day by day."

"Then how do they propose to go about it?"

He smiles slightly at the permission granted. "They left that largely to me." If they are already taking him as de facto Governor, he takes care not to show any consciousness of the fact. "My suggestion is that we add two department heads to the group. After we have surveyed the site, we send them north to work with Edward and Shi Wa in drawing up a proposal for the physical development."

"And which department heads do you propose?" The question is neither idle nor a matter of curiosity. Nasser knows very well that there are more dangers ahead than Yori can know and has a fair idea what some of them will be.

"For construction projects Lars Hanssen and for water and agriculture Véronique Dumas."

The Governor's face grows more lively than at any time since their meeting in the Chamber of Names. He looks hard into Yori's eyes as though what he just said might trouble him. "I suppose you know that you and Lars Hanssen have been traveling different roads for a long time. You both may have mellowed, but your compasses are still trained on different stars."

He pauses as though considering, then continues. "One fact you should know, but you must accept this in complete disinterest: Lars was the one who first dropped hints to me about your subversive views. It's how you got on my radar screen. Now don't let yourself feel it as disloyalty in him. By his lights he was being true to a higher allegiance."

Far from taking offense, Yori accepts the point eagerly. "I understand. But since it's not avoidable anyway, don't you think it's better to include him in the vanguard of the project and deal with issues as they arise? The others all understand the risk and will mediate between Lars and me. I know you trust Véronique. It was a stroke of brilliance to set her in contact with Paola. You know, don't you, that she and Paola have become friends and allies? She, too, is good at handling Lars. If she is Lars' technical counterpart as Edward will be his counterpart on matters of construction, then add Shi Wa and Paola as mediators, and there should be little occasion for direct conflict between him and me."

The Governor seems to approve what he has heard so far but he has a further question. "Does it worry you that you and your circle of outlaws may appear too secretive? Creating suspicion on the Council if not in the populace. You are contemplating an oligarchy, you know."

Years of reading and thinking about the rewards and risks of all kinds of political organization have taught Yori that action is always a walk on a tightrope, and one needs criticism. "Yes," he answers thoughtfully. "Too much secrecy encourages suspicion and too much talk encourages uninformed opinion. In this case, isn't the possibility of the settlement's becoming a Tower of Babel the greater risk? What would you advise?"

The Governor answers the question by ignoring it. Instead, he asks, "I know you understand the dangers of letting partisan opinions rule, but isn't your group subject to the same criticism? Isn't this another instance of rule by the interest of a few?"

Yori smiles at that. He is being warned about a risk that the Governor has himself accepted for many years in the colony. "Our view will appear partisan to some. In fact we have all arrived at approximately the same place by quite different paths. Did you ever hear of a book compiled by the Council of Elders on the starship?"

Nasser studies the question a moment, searching memory. "Can't say that I did. How is that relevant?"

"It's called *Starship Galatea*. Paola's father had it smuggled from the starship to my father on the ground to pass on to her. But that's another story. The book contains a history of the starship mission along with Council debates occurring over two centuries, often about just such political questions. For Paola first, and later for me, it was a political education. As far as I know there was only one copy."

The Governor acknowledges that he knows about the debates among the Elders. Everyone does, or did. "I have read some of them. They are voluminous and all on Alexandros."

With another ironic chuckle, he adds, "Of course that was also a way of hiding them. Hide a thing in the open where everyone can see it." Then a digression: "Do you know a story by E. A. Poe about a stolen letter? This detective is called in to find a letter that compromises the Queen of France. The police take the house apart and can't find it because it's been exposed on the mantelpiece the whole time. Total information, universally available, is like looking with the naked eye for a single star in the universe. The first trick is to find it and the second is to understand that you have found it. Those old dialogues were intended to be lost in broad daylight."

In acknowledging the point, Yori sees that it's discreet political advice. "Someone once said that wisdom is sold in the market where few come to buy."

He stops as though enthusiasm might be unseemly just now. "The book is a storehouse of ideas and models for whatever needs to be done." Then, after another moment, "It may, that book, have been what subverted the landing party. But to come back to your point about its present relevance, the book is surety that no one is inventing anything out of self-interest."

Some long thought, opaque to Yori, causes Nasser to answer slowly. "What does your book have to say about oligarchy?"

"It says: Think provisional ideas quietly while working away on the practical in broad daylight. And our primary recommendation to you is that we let the settlers build their houses slowly so that their lives will be well built. Things can be manufactured overnight, but lives have to grow."

"No one is likely to disagree with that so long as you don't explain it to them. Meanwhile, I'd like to read your book."

Yori went away from this conversation in a quandary without any idea what the quandary was. He stored it up to review in bed after the other concerns of the day. When the time came, he reviewed the meeting with the Governor and found it satisfactory in every respect. Thanks to Paola, he knew better than most what good conversation was and had already benefited from more of it that most people can expect in a lifetime. In this talk the meeting of moods and minds had been exemplary.

And yet somewhere toward the end a shadow had fallen across it. Not a shadow exactly, but even as the Governor spoke as congenially and wisely as ever, something behind his eyes had gone ever so slightly awry. Did it coincide with his bringing up The Book? Not so much as a change in tone but a slight alteration, as when the timbre of a singer's voice alters by covering. Then, just for an instant, as Nasser delivered that last casual remark about reading The Book, something that was anything but casual had flashed across his face.

Having nothing more substantial to go on, Yori laid the question aside without surrendering the conviction that something had taken the Governor by surprise.

22

P<small>AOLA</small> WAS INVITED INTO the colony at the same time as Yori and, like him, given permanent lodging in Colony House. Aside from the strange woman from the hills, passing through the paths and lanes in a homemade shift that she refused to exchange for the establishment uniform, no one notices. What Yori sees is that the Governor is careful not to "pardon" her or to "restore" him, presumably because pardon or restoration would reassert the authority of a command structure that Governor Nasser has outgrown. Instead, he "welcomes" them because, however the colony might be described, they are already included "by nature."

"Nothing here is real," Paola complains. She means that inside all is clean and new and artificial. A cookie-cutter existence in which she can keep to the order of the day only by an act of will. Through the distorting transparency of the domes and arcades one can look out *at* the earth and sky as distant objects but not *belong* to them. Even the colonials, protected by their shell, seem vaguely counterfeit as though the good life requires pretense even where the pretending is a way of not looking themselves in the face. And the incessant mechanical hum! It keeps her awake nights. No one else notices, but it makes her yearn for the naked truth of life in the hills.

Though she takes satisfaction in watching Yori expand daily into his new place, she feels cut off. A dwelling requires locations—a dark Chamber of Names where one can appreciate the light, a temple on the brown hillside, a cistern of cool clear water, a Chamber of the Hearth, a garden straining upward toward a gash of sunlight falling down sheer canyon walls. *Locations* add up to *places*, as measured space does not. And so, when opportunity offers, she is always happy to set off on foot across the plateau—going home.

For a considerable period her time is rather evenly divided between the two. There are reasons other than Yori for spending time in the colony. She has become the maiden aunt for Shi Wa's children and takes them often to the caves for weekends. She also has friends among the members of the starship Elders who now live in the colony, all well-known to her as her father's friends. The biologist Ang Yimou, for example, had once been her teacher and Edward Hamilton's research advisor until the two of them signed up for the landing party.

Another, Hans Rückert, a political scientist turned philosopher, used to have long discussions with her father at their apartment when he was a student and she was a child. She had been allowed to stay up very late on those nights just to listen to the intellectual war games between those ancient heroes. Once she was established at Government House she also fell into immediate friendship with the other "Elders," whom she knew less well. The result of these old connections was that she was accepted as a natural member of an informal circle that was destined to be one of the greatest benefits to Yori's governorship.

Governor Nasser had encouraged this group but done nothing to give them a formal role in the colony. The relation between him and them was politely distant. Although he had invited them to take up residence and treated them with respect, they had well-founded suspicions about the role of starship First Mate Talib Nasser in the founding of the colony. Paola, foreseeing that Yori would eventually need to constitute (or reconstitute) the group in the style of their fathers' day, gave an occasional gentle nudge toward regular discussions with them on issues suitable to a governor's "brain trust." Nothing shows her disposition toward them so well as the fact that when she's away either in the hills or in the North, she makes a point of returning for these sessions, thereby quietly insisting on their importance.

Yet she still looks for excuses to "go home." After the memorable day of that first Governor's meeting, followed in the evening by the brainstorming about a satellite settlement, she had left with Edward and Shi Wa for the caves. It had been many years since those two had seen their first terrestrial home, and the children had only heard romantic stories about their parents' early days as explorers. In light of recent developments, the three old friends had much more than nostalgia to discuss among themselves. Judging from consequences, these conversations must have ranged far indeed.

Had they not withdrawn precipitously to the hills, Yori might have gone too. With conditions changing so fast, he could have used time and space to think, and thinking remains more natural for him in the hills than in the colonial "keep." As it is, the best he can do is ramble through the arcades as inconspicuously as possible, alone with his thoughts, enjoying what passes for fresh air in a sealed box.

And so it happens that, crossing from Government House into the central square one day, he discovers that a crowd has gathered. He has seen that only once and that was before he was banished. At the time Sandra Mohr was playing a concert, and he had felt a subtle shift of mood among the people who had gathered to listen. It was a barely detectable pulse, a hesitant stirring of consciousness that didn't outlive the music, but now that lethargic spirit with its false intimations of life comes to mind again in the torpid warmth of the dome.

Tonight he finds something new. People gathering spontaneously as they never used to do. Nothing explicit, but unmistakable signs of expectation among small groups huddled together to exchange remarks on some clandestine subject in a place where there are no secrets. Passing more or less randomly through the crowds without drawing attention to himself, he tries to catch the tone if not the subject of the muffled voices.

He catches both. There is no secret. A rumor has begun to spread about a new settlement related somehow to those visitors from the past. Here and there arguments erupt over whether there already is such a place or one is to be built. As always with rumor, by the subtlest shifts in words, fantasies slip into certainties. The astonishing thing is that so many have been roused by curiosity and drawn to Government Square as though to feel physically close to some important event, anxious to learn—or invent—more for passing on to others.

To Yori's ears it's all about mood and the time for action. The sight of faces however briefly reanimated, eyes in focus, bodies stirred by a memory of purpose, fills him with hope. Droplets of news, trickling from a single Council meeting, have been enough to nurture interest in the future. Something is coming!

Since Yori is still unrecognized, he joins one group and listens a few moments. The questions may be random and the answers incoherent, but it's the music that matters.

"Who gets to go to the new colony?"

"Where did you say it's to be built?"

"I heard it's already built by those old explorers."

"When is it to open?"

"Wouldn't it be exciting to live in the wilderness like that woman in the caves?"

"Who did you say gets to go?"

Yori leaves the Square and returns to his rooms having forgotten all about his intended walk.

A few days later when the outlaws return from the caves, he convenes the first formal planning session. He prefaces the discussion with remarks on the late changes in the public disposition. "While you were away, I made some random observations related to our project that may interest you. Strolling through the lanes listening to the voices, I discovered something astonishing. Peoples' tone has suddenly modulated into a brighter key, all because of a rumor about a satellite colony. Hope has sprung up before there's anything to hope for. Now we must make use of this new energy and the change in public mood."

Considerable talk follows in which opinion is divided. Is the feverish murmur in the lanes a promising omen of support for the project? Or might expectations be roused then dashed by the slow pace of sensible development?

When this equally energetic debate dies down, Yori lays out an agenda. They must decide which initial surveys of the site are needed, who should be involved in drawing up the first plans, and what the general order of priorities is to be.

After much discussion, it's decided that when the surveys are completed, construction can begin with housing and a central public building to serve as a school, Shi Wa's clinic, and a communal meeting place. As soon as the settlers begin arriving, Edward can organize an informal council along the lines of the present colonial Corps of Governors to deal with practical matters, deferring questions of long-range objectives for consultation here in the colony.

When Yori suggests that Lars and Véronique be included in their group as technical advisors, Edward again raises an objection to Lars. To him Lars personifies the technocratic ideal three of them nearly lost their lives opposing. The intention to give him any authority in the construction of the settlement raises Edward's suspicions.

Yori ironically acknowledges the point: "Yes, Lars' instinct will be to pave the planet over for a transportation system, mine all its resources, and build industrial plants wherever is most convenient. Then once the planet has been trashed, he'll build a starship to repeat the same process all over again. Lars' political principle is never to let human beings get in the way of 'material progress.'"

The satire is good-humored, even affectionate toward his old friend, but he adds more gravely, "We all know the danger comes from a disposition that isn't unique to Lars. The disposition to mastery belongs to the legions of the sons of Adam."

He explains that Lars' appointment is intended to protect against just the contingency Edward foresees. "None of what you fear will happen, but we must agree on *how* it will not happen. The political tactic must be to overcome by yielding. We don't want to reignite the old opposition between the Starship Command and the Elders. The conflict between Lars and me always was a personal version of that. So I will need your help in limiting it to the personal." Yori's face brightens with uncharacteristic enjoyment. "When I imagine Lars up north with you three or"—he looks at Paola—"perhaps four, I almost feel sympathy for him."

Then a new issue from Edward. "When the Galatea left, what happened to the DNA archive from Ulro?"

Yori, completely at a loss, sits for several moments staring at the question. "I don't know what you mean."

"Did you learn in school that the original plan for the mission included a complete archive of Ulro's genetic codes? Once human DNA had been mapped, researchers spent years decoding the family trees of the flora and fauna. That archive, along with preserved tissue samples for each phylum, was deposited on the ship. The idea was that once the species of a host planet had been mapped, the local ecosystem could be expanded by introducing appropriate species into the chain.

Exemplary members of a phylum were preserved so they could be rejuvenated, and other members resurrected by mutation from the organic samples.

"Paola's work on the phylogenic groups in botany and mine with the animals were the heart of our research back on the ship, and that's one reason why your father and her father got us included in the original landing party. The technocrats with their short-term perspectives were not much interested in the 'theoretical' science, but the Elders always understood that anything that could be done would be done.

"Later the fate of the landing party appeared to put that line of research in zoology out of reach forever. Only what Paola retrieved from Alexandros and the few plant specimens from the ship seemed likely to survive here. I only told her about the DNA of the fauna after we were left for dead. Now the rudimentary studies I have made of the bio-system in the North could be immensely expanded if we discovered that the archives on the ship were shared with the colony. By training a new generation of biologists and with requisite caution, this understanding might eventually be expanded planet-wide."

Yori says simply, "I'm afraid I can't tell you. I do remember hearing about some archive in school, but I've never heard it mentioned since and I don't know what happened to it."

For the first time Paola speaks. "When I came north with the Governor, I was able to broach this topic distantly by inquiring about information resources the Galatea had left to the colony. I didn't mention the phylogenetic archive directly, but I learned enough to put Véronique on the scent. She has discovered that a copy of the DNA maps was included with a few specimens—I don't know in what quantity. It now appears that after Nasser's change of heart, he quietly managed the whole thing himself and for safety kept it secret."

Then she adds, aside to Yori, "Curious that he hasn't told you about it. Maybe he thinks it is better to let it surface later when the colony is sufficiently stable to make wise use of it." Then she addresses the others. "Anyway, the zoological files should be available. You know I have been working with a few Ulro phyla for years, but Véronique's experiments are much further along. At least we know that the original theory works for the flora, though experiments with more complex organisms would be difficult. They would certainly require greater caution. Such work, if undertaken at all, should be done far from the public eye. Otherwise, we may find that we've brought the Ulro plague with us."

When Edward asks how all this caution and secrecy might be managed, she speaks again to Yori. "What if you raise the topic with the Governor? If he will tell you and give you access, you could arrange for Edward to set up a lab somewhere in the mountains without any publicity. We four could share responsibility for the risks ad hoc until appropriate oversight is in place. Then Edward can begin training assistants here in the colony."

Paola's idea sounds feasible and the discussion drifts in a different direction while Yori sits on abstracted, revolving this new issue in mind. Presently, he interrupts, "I understand the idea of expanding the ecology of the planet, but one thing bothers me: On what *basis* would we decide that this or any other bio-system *should* be expanded?"

The question is addressed to Paola as the one most likely to provide an answer, but when she doesn't reply, he continues. "I see that it might be argued on practical grounds like expanding the food supply to include dairy products. That's exactly why it must not be put in the hands of those who *know how* to do things but not *why* they should or should not be done. Meanwhile, how would we justify taking any action of the kind?"

Edward surprises them all with a cautious and unusual answer. Scratching his head awkwardly, he replies, "Aside from the biology, there is an ancient philosophical reason. It is that we need the animals as a boundary marker of the human. We understand vegetative life by reference to the inorganic on one side and sensate organisms on the other side. Similarly, to know the human, to take its measure and specify its field of action, we must consult non-human beings. During the expansion of biological science in the nineteenth century, humans identified themselves more and more as an animal species, with good scientific reason, especially the evidence of evolution. An explosion of knowledge resulted: brain science, the mapping of the genome, and a hundred other revolutionary developments associated with evolution. But something was also forgotten: the non-animal character of the human dropped out of sight."

Edward stops there and Paola, who has an expression of total surprise and amusement on her face, responds. "You have been thinking long thoughts up there in your mountains. Not the old *thinking man* I once knew but *man thinking*!"

They all laugh as she adds, "To finish the idea let's add that the explosion of science taught us brilliantly *what* we were, but at the cost of the *who* and the *how* of our modes of being. Eventually, by studying the limited world of sensation and instinct in the animal kingdom, we got around to the 'human surplus' beyond biology. Reflective people could always look at the house pets that were so popular during the last days of Ulro and see that humans were 'such stuff as dreams are made on.' Not many will try to understand this idea since it comes with tough responsibilities, but you, Yori, must understand it because you will be responsible for cultivating the uniquely human capacity for wonder. In *Starship Galatea* there is a venerable old colloquy on this subject. Go read it again."

Those two speeches were conversation stoppers, but Yori was quick to recognize the kind of obscurities that, taken to heart, had a way of shedding light in the darkest corners of perplexity. For him at least these ideas were to become a beginning rather than an end.

23

To GRASP THE SPIRIT and driving force of the northern project one needs a face. Yang Shi Wa's is such a face. In fact she's the soul of place. It all belongs to the extraordinary arc of her life and to her mode of facing hardship. After being trained in medicine and becoming one of the explorers, after surviving the purge and living off the land for more than a decade with Edward and Paola—after all that, she and Edward were forced by his injury into deeper exile, not knowing but what they were the only survivors on the planet. By what unimaginable endowment of strength or grace does one maintain a balanced life under such conditions? The "how" aside, here in the northern wilderness an ideal of character was forged that would become exemplary.

After the birth and early death of their first child, unable still to rejoin Paola in the South because of Edward's accident, they eventually found a cave large and convenient enough for permanent dwelling. Some fifteen years further on when Governor Nasser and Paola rediscovered them, they had water and food enough, wood for their fire, and two other children, a son and a daughter in their early teens—even a "happy'" life if one uses that word for a strenuously inventive existence.

Paola, whose stark existence underground was far less comfortable than theirs, was not one to romanticize the rudimentary life of nature, though to the Governor, accustomed to a colony sprawling lazily over a desiccated equatorial plateau, their domestic scene may have had a utopian hue. In truth the only ideal thing about it was the grit of a woman whose hard experience would have destroyed most.

"Kwan," her family name, means "mountain pass," and she knows the raw stones and shallow soil of this landscape with an intimacy that counts as kinship. While her laborer's hands mix with the earth and bring forth food for her family, she belongs no less to the sky above than the earth below. In this respect she is as close as one will easily come to a standard of unobstructed human character in which "character" names affiliation and modes of relation.

Originally the man and the woman survived in a small cave at some distance along the base of the hill from their permanent dwelling. It was little more than a niche in the face of the rock where a damp spot in the floor promised survival. In this place where expedients had to be as simple as the circumstances were primitive, days were spent scratching at that damp spot with rudimentary tools of wood and stone until a small crevice opened in the rock. Days of backbreaking labor were rewarded with a first trickle of groundwater. Gradually the opening was expanded and, thanks to some unknown geological structure, there was pressure enough to make a small stream from that trickle.

Thereafter Edward cleared a stone channel, and in time the precious liquid began flowing down the valley to the mouth of the larger cave. Eventually he hollowed out a basin for "house use" and allowed the surplus to flow over a table rock and fall into Shi Wa's garden. As it happened, the stream that had begun so hesitantly increased until it was more than sufficient for growing their food.

As a gardener, as in all other things, Shi Wa welcomed necessity and put it to good use. Slowly she improved the thin soil in her valley plot and began transplanting and cultivating edible species in the fertile patch at the bottom of the hill. Years before she had learned from Paola about domesticating indigenous plants, and by the time the second and third children came along, the hardest times were behind. The children learned from their parents to live by their own hands, to participate inventively in the simplest processes of life, and to accept in gratitude the blessings of the earth. After the roots and berries and fruit, they grew flowers that made their cave the closest thing to a home any of their peregrine species had known for three centuries.

The high point, the ritual of their day, came when the four sat down together to tell stories. Stories of the literary kind in the evenings before the fire, but stories of natural processes too, recounted sometimes during rest periods in the garden and on hikes in the mountains. Shi Wa and Edward, being Level I graduates of the Galatea Academy, were well-grounded in all the intellectual disciplines, but knowing some things well, they understood how poor a substitute two specialists were for the diversity of a faculty. Living banished and forgotten by a distant colony they didn't know existed, there was no Alexandros with its memory banks, no books, no labs. As there was nothing to read, there were no materials for writing. However well-stocked the parents' minds, however active their memories, instruction had to be oral.

There is an old saying about necessity and invention, and Shi Wa applied it well. From writing with a stick on the ground to homemade pens and ink and the bark of trees for paper; from brushes and paints for drawing on cave walls to collecting plant specimen and rocks and studying the stars—however clever her inventions, she measured the children's education by her own student years. The ratio of students to teachers may have been 1:1, but they were two scientists who had not seen so much as a primitive microscope or a book in a quarter of a century.

But what makes Shi Wa an exemplary denizen of a new earth is less her heroic response to desperate circumstances than something too demanding for words. She is not a free-standing "real thing" one might come across in a full world like one among a bag of marbles. It's exactly that fantasy of "thingliness" that has been worn away until her name is more verb than noun. Her "substance" consists in the color of her relations as if she were a knot in the weave of the tapestry that gives her being. As inseparable from earth and sky or from darkness and light as from garden and family, she differs from the other elements in this kaleidoscope of relations only in knowing it and reflecting on it as in a looking glass.

If Shi Wa "knows" herself as a figure in the constellation of these relations, it's because she is disposed to hold it all in mind and welcome it. These coinciding elements emit the force or spirit—call it Eros—of a living "soul," for that ancient word remains the most economical way of naming how, beyond biology, a person *is*. Difficult as it may be to conceive, the point is essential because, with no fanfare whatever, Shi Wa's way of life was destined to become exemplary for the citizen of a New Earth, and her difference is nowhere more evident than in the contrast with Lars Hanssen.

The two names, Yang Shi Wa and Lars Hanssen, embody the contending loyalties that define Yori's political task: an atom with a core of autonomous interests versus a stable wave of energy interacting with other elements, themselves nothing but other energies in the single field. Rival ideals from which Yori must configure a city.

After the outlaws' belated reinstatement in a community of kindred beings, the months passed, the settlement got underway, and the first settlers came to stay. The four couples were quartered temporarily in caves near Edward and Shi Wa, across the valley from the site selected for building. Little was done to reduce the challenges of their rudimentary life except for a regular flow of supplies from the colony. The whole object had been for them to construct their own life, but conditions were hardly what Edward and Shi Wa had faced. Survival was not at risk. In fact, they were immediately initiated into the existing plan for constructing living spaces and consulted on how the plan would proceed. As drawn up, a single building would be set into the side of the opposite hill across the small valley from Shi Wa's garden. It was to be a row of four units like the ones in the colony but made of local stone rather than the prefabricated materials. The settlers were to learn the requisite skills and contribute their labor.

Two of them were well-qualified for the task and another, David Laroche by name, had a good eye for design. It was he who suggested that the building be turned ninety degrees from the valley, toward its own eventual community, and that the units be arranged like stairsteps, one a bit above the next to honor the shape of the landscape. The virtues of the idea convinced everyone, and the ten residents got the building underway. The colony dispatched engineers and equipment sufficient for quarrying and moving stone. These people were assigned to oversee the technical aspects of building and offer advice on construction.

In the first stages the work progressed more smoothly than might have been expected largely because the settlers with experience mediated between the technicians and the novices. All being young, energetic, and capable of learning quickly, the walls of the dwellings went up with remarkable speed.

During this phase, Lars was back in the colony attending to the routine duties of his department and monitoring progress at a distance. Once the shell of the buildings was enclosed and work began on the interior, the engineers turned their attention from the houses to the water supply. In preparation for this second phase Lars returned to help settle on a suitable plan.

Thus it happened that the three—Lars, Edward, and Shi Wa—were sitting one evening around the hearth fire in their cave discussing possible designs. The background irritation in the engineer owes something to the progress of the building that had gone better in his absence than he may have hoped. His tone of authority in laying out his idea for the waterworks suggests that, having lost the building round, he intends this time to win.

And so he describes a pipeline extending from Edward's channel across the valley and up the hill to a cistern above the houses, all to be powered by solar pumps large and adaptable enough to meet all contingencies. Because now people must haul water up in buckets, he will provide a temporary line and pump within a week that will tide them over until the permanent line can be installed and a cistern built. Edward patiently hears him out, though at one point Shi Wa wonders aloud about defacing the hillside with a giant pipe and disturbing the quiet with the sound of pumps.

When Lars has laid out his plan, Edward asks, "Do you know a man named David Laroche?"

"Don't remember him, but I've heard the name. You can imagine that the people chosen as settlers became instant celebrities in the colony. I think that name may have been one of them."

Edward continues. "David isn't an engineer, he has a flair for design. He is the one who convinced us all to reorient the row houses in harmony with the terrain. Anyway, I want to show you several things. First, this picture of the end of the valley where the hills join." And he passes Lars a photograph of the roughly V-shaped landscape. "Now look at this." He hands him another of an ancient aqueduct that he has discovered on Alexandros. "Finally, look at this drawing of the same spot in the landscape." The drawing shows a gently descending ribbon of stone supported intermittently by vertical pillars. It begins at a point somewhat higher up this side of the hill and extends around the joining of the hills to a point opposite and above the building site.

"David's idea is that we build an aqueduct and let gravity do the work. One of your engineers and I discovered accessible water deep in another cave near the end of the valley. There is ample supply and a favorable grade for letting it flow into the aqueduct. Laroche has explored the whole course. We would have to build only three short spans, drawn here"—he spots them on the paper—"and each would be only a few feet off the ground. All natural. No pumps."

Lars is speechless. He stares for what seems minutes, completely mystified. "You're serious! I can't believe it!" And he stares a while longer.

When he is able to speak again, he recurs to the topic of the houses. "You had your way with the houses, and I admit that it has worked out pretty well so far, probably because the settlers were willing to do the physical labor and haven't yet lost their enthusiasm. Still, it was a blatantly inefficient process. We could have done the job in half the time with much less labor. But what you're proposing now differs by many magnitudes. It's madness!"

No one speaks for some moments. Then Lars continues, "For starts, you'd have to move a small mountain of stone. The labor would be backbreaking and would take months, maybe years, even with the aid of our machines. If it wasn't abandoned along the way, your water supply would be open to contamination from the air. The trough would require seasonal cleaning and occasional repair that would be labor-intensive. And those are just a few items off the top of my head. In my plan we use prefabricated pipe and solar pumps. The whole job is done in no time and with very little inconvenience to anyone. After building a cistern that will be needed in any case, we can install a pipeline in two weeks and have it operational within a month. It's just common sense. I can't believe you've wasted time on this crazy notion."

Edward takes a deep breath as though preparing for an extended oration of his own when Shi Wa waves him aside and says, "You make good points, Lars. You have imagination."

He replies sharply, "Imagination is exactly what we don't need here. This . . ." he waves David Laroche's drawing in the air . . . "this is imagination! What we need is common sense. We need to adapt to the situation and solve the problem with the least possible hullabaloo. Doesn't the mission show we're the most adaptable of species? Imagination wastes time on the unreal. It's a waste unless you're trying to rebuild Rome on P2314. Common sense is what we need!"

Shi Wa ignores this outburst. "What you say is completely logical, except for one thing."

"What's that?"

"You're leaving the human out. Whether water comes through a pipeline or an aqueduct is secondary. It isn't finally about the most efficient way to water our gardens. We're growing healthy people here, not efficient waterworks. Healthy people thrive on remembering!"

Edward can't resist adding, "To you lot the settlement is not for the settlers. It's an opiate for the restlessness of the builders."

Lars responds, "Apparently you're growing serfs who will waste their lives in manual labor! How can you think that doing things in impossibly hard ways produces a better quality of life then being served by impersonal power?"

The next morning Edward and Lars make a walking survey of the rough landscape, marking additional building sites, exploring nearby caves for water, examining indigenous building materials, and considering how they can be moved—these and a hundred other things. From training and ingrained habit of mind, Lars sees the land—and sees it well—through the grid of a master plan and contemplates its swift and efficient execution, while Edward regards their deliberations as life itself. The difference is a bit like the proverbial tree and forest: One man sees particular trees in the green swath of forest and tries to get the other to look away from mental blueprints and take account of what's in front of his eyes. Even if Lars had the disposition, it's an altogether harder thing to do, requiring initiation, and so he looks away from the earth toward the plans in his head and misses what's under his feet.

Later in the morning Lars leads the march forward, reciting a list of tasks he has set for the remainder of the day, while Edward ambles along at his side attending to the little accidental things in their path. At one point, lagging just behind, he asks, "You know, don't you, that only the person who takes the time to love this land can build a good house and a good life?"

Lars stops, turns around, and stares at him as though he, Edward, has lost his way. "If we follow that philosophy, it'll take forever to turn this wasteland into a settlement."

"Life takes forever," Edward answers. "If we aren't careful, the time of life will be like the track of a rocket. It will pass through a series of points without occupying any of them. If we conceive the moment as the hair's breadth between what is already gone and what hasn't yet arrived, we'll never find the expansive, hollow moment where we can live." Lars' stubborn resistance so exasperates him that in sharpening the point he makes it obscure. "The only life you ever have is today!"

"I didn't invent the universe," the other answers resentfully. "My job is just to get on with it."

Edward continues as though randomly musing. "I think my life—my time—is a broken line. Not a narrative with a plot. The only place it leads is to here and now, to us together on this hillside, to the crunch of the gravel under our boots and the sun over our heads. This is the only day that can be lived. The thing is to live it well. Your continuous line of relentless progress ends up nowhere, nothing, *nihil*—like a starship rushing at warp speed . . . where? How many generations lived in that tin can with no destination in mind? Life on hold while we chased a fantasy. No wonder they were bored. Boredom was their promise of salvation!"

Edward is a brusque man, certainly no diplomat. But neither is he the belligerent opponent Yori had once been, and so the exchanges with Lars rarely get overheated. Nevertheless it is Shi Wa who has the skill to draw Lars by sometimes devious routes into their vision of the settlement. When he gets carried away by the ambition to build, she is careful to raise practical rather than visionary objections and to keep the discussion from becoming a competitive struggle to be won or lost.

One evening she drops the chance suggestion that it would be convenient if two more settlers, possibly teachers, came immediately. She and Edward could easily arrange space for two.

Edward agrees. "Two would adapt faster than a dozen strangers at once. They would ease the way for the next lot of maybe eight or ten."

"Immediately?" Lars explodes. "Two? Then eight or ten?" he protests. "At that rate it will take forty years to get anything done! It'll take a year even with our technology to fabricate and install quarters, establish a food supply, water distribution, and a hundred other things. But by that time, we could have the infrastructure in place and you would have your settlement. Then bring in the settlers."

"Dear Lars," Shi Wa replies, "you're right of course. But what we're doing here is more like a science experiment than an industrial production. There's a difference between *settling* a way of life and assembling a support system. I know you want to do what's good for the settlers, but that won't get done if we decide *for* them. They must live into it along with all the frustrations of bringing it about. As they build a house and a village, they also build relations with the earth, the climate, the elements. Build it and give it to them and they'll *own* it, but they won't *have* it. It's the difference between giving a child a toy and letting the child invent the toy. If it's the child we care about rather than our pleasure in knowing-how, we help the child acquire that know-how. Surely you agree that if we care about them, we will make them inventive, not fill their closet with toys?"

Lars doesn't answer with his usual promptness so she gives him another long, affectionate look. "You watch. When this self-reliant way of life is described in the colony, we'll have to turn the volunteers away. There will be competition to give up the easy life and come up here for a real life. That will make the settlement an even stronger ideal. Maybe we should think about why that is."

Then an addendum that comes as lightly as a joke, "Afterward, you and I will have a long conversation about what life really is."

In just such a manner Shi Wa revives the discussion of the aqueduct that she had let die away the night before. She touches the subject gently, even affectionately. That's not difficult since, Lars' rigidities aside, he is a likeable fellow. "I know we don't all agree on how things should be done here, Lars, and that's fine. We can live on affectionate terms with people whom we seriously disagree with. And we care about you especially and want you to understand something."

She picks up two of the exhibits Edward used the night before. "I want you to take a slow look at this picture of the bare hill." She uses silence to force him to give attention to a picture that holds no practical interest for him. Then she hands him David Laroche's drawing.

"Now look at how that line of stone makes a visual cut across the natural gash in the landscape. Compare it to the photograph. See how the gradually descending line of stone turns the wilderness of barren rocks and scattered bushes into *a place*? It joins the hills and the valley and creates a location, as it unites earth and sky and water and the fire of the sun, into a human place where now there are only bits of geology and plant life. Your pumping station will deliver X number of gallons of water per day from the valley to the hill opposite, but this aqueduct will make a place of these space rocks and bind the human generations together for a thousand years. The water supply isn't just about growing vegetables. That's survival, but life must be *for something* greater than itself. The decision between a few stones and a pipe is a decision about the ultimate goods."

There is a sad fact here, with endless consequences. It is that however much time Lars spends with these people, however closely he listens to their conversation, none of it seems to stick. When forced to listen, as Shi Wa forces him, he will take her point for the moment. But the next day he will have snapped back like a bungee cord to yesterday's state of mind, leaving not a trace behind. Why in a man who is not at all stupid, who is grounded in all the same intellectual disciplines as they and quite as capable of considering a question from various points of view at the same time—why should such a man be captured by narrow interests? Why refuse to take the long view? The still more solemn question is what kind of polity can there be with people who understand but will not take the trouble to act on what they can see as good? On this occasion at least it is agreed to submit two plans for the waterworks to Yori and the Governor for a decision.

And so they did. Lars took them back to the colony and laid the drawings out on a table in Yori's office. He gave a fair description of each as Yori, leaning over the table, studied them, quick to see the elegance and impracticality of the one and the efficiency of the other. After studying them for a while, he straightened up and said with the old fraternal smile, "I admire the practicality of your solution. It seems straightforward and easy enough to do. I especially like how you have buried the pipeline and restored the surface of the ground so that nothing is spoiled. That, I suppose, will take some channeling out of the rock but it looks good."

Lars, gratified, expressed wonder that the settlers who would have to do most of the work if it went their way still preferred the aqueduct. "How much of life, after all, do people want to spend lining a wilderness hillside with boulders, however nicely they sparkle in the morning sun?"

Yori replied, "Yes, what *do* they want? Things do tend to come down to desire, don't they?" He waved the thought aside, "I guess there's no point in delaying the decision since the information is all in. Subject of course to the Governor's approval. Let's sit down and think this through carefully." So the two ancient friends and modern opponents sat down to consider.

Never one to beat about the bush, Lars began. "Well, you know what I think. I don't see that there is much more to be said. So what do you think?"

Yori took his time. "Well, it is beautiful. Laroche's drawing, I mean. Look at how the colony here was plopped down on a convenient flat spot. After all these years that sea of rocks out there is still nowhere. In a few hours of work one drawing has created a habitable site on this planet except for Paola's caves. To think that a simple arrangement of native rocks could turn those random hills into a human habitation! Compare that to this artificial environment"—with the gesture of one hand he put his own office in evidence —"or compare it to the life-support capsule of the starship."

Lars said nothing. Yori remained pensive for a few moments before continuing. "And yet, there's the cost. Life is concrete and local. Why should we sit down here at a distance and decide what the settlers up there should do with their lives? Mind you, I'm not being a libertarian. There's nothing more abstract and dangerous than the idea that people are Robinson Crusoes limited to their private interests. But universal issues aside, why shouldn't we help those pioneers do what they decide together? If they want to break their backs building their aqueduct, why shouldn't they? Meanwhile we'll look out on our nondescript plateau and envy them for having made a home where we have made none. It's true that they would be obligating themselves and others to maintain that thing, perhaps for generations to come."

Lars didn't care much for the direction Yori was going. "You sound homesick. Isn't all that romantic nonsense?"

Yori chose not to reply to the provocation. "I'm not trying to compromise the issue, but in this case why couldn't we lay the pipeline along the path of the aqueduct? They would be free to put it inside the stonework. If they actually do it, they get what they want and the maintenance issue is addressed. Your good idea of a temporary line from below to the cistern would still serve until the work is done. Meanwhile, their industry may surprise us."

And, with the Governor's approval, that's what was done, though it was not without a considerable expenditure of what is called political capital. Lars' technicians were deployed to quarry the stone for the aqueduct and distribute it along the way as planned. When construction began, it was a shaky beginning. No one had any experience building such an ancient structure. The engineers, instead of using their skill to help solve a curious problem, only saw how silly it was to build a bridge for water when water could be made to flow anywhere on command by pushing a button. And Edward didn't help. Instead of letting the engineers get on with their part of the work, he insisted they provide advice to the settlers on the theory, as he never tired of saying, that "growing people" is more cost-effective than efficiency. The young technicians, standing idly by watching a painful and unnecessarily slow process, complained of being reduced to teachers.

The result was that Lars' people revolted. They protested loudly and then, when he said his hands were tied, refused to work until he found a solution. By the time this first protest in the history of the colony was resolved the settlers had learned how to build an aqueduct, and relations in the North returned to normal.

But Lars Hanssen was the last person to sit still when he was made to look weak in the eyes of his subordinates. He threatened to go to the Council with his complaints if the Governor didn't intervene. Well, Governor Nasser did intervene in his benign, temporizing way and, if the problems were not resolved, at least they were postponed. But Lars was left smarting from embarrassment, and the event contributed to a store of resentment with implications that would reach into the distant future. He began to collect his weapons for ambushing Yori once Nasser was out of the way, and thus, before Yori even became Governor, colonial life took a turn toward political history.

24

YORI IS AWAKENED ONE morning in the early hours by a sharp rap on his door and summoned to the Governor's quarters. The old man has been taken ill and Yori finds him waiting, clinging to life long enough to say whatever he has to say.

Obeying a gesture to sit close by the bed, Yori waits until a few words begin to trickle out between laborious breaths. In a weak but steady voice he says, "In the cave . . . when I told you my name . . . I saw you had never known me. I was glad." Then a spasm of coughing before he can continue. "Take that paper." He stops to let his breath catch up with his words, then gestures feebly toward a side table. "Take that paper when you go . . . Read it later . . . I have difficult things to tell you . . . Then I'll ask for your blessing."

Continuing intermittently, in broken breaths he confesses that it was *he* who destroyed the landing party—acting under orders, but orders that he had approved without foreseeing the consequences. Weak as the dying man is, he calls up all his remaining energy to tell a story that recapitulates his life on Planet 2314. "Your father died by these hands." Raising them with difficulty from his chest, he holds them unsteadily before Yori. Slowly, painfully, it emerges that later, under the stresses of governing, he had come to appreciate the greatness of the man he had destroyed.

It's a confession, and confession throws Yori into a mael-strom of contrary feelings. At last, when all has been said that can be, he lays aside his own turbulent feelings and performs a paradigmatic political act: He lays the palm of his hand gently on the old man's head in a gesture of forgiveness.

Apparently it's enough. With a final surge of energy Nasser fixes him in a gaze that seems half pathos and half irony: "All will be well. Akira has won."

And with this benedictory invocation of the name of the father, responsibility for the colony passes to Yori.

Within hours he is quietly moved into the Governor's office where his first thought is of Paola. At the moment of greatest need she is far away. He sits for the first time at the big desk in that hollow cell and stares at all those monitors on the wall. During the months since Nasser announced his appointment to the Council and put the settlement in his hands, he has been initiated into the smooth operation of the colonial machine. By now the cooperation of the department heads is assured and, by a transition that has never occurred before, they will find themselves under his authority today. Another fortuity is that the sleepy colony with its loyalty to traditional organization will have no incentive to question the Governor's judgment in appointing him. Governor Nasser did it; therefore it was the right thing to do. That for any new official is an incalculable gift . . . and challenge.

And yet the Governor's death leaves Yori stirred to the lees and divided against himself. He has none of the positive feelings with which he might have welcomed this turn of fate in suddenly, after years of banishment, being restored and, within weeks, advanced to supreme authority. None of that touches him. He can form no distinct idea of his feelings except to repeat over and over to himself, "I don't want to be Governor."

The fact is that his unusual training for the post has left him with monkish tastes. He would much rather return to the caves and continue the contemplative life than attend endless meetings, read numbers on dials, and mediate between contrary opinions about where buildings should be built.

His first act is to call Paola in the North. Even her solemn face on the screen is a comfort. "The Governor just died."

"Long live the Governor." The cliché resurrected by an act of fate, neither playful nor gloomy. "I understand your misgivings but I congratulate you. This is the moment of your destiny. I'm sorry I can't be with you just now."

He swallows his doubts and says almost nostalgically, "Governor Nasser has been very good to me. I am sorry he is gone. But I don't want this. I know it's my fate, but I wish we could return to the hills and live like the gods."

The reply comes in the old, oracular voice. "What you want is irrelevant. That's where you differ from Lars. *He* thinks what he wants matters, but you understand that's life-denying. It's a death wish." Then dropping the prophetic tone, she directs his attention elsewhere. "Before you grieve too much, I promise to tell you when we meet of how much more harm Governor Nasser did to us all than you yet know. But for that you must wait. Meanwhile there is work to do. At the moment we're having a little power struggle here."

He makes an effort to answer lightly. "Let me guess. Slow human development against twenty-fourth-century technological revolution, and Lars is the hero!"

"It's just the new community building for the village. Véronique is carrying the burden of it, but I can't leave her just now. She's doing two important things at once: absorbing an entirely new ideal of life like a sponge from Shi Wa and keeping the peace between Edward and Lars. She's an extraordinary young woman. You know what a quick mind she has. You can rely on her resourcefulness and patience. Someday your city will know how blessed by destiny it will have been to have her and Edward and Shi Wa just where they are at this moment."

"And one other!"

Now he has to put all that aside and receive Council members who drop by to offer condolences and best wishes, unaware perhaps that their real need is to take a fresh look at the man who is now in charge. His calm attention betrays no consciousness of himself or that his relation to others is altered. The visitors appear to be reassured by gravitas in so young a man at such a moment. The Asian features also set him apart, of course, but the greater effect is of unfathomable character in one who has lived apart and been irrevocably changed by a decade in the wilderness. He bears a trait of mystery that will never leave him. If Paola had been there, she would see that something has indeed changed overnight, something more important than assuming the highest colonial office. She would see that quite suddenly the inherited face and the eyes have become his, that he has settled at last into the person whom only she and perhaps Governor Nasser had known was there.

At the end of the day he wants nothing so much as to get out. Before, in the world as it was yesterday, when he wanted to escape he could go to the hills. But now he can do nothing but ramble about in the colony enclosure. Although news of the Governor's death has spread quickly, public consciousness has not caught up with the consequences, and he is aware that this is his last ramble through the lanes under cover of anonymity.

There is a memorial for Governor Nasser, but Paola does not return immediately. She stays in the North until she can complete a public garden project she has in hand so that when she does return, her stay can be for some duration. Thus it is several weeks before she resumes her residency in Colony House. Once installed there, she's as unlikely to venture out into the colony as the colonials are to venture into the wilderness. Not that she has lost interest. She's invested as always in the expansion of her gardens in the canyon, invested in the village and her friends, and invested in Yori, but she has little curiosity about life in the colony otherwise. Somehow it just doesn't fit. The body accustomed to a lotus position on a rock does not adapt comfortably to form-fitted furniture. Generic food prepared by anonymous hands and labor-saving devices is tasteless. The garish light of a colonial enclosure that forbids dark corners makes her feel intruded upon. By preference, she would return immediately to her hills and caves except that she, too, has a destiny to serve.

Though she and Yori are free to resume the old habit of spending evenings together, on the second day after her return he asks her to come to the Governor's office. It's an odd request. Neither much likes the place, and both prefer to meet in his rooms or hers. She enters silently the room where reality has been digested into numbers and graphs on a wall of flickering monitors. Without a word the two sit down together as far as they can get from the electronic screens.

Conversation never comes easily in a place so empty, but there is something more than the alien setting. An ominous spirit, having nothing to do with officialdom, throws a heavy shadow across Yori's face and his mood. They remain silent for a few moments as of old to let their feelings come into harmony, but it doesn't work. As Paola cannot account for the heaviness, she waits for him to speak.

Eventually he does, laboriously. "There would seem to be many things to say. We haven't had a good talk in a long while." His gesture marks the unacknowledged reversal of roles, the novice having become ruler and the master having become subject. The fact is silently acknowledged and dismissed by both as insignificant.

"Shall I begin?" she asks, then begins, knowing it's all filler, biding the time, waiting for him to find the words for whatever she is there to hear. "You know all that's happening up North so I have only impressions to report. We can have high hopes for the village. There will always be crosscurrents portending different destinies as in an old Greek play. It's Edward I'd like to speak of. His only real political experience was during those few months when we were all together in the landing party. Otherwise he went directly from student to outlaw. Since then he has had only the private life of his family, and that has little to teach about political life. But he learns as fast as ever."

"What is he learning?"

"Thanks to Lars' intransigence, he has learned that conflicts over values are dangerous because they belong to unthinking moralism. Recently he observed that 'fraternal enemies cut the world in two and make one-half good and the other evil.' He went on to explain, 'They don't notice that they see the same issue in opposite ways.' More and more Edward is searching for the concrete phenomena behind our differences and letting discussions start there. Disappointments will come when he discovers how most people resist examining what they hold onto without thinking. But you see the promise."

Yori answers on subject, though his heart is elsewhere. "It's a good sign. Edward needs the company of you and your friends from the Elders." He stops and looks out across the room at Governor Nasser's little derelict garden and thinks, irrelevantly, that he should ask Véronique what can be done with it. Then he adds, "Edward and Shi Wa have completely altered the future as anyone could have foreseen it."

Paola replies with a touch of reluctance that is new between them. "There is a thing you might consider when the time is right. You might find a way of including the four remaining Elders in the planning loop. It would give you allies outside the means-and-ends Corps of Governors. In any struggle with the technocrats, you will need people who are capable of taking the broadest view. For example, Edward's research, if it leads anywhere, can't be shared with the department heads. Yet it needs oversight. No one with important—and dangerous—responsibilities should be left to his private judgment."

Though distracted still, Yori appears to turn the idea over in his mind. "I've just been introduced to them, aside from what we know from The Book, but that was who they were in a different world twenty-five years ago. We should talk about this idea again soon." Then he drops the subject.

After another pause he continues, "Now I have something I need to tell you. Not about us. More or less official. It's why we're meeting here in this broom closet for androids." Then instead of telling her, he stops short and even gets up again to pace the floor. She has not seen that since the day when a mere boy bearing his name walked up and down by the cistern in the hills raging against his banishment. Eventually, he sits down again with his back to the monitors, apparently ready at last to face whatever he has to say.

"I have told you only a little about the night the Governor died, the part about killing my father. I was summoned to his rooms at—I don't know—maybe three o'clock in the morning. He wanted to talk. And he did talk, intermittently. He talked for what seemed like an eternity. From time to time he would pause to gather his strength or renew his resolve. Then, propped up on pillows nearly in sitting position and looking at me from dark, sunken eyes, he would go slowly on, the hands folded on the cover in front as though they would not be needed again and had already been put away. In a weak but steady voice he said:

"'When the sun rises, you'll be governor of the last human outpost in history. But first you must hear things that will make you a better ruler. Some of it you will have had already from Paola Rucai, but most of it she doesn't know.' And again he had to stop and wait for breath to go on."

Yori stopped too and sat distracted for a few moments as though there was a wrinkle in the narrative he hadn't seen before. "Maybe it wasn't for breath he stopped. He had been rehearsing this story for twenty-five years, waiting for the person who would have to receive it, and now for some reason he was having trouble getting it right. The rest had been scrawled on paper, probably over several days. He had me take it away to read later. I *have* read it. Over and over. Now you must hear it too."

Yori unfolds the paper and begins reading:

> By the time you read this I will have told you that I knew and admired Akira, your father, but there is more to tell than I will be able to say. You must know I was an enemy of Akira's scheme to hijack the colony, and it was my job to hunt him down. This is not a deathbed confession or an apology. I am not culpable. I was acting under orders. Every established authority, every rule, every right was on my side, or so I thought. Akira had instigated the rebellion and the rest were killed for what his words and his ideas had made of them. Cleverly he got out ahead of us and loaded the landing party with their own disciples. For the sake of the colony as we saw it, the teacher and the disciples had to be purged and we had to start over.

Yori pauses along enough to glance aside at Paola. She isn't looking at him or at anything else in the room, and he reads volumes in that absence of response. He knows that gaze into the nothing, beyond the room and its banalities, despising whatever is there to be seen. She is holding herself open, whether in wonder or hate or indifference, for whatever may be approaching from beyond, not knowing what she will find—or what will find her—at the extremity of that empty and expectant squinting of the eyes. Discreetly he returns his eyes to the paper and continues.

> *What I must get you to see is that it was not between him and me or between Command and the rebels. It was like two of those old gods we read about in school who were driven by fate to destroy each other—or try. We were all trying to do the same thing in different ways. The species had to be saved. But it wasn't the same thing after all. For Akira and all the other dreamers—God bless them now—the point wasn't a goal at the end of a process, not even the salvation of humanity. He had come to think that trying to save the species was the sure way to lose the human—to have already lost it. Your father wanted humanity to* deserve *to survive! I still don't completely understand that, but it's what he said on the day he died.*

> *I entered the caves that day with my band of storm troopers—the cave you call the Chamber of Names. We were more like a posse from an old western, there to enforce the law because without law there is chaos. The others were all there—or so we thought—like Robin Hood's men in Sherwood Forest carving their eternal names on that damned wall. A bunch of lunatics*

suffering from some exotic fever. That's what we had been told.

Akira knew instantly why we were there. He was anything but a lunatic and he certainly wasn't sick. He asked me to send all the others outside so we could talk. Just the two of us. Not that he was going to try to talk me out of it. He was the last person who would have groveled and pled for his precious self. Too noble for that. Knew better than to waste the time too. No. He wanted to use the moment he knew I would never forget to speak for all futurity, to plant the seeds in my mind that he had planted in the others. He stood there in that dark cave facing certain death, knowing that all futures depended on his words. It was not a conversation. It was a monologue, a homily, a blessing, a curse. I don't rightly know what it was. I do know it was a leap of faith. Not in me. I understood very little at the time and he knew it. But he had that much faith in words. He loved existence by loving words and he could use them like Orpheus.

I let him finish, then he died knowing those words would lie in some out-of-the-way corner of my mind until they changed me utterly. That's what had happened with Paola Rucai and Edward Hamilton and Kwan Shi Wa and the rest. He was a soothsayer who could use words to reshape the world. And he knew they would. I saw it in his face as he went down.

Again Yori glances in Paola's direction, where nothing has changed. Not so much as a blink of an eye.

It wasn't two factions against each other. It was the crucible of history. Not strife exactly, because the two parties, the Elders and Command, didn't even coincide in opposing each other. One side bet everything on fabricating a human world as it had fabricated a starship, while Akira knew—as over the years I would come to know—that some things can't be made. They have to be accepted as given and nurtured. You'll see.

You'll have your city—and your father's—so long as you don't decide what a city is and set out to make it. It must happen as a collateral effect of tending to the little everyday things. Your job will be to recognize it when it becomes possible. It won't look like you expect it to look. All you can do is care for whatever turns up. It can't be made, but it can be destroyed before it's born.

"That's all." Yori continues to stare at the paper in his hand. "He stops there as if he has told everything. How often do we get to see a man sum up his life on his last day and in his last hour? That's what the Governor said, and it was enough for a lifetime."

He looks up to meet Paola's eye, but what he meets instead is a face so pale, so stricken, that he moves to her side. "I've been stupid," he adds. "I saw that this was your story as much as mine. I didn't see how much more closely it touches you than me."

In a few moments she composes herself. "It's Shi Wa's and Edward's story too. When the time is right, I must find a way to tell them."

245

25

YORI, NOW GOVERNOR KASHIMOTO, had been asking one question since his student days: How is a life-support system ever to become a city? When he had been stung by ridicule at the Academy, Paola had pointed him toward the words of the young Hans Rückert in *Starship Galatea*. Those words had given him a head full of baffling questions that returned like old scores that had to be settled now. He needed nothing so much as the conversation of people with greater experience. Who better than the older Rückert himself?

Paola's suggestion about the four émigré Elders came at an opportune moment. If the moment of transition to a new governor were allowed to pass, the colony would settle back into routine and Yori would have missed the only chance he might ever have to give the essential nudge in the direction of a polity. So if he hadn't exactly leapt at Paola's idea of calling on the old Elders, he hadn't forgotten it. In fact he thought of little else.

There were practical difficulties, however. He would need to get to know the four people well, to persuade them to accept a formal role in governance, and then cope with the resulting strains in the Corps of Governors. The direction of Yori's thinking went something like this: It might just be possible to establish a Council of Elders as a complement to the Corps of Governors. It's approximately what the designers of the mission had in mind nearly three centuries ago: a Council as counterweight to Starship Command.

The primary responsibility of such a group might be the schools and the perpetual education of the public. At the present stage of development that might not be controversial, but the essential point would be to give them a voice in policy. He imagined, as half of a bicameral advisory structure, the Corps concerned with practical operations, the Elders with critical exploration of contexts and coherences. With these sketchy ideas in view, Yori waited for another conversation with Paola.

The occasion was a simple evening meal together in her apartment. According to the Rule, still honored between them, the real talk had to wait until after eating and restoring domestic order. Then they settled down together and he opened the topic.

"I have been considering your suggestion about the Elders. You know them and I don't, so I'd like you to tell me about them, especially why they chose the colony rather than remaining on the ship."

"Here's what I know," she answers. "First Ava Sarosh. She's a sociologist from a distinguished family of Persian descent. She followed in the footsteps of her great-grandmother, who was a member of the Council three generations before her. Her primary connection to the colony is her late brother Barham Sarosh. You remember him as the member of the ill-fated landing party who designed the present colony buildings. At least"—she waves a hand in an arc to indicate the whole of the enclosure—"this is what Command did with his ideas after he was dead. You know that he and I were in love and hoped to become permanent members of the colony. Ava hasn't mentioned her motives to me, but I suspect Barham had something to do with her decision."

Satisfied to learn that Sarosh is much the person she was in The Book years ago, Yori passes to the next person on the list. "Leaving aside Ang Yimou for a moment—there's a mystery about him—what about Joseph Kern? Why is he here?"

Paola continues in the same relaxed, almost gossipy spirit. "Joseph is here for the most ordinary of motives. Except for your father, he was the one closest to my father. He read classics with him in his youth, though he specialized in a different area of European literature. After the disaster of the landing party, when the Council had lost its influence on the ship—what he calls the passing of the Rucai-Kashimoto era—he had no desire to spend the rest of his life on the Galatea. He gambled that once the influence of Starship Command was removed from the colony, there might be a chance—the only chance remaining in his lifetime—to help realize the Elders' dream."

Yori nods and moves on. "You directed me to Rückert's political ideas some years ago and I presume from your present regard for him that he isn't a disappointment in that field. That's recommendation enough, but why is he here? Were his motives for choosing the colony similar to Kern's?"

"Yes, but there's an untold story. I suspect his state of mind was quite different from Joseph's. The most important person in Hans' life was the political theorist Oleksiy Hunenko. You know Hunenko too from Kahn's book. He was Rückert's teacher, a generation older, and his companion for life. The additional factor in Hans' case may have been Hunenko's death. He would have decided that a complete break was preferable to nostalgia and hopelessness. It's what you might expect from the Rückert you meet in the Colloquies, though you'll find him changed." Her eyes narrow and her tone modulates to a darker key. "That brings us to the mystery."

Yori marks the change. "Yes. Much depends on Ang Yimou."

Paola takes her time as though making an inventory of what she knows and finding it thin. "I don't *know* anything. All this is surmise, but surmise is necessary here. You know that in their youth he and Rückert were a bit like Lars and you. And much for the same reasons. They straddled—from opposite directions—the two cultures that extend back into Ulro history."

She pauses again as Yori takes the measure of the political risks that might follow any effort to give these two, even these four—with Paola, five—a formal role in governance.

She resumes, "We know several things, and the DNA project is central. Ang was Edward's teacher and directed his research on the Galatea. But for him, Edward would never even have learned about the DNA project since it was the best-kept secret on the ship. The fact that the files got here at all seems to prove that the starship commander didn't know they were on board. The knowledge had been passed down the generations of chief biologists and was shared with no one else until our generation. That indicates that Ang expected Edward to be his successor."

Yori speculates, "Then if First Mate Nasser and Ang Yimou had largely shared the idolatry of technological progress, Governor Nasser's change of heart might have left him reluctant about inviting his old friend into the colony?"

"Yes," she answers, "unless the research project was his bargaining chip! On this account the Governor may have learned about it from Ang when the ship began preparing to leave the planet. At the time Nasser invited him, neither of them could have known Edward was alive, as Edward didn't know the colony existed."

Paola stops again to look for possibilities she might have missed in the morass of detail, as Yori observes, "And, once here, the project remained completely secret."

Paola, still looking for consistency in the facts as they know them, asks, "But then, why wasn't Ang allowed to continue his research in secret?"

"Maybe the Governor, or he, or both, saw that the time wasn't right. Only the two of them stood between the status quo and a Dr. Frankenstein nightmare being loosed on the planet."

Yori finds humor in that idea and what happened next: "Then I turned up with the news and Nasser, the wily old fox, never said a word. Just consented to let Edward work on the project in the northern mountains far from prying colonial eyes."

Paola gives him a broad grin in response, to this new and surprising intelligence. "You think Nasser was playing a cloak, if not a dagger, game all along? Perhaps. Once real life had inspired his political conversion, he might have invited Ang to the colony *in order* to get those materials off the ship. Knowing Ang's predisposition to the best and worst sides of specialization—all his students knew that about him—Nasser managed to gain control *and* to control Ang. Nothing interested Ang anyway but his project. Even Edward, his best and most advanced student, was never close to him personally. We always wondered why Ang was chosen to join the Elders in the first place. He wasn't the type."

That opens another line of speculation, and she continues. "If Akira and Claudio had known somehow about the DNA, they might have gotten Ang on the Council to safeguard the secret by keeping him close. We have no evidence of that, but, knowing them, we can imagine they saw some reason to expand his horizons."

To which Yori adds a further speculation: "So, when I approached the Governor on the subject and got permission to share the files with Edward, he, Nasser, wouldn't even have consulted Ang!" Yori studies that set of improbabilities for a few moments, then pushes the theory ahead another degree. "That means that when Edward showed up in the Council meeting with Ang present, all the information for solving the riddle was in that room."

"Yes," Paola replies. "And Ang would not have shown a thing. Just taken it all in and waited to see where the mystery would lead. But Edward's not at all like that. He doesn't have the same craftiness."

"Edward would just have thought that Ang was in the secret with the Governor and with me."

Paola is still skeptical. "But, suddenly finding Ang in the room, Edward must have wondered why Ang's name had never even been mentioned in his presence. And how is it that they had no personal contact after that unexpected encounter?"

In this search for consistency Yori has to back up. "Or maybe we've got it all wrong. Maybe Ang's horizons expanded under the influence of the new Nasser and colonial reality. However complicated, Edward's sudden appearance and the prospect of his research being shared without his knowledge, Ang might have done exactly what our fathers would have done: set his own interests aside for the greater political good and bided his time."

"If that's who Ang has become, he's now ready for appointment to your Council of Elders."

Having inferred so much from so little, they turn to the political risks, and Yori slants the question differently. "On the view that Nasser didn't trust Ang but did trust Edward, why would I put Ang on a small council that Edward might later join? Wouldn't that be asking for trouble?"

"Why should you add Edward?"

"Because four people can't provide the diversity of a council of twenty. Even though one may count for more than one."

Paola emends the arithmetic: "As in a conversation each additional person expands the group exponentially."

"True. And these councils don't vote on things anyway. They argue as in an old law court. So even in the worst case, Ang would provide diversity."

Having exhausted their speculations on these topics, the two sit on together in silence much as in the periods of ritual contemplation in her gardens. She had tried, not very successfully, to make her apartment as much like the Chamber of the Hearth as possible, mainly by dispensing with conveniences. Besides using a straw mat on the floor for sleeping, the only visible success was the small table. She had cut the legs off so it could be used while sitting on the floor. And there they sat, these two, as though across the hearth in the cave, she in lotus position on one side, hands resting in her lap, and he, in Japanese seiza-style, kneeling on the mat, thighs resting on his calves and the tops of his feet. And nothing more was said that evening.

When Yori returns to his quarters, he spends much of the rest of that night in reflections on his new responsibilities. He had had little time to anticipate becoming Governor before the reality overtook him, but he feels poignantly how little the most careful plans would have coincided with the thing itself anyway. To whatever degree he may fancy that he is the same person as before, his place in the world and all his connections are unimaginably altered. Not dramatically in all cases but decisively.

26

AFTER ALL THEIR SPECULATIONS, when Paola and Yori meet the four Elders in the Council room of Government House, events turn out much as she had foreseen.

Having done his homework, Yori is free to gather first impressions. Once the six are seated toward one end of that big conference table, he is startled by how old these people are. The youngest is a generation older than Paola. On the ship, in Ishmael Kahn's account, the four were young members of a small circle of wise elders when he was still a child. And age may be related to the unexpected ambiance of the group. The tone is quiet and respectful toward Paola and him, apparently for their having sacrificed everything for the mission.

But what strikes Yori most is the room, the difference in the mood of the place now and the mood when the Corps of Governors meets here. On all other occasions when he has been present the space has been full of people and charged with what is called "strong personalities." Interests, all competing across the flat plane of that huge table, all filled with self-consciousness and ambition. The Corps of Governors may be civil and cooperative as far as their common interest in the colony extends, but here the atmosphere is quite different. The disposition the Elders bring with them is replete with purpose.

Yet something is wrong. Yori scans the room looking for an answer. Then, as soon as he moves on to other considerations, he sees what it is. The room itself is wrong. It's alien to the spirit of reflection and much too big for the six people spread around a table that would be ample for thirty. The rigidity of that object between them pushes them apart even as their words pull them together. It's exactly the wrong spirit, and he makes a mental note to find a more appropriate place.

All this aside, he is inspired with confidence that things said here and now will be said for truth, not advantage.

Before he can speak, however, Ava Sarosh addresses him quite informally, no doubt to establish a tone: "I wonder if you know that you are an exact image of your father. He, along with Claudio Rucai"—she glances at Paola sitting next to her—"were the most respected men on our Council, and we have never forgotten Akira's loss." Sarosh, now in her sixties, bears still the charm and the handsome features of her Persian heritage.

Yori is strangely moved by this unexpected and gracious tribute to his father. He shows as much, as he thanks her—a bit awkwardly. Then, after a pause, he addresses them all. "I know you all best as characters in a chronicle that you commissioned Ishmael Kahn to assemble about life on the Galatea. You may not know it since there was only one copy and it was smuggled down to Paola by her father and mine."

Sarosh interjects, "Thanks to Paola, we have all read it."

After his restoration Yori had met these people but only in passing, and so he now looks slowly from face to face as though trying to close the gap of twenty years between the characters in a book and their presence in the flesh. Then he says, "I've asked you to meet here to offer advice on establishing a new Council. It would make you collectively part of the governing structure."

He goes on to specify that first they might assume oversight of the schools as on the starship. Who but the most learned should do so? But the more vital task would be as part of the governing structure of the colony. Here he cites as inspiration the Roman Tribunes, who could legislate nothing but propose anything, except that their role would be more like a think tank responsible for exploring the implications and consistencies of all plans and proposals and advising the Governor.

Immediately Joseph Kern is skeptical about so small a council. He leans as far as he can across that expanse of table and responds. "If you mean we five"—Yori notices that he tacitly includes Paola—"five can hardly encompass the breadth of learning and experience of twenty. We could hardly pick up here where we left off on the ship."

Yori responds, "Twenty advisors may be better than five but five are better than none. Didn't someone on your council once say, 'What is necessary is usually impossible'?"

When no one replies immediately, he drops another remark into the silence. "If you were favorably disposed toward the general idea, I would offer a related one."

By a cautious glance in Hans Rückert's direction he tries to judge just how favorable the mood is. Rückert is known to have the keenest political instincts in the group, and he has said nothing so far. He would be looking ahead for implications. Whatever Yori reads in Rückert's face, it inspires him with a daring move. He goes on to speak openly of Edward Hamilton's DNA project, now in the planning stages, making a point of how any expansion of the ecosystem would need critical oversight. "It's a task for disinterested scrutiny by other good minds. I hope you will meet with him and discuss where to go from here. I think he will value your council as much as I will rely on it."

Ang shows nothing!

Meanwhile the proposed council inspires questions about the duties he foresees them assuming, their range of topics, and how they would relate to the Corps of Governors. They remember very well that only once had the Commander of the Galatea sought the advice of the Elders and that only for reasons of public relations. The Council of Elders could influence social life on board and discuss whatever arcane topics they liked, but they had no voice in decisions about the mission.

Yori replies to these general concerns, "Responsibility for the schools, because any polity begins with the young, and a public that can participate in the colony must be enlightened by more than information. They must know how to think. Beyond that, if you're wondering what master plan I have in mind, I can only say I come empty-handed. Isn't that governance best that concentrates on the needs of the day?"

Through this and much more Paola sits silently by, observing, taking the auspices of the quickly developing relation between Yori and the others. She studies the faces, their patterns of attention, the absence of self-conscious reserve. It's as though everything happening is happening without distraction, on the picture plane, at the front of the stage. In fact, even if they do look trapped in their chairs by the table, everyone present is so engaged that no one but she, Paola, notices that they are in agreement and the new Council of Elders is already at work.

Though Yori shows little on his impassive face, she watches him wait for Rückert to speak. The precocious and impatient young man he so admires in The Book isn't here, and Yori is having trouble fitting the present Rückert to him. Gradually he adjusts to the gravitas of this quiet older man to the pursed lips and slight frown. When he finally speaks it's with apparent irrelevance. "I suppose we're stuck with the name Corps of Governors? It gives the impression that governing is about housekeeping. That, I suppose, is not what you mean by caring for the needs of the day."

"Correct." Yori gives his Japanese smile, leaving the impression that on questions of governance they understand each other very well.

Ang Yimou, who has also said nothing and shown nothing on his face, now offers a more concrete version of Rückert's question about authority, again without a trace of self-consciousness. "You mentioned Edward Hamilton's DNA research. Who has final authority there? I see that you're looking for shared responsibility because of the sensitivity of the project, but the buck always stops somewhere. Where?" The tone is not as sharp as it sounds. It's an uncompromising question but carefully controlled and inoffensive.

At this Paola feels reassured and sees Yori almost visibly sigh with relief. There are two reasons: The political subtlety of

Ang's question is very different from what they both know of the much younger Ang Yimou. And, for whatever reason, Ang is letting himself be seen as not making trouble over Edward's having, in a sense, supplanted him in his own research.

She knows in advance how Yori will respond. He has been living with the question for years and it has become second nature. And yet he takes his time to consider how to respond without beginning that infinite conversation tonight.

He says, "Think of two councils along with the Governor as three intersecting circles. A Venn diagram. In the quest for the broadest and clearest vision, one council considers practicality, the other imagines where possibilities might lead. As they overlap with each other, the Governor overlaps with both and finally decides. Then, for realism, redraw the Venn diagram as a knot composed of dotted lines."

To which Ang asks, "And who wields the knife that cuts the knot?"

He chuckles. "Knots made of broken lines are not famous for their strength. But to answer your question, as things now stand, the Governor wields the knife." He continues to grin good-humoredly. "But we're not trying to take away tomorrow's freedom for making its own mistakes. Just not to encumber it with our mistakes."

As all five appear to wait for him to say more, he adds, "Is the question really about who has the power to choose or is it about the basis of the choice? The Colloquies of the Elders show that responsible judgment moves in the largest circle of influences. I would hope for a council devoted to the widest possible speculation."

Sarosh observes with a warm smile, "You're imagining a large agenda for a small group. Twenty of us often had our hands full with the schools alone."

To which Yori replies, "Shouldn't we start by lodging authority where it belongs, then find ways of making the impossible possible? You can expand your ranks as opportunity offers. For starts you might find Edward Hamilton a worthy and compatible colleague."

At this point the exchange might have become general except that Rückert hangs fire as though he has something else in mind. Everyone waits until he says, "I think you will all agree that nothing much has been decided tonight except perhaps the governance of this colony for the foreseeable future."

He raises his bushy eyebrows in something approximating a smile. "I propose we end with a firm recommendation to the Governor. One thing has been tacit in all we have said: The first time his authority is challenged—and it soon will happen in the Corps of Governors—he must firmly maintain the integrity of his office. That will be decisive for years to come."

Kern asks facetiously, "And why shouldn't his authority be challenged?"

"Because," Paola answers in her mock-sibylline voice, "he isn't an individual; he's an operation." And that was sufficient to terminate even a discussion among people whose new job it was to sit in a council room endlessly talking.

After this meeting, back in Yori's apartment, Paola asks, "Did you see how your gambit rattled Ang? As you intended it to, of course. He almost noticeably smiled! For him that counts as rattled . . . and it's a good omen."

"I hadn't planned to move so fast, but on the spur of the moment it seemed like a good test and a shortcut. Now we should keep our ears to the ground. You with Edward. He will listen to you. And, if necessary, I might talk with Ang."

"Let me broach the matter with Edward first. In his student days Ang respected him as a scientist, and they worked well together. Chances are he would be thrilled to have his teacher as a colleague in the project."

Then for a while longer Paola and Yori sat on in silence considering a range of new possibilities opened by the innovation in the governance. For Paola, the interesting question followed from the last point Hans Rückert had raised: How would the Council of Elders respond when inevitable discontents set in. Not disagreements with each other. They had lived with thrived on controversy for most of their lives. But what would happen when they met the first opposition from the Corps of Governors, whom they would see, however charitably, as lightweights? And how would Yori respond when he was caught in the middle?

27

THEN CAME A PROBLEM: the incalculable that always follows the best-laid plans. After the colony became self-sustaining and the Galatea left this solar system, the growth in population began to strain production of goods and services. On the starship, given unlimited energy sources, materials had been fabricated from radical elements, and that capacity had been duplicated on the ground. But the capacity was always limited. With population growth the burden on infrastructure required changes or feasible alternatives. The only alternative was the ancient and far simpler process of mining heavy metals for new machinery.

Governor Nasser had prepared the way for the project with considerable care. As early as his first year in office he had taken a turn toward responsible management of the planet, and that change of heart had endured. His instinct for conservation may have been negative, along the line of twentieth-century ecology: management still, but careful management with an increasingly strong sense of not disrupting nature needlessly.

"Do no permanent damage," he might have said. "Walk without leaving footprints." That bore little resemblance to Paola's and Shi Wa's sense of earth as interwoven with individual and collective human existence, but it was enough to raise an eyebrow among the pragmatists and lighten their steps.

For as long as possible Nasser held the project in abeyance, hoping against hope that a third way would turn up. When it didn't, the moment for choice arrived and forced him either to renew constraints on human reproduction or begin exploring for raw materials. So he relented. Lars Hanssen got the nod, the Governor died, and Yori didn't interfere.

After surveys showing substantial deposits of iron, copper, and other heavy elements far south of the equatorial plateau, Lars chooses a younger engineer named Roger Portman to accompany him by land rover to several sites. Portman is a recent graduate and an outstanding student of the physical sciences, assigned to metallurgy. Unlike Lars, who came up in the ambitious curriculum of the Galatea Academy, he is more narrowly educated along the lines of specialization Starship Command had expected the colonial schools to produce. The result is that he is at once the person best qualified to take samples of the crust of the planet and analyze them and least qualified to influence public policy. So as the two set off across country where no one has been before, the younger is prepared to give the older a lesson in mining and accept (or not) a political lesson in turn.

The first leg of the trip is over land that looks very much like the desert except for a slow rise of the ground and increasing vegetation of kinds that they wouldn't recognize even if they took the time to notice. On the second day the rocky landscape slowly turns to fine red sand that impedes their progress. It is slowed again when they reach a landscape punctuated by dunes that, for safety, they must go around rather than over.

When eventually they reach the first set of designated coordinates, there is nothing to see. The numbers are right but there's no place there. The only thing to consult in selecting a spot for camping is the scattered patches of brush useful for a campfire. So they pull the land rover close to some brush in the shadow of one of the smaller dunes and unpack their gear. After gathering fuel for an evening fire, the remaining daylight is spent staking points where they will take samples of the planet shell.

The evening is filled with enthusiastic discussion about the technical challenges of mining such a landscape, what equipment would be needed, how large a team of workers, and a dozen related topics. What, after all, is there to do in such an inhospitable and monotonous place? In fact there is much to do. There is more to see in the landscape than they take time for. It's a picturesque scene, a vast red sea of windswept sand. Between the great dunes, the wind has sculpted intricate repetitive patterns like a moderate chop on the surface of a red sea.

Lounging on their folding camp stools by the smoldering brush, they dream of mining and refining and of building a human world. They miss many things that more receptive spirits wouldn't miss: the red sun hanging above the horizon trying not to set, the modulations of color in shadows of the dunes, the luxuriant cooling of the air on their skin, even the smell of the burning brush. But most of all they miss the incomprehensible vastness of land and sky that has been here morning and night for billions of years with barely a trace of life. Why do they not, these first two explorers, take a new measure of human ambition and its rage for certainty? No answer except that they do not.

After eating their rations, there is time for conversation. Young Portman has already heard about possible ecological restrictions on any plan for development. Why, he wonders, choose harder, slower, and more wasteful ways of developing the mines? "Why don't they draw a straight line between A and B? Why waste time preserving land where nobody has ever been? Nobody will ever see it. What difference can it make out here?"

Lars replies in the paternal voice that he enjoys using. "You will learn that political decisions are never efficient. You have to be patient with people who don't want a rock disturbed. It's a kind of romantic illusion. Efficiency will eventually win. Already is winning, actually. The fact that we're here is a concession to practicality. But they'll learn better in the new settlement. If not in that one, then the next one. Not fast enough for us, but they'll learn. Meanwhile we have to put up with this sentimentality about not disturbing nature in the raw."

But Portman isn't thinking on so wide a scale. "Will they put the manufacturing facilities out here with the mines"—he points in the direction of the spot where they have been drilling—"or will they haul the raw materials back to the colony for processing? Either way the land between will be disturbed. There will have to be a corridor of some kind for industrial traffic."

"If I know them," Lars replies, "they will end up doing the opposite of whatever is expedient. My guess is they will haul the raw materials to the plateau because some people won't want to isolate the workers out here in an industrial camp. That might lead to a permanent settlement under circumstances regarded as too primitive."

"What's too primitive for a mining camp?" Portman looks around vacantly as though his own blindness proves something. "What do you need? Food, shelter, and work. What else is there?"

Lars may look on Portman's idea favorably, and at that moment his face reflects as much. But he answers in a different spirit. "The view is—and if I read the cards right, this view is likely to get stronger—that people should not live without the cultural amenities of schools and music and gardens and all that. Don't get me wrong. All that's good in its way. You know that Sandra Mohr, my girlfriend, is a musician and I'm very proud of her, but when it comes to progress, we can't always afford the niceties until the hard work is done. Comfort and well-being come first so people can enjoy the niceties."

"You're right. How long is it going to take to get back to those fundamentals?"

The expedient Lars, sensing that it may not be particularly useful to imply criticism of the governors, wisely backs off. After all, Lars is no Portman. He is a more complicated person, educated in the ancient tradition of the arts and sciences on the starship; and the person he has always respected most, his oldest friend and enemy, is the new governor. Nor is it accidental that the woman he loves is an artist. Lars Hanssen is a different being than his companion, and at their next stop that divided consciousness begins to show.

The second site among is entirely different from the first. It's on a gently undulating plane with patches of greenery unlike anything recorded so far on the planet. By this time exploration is settling into routine, and Lars can spare a little attention for the surroundings. Not going so far as to measure human capacities against infinity, perhaps, but he does look closely at several varieties of plant life different from anything in Yori's hills or in the North. He even collects a few samples for Véronique.

As usual they set up their equipment and continue boring into the surface, drawing up samples from great depths and examining their composition curiously. During working hours they are absorbed in the task at hand and miss both the earth under their feet and a softness of a light they have never seen before. But Lars is not blind. Just distracted. Occasionally, after work and after planning the next day, he gives a little attention to the landscapes, comparing this more gentle terrain to that sea of red sand and to the hostile desert environment of the colonial plateau. If he stopped to reflect, he would surely see that he has begun to enjoy these vast open landscapes, the undulating surface, the grandeur of the planet and its sky. But Lars rarely has time to reflect.

So it goes for days, place after place, keeping progress in sight until, replete with data and enthusiastic recommendations for the improvement of life, they retrace their tracks to the colony.

When Yori convenes his first session of the Corps of Governors, one might expect all eyes to be on him. But as he takes his seat at the head of the big table in the council room of Government House, all eyes are not on him. Not exactly. There are traces of discontent in the room, and they confirm his resolve to hold the agenda as close as possible to routine operations. He will make no waves except for one detail at the end.

His first intention is to relieve whatever anxiety the department heads may feel about his intervening in their daily operations. To that end he begins with procedures related to the settlement, since it is everyone's preoccupation. All the departments are at least remotely involved with activities in the North, and since operations in that quarter are far from routine, matters of coordination need to be settled at these meetings.

When the topic comes up, Lars apparently judges it both appropriate and timely to air his grievances over the management of affairs in the settlement. Appropriate, in that by tradition members are free to raise any subject of common concern in this forum, and timely, in that most members remain out of the planning loop. If changes of direction are to occur, when better than at the changing of the guard? It turns out that Lars has even solicited some support for his ideas in advance and brought one of his subordinates along for good measure. The gamble apparently is that he has more to gain from attacking the *idea* of inefficiency early on than waiting until all present are closely involved enough to judge for themselves. Thus a meeting intended to be routine takes a different turn.

Lars' discontent may have most to do with the settlement, but the mines also feed it. So, perhaps emboldened by subordinates like Portman, he decides in advance to lodge a complaint at this first meeting of the Corps with "Governor Yori," as he calls him privately. Unbidden, he rises from his place far down the council table. Nothing unusual there. It's practical for formal presentations in such a large group. Lars casts his remarks as an argument against the way expansion in the North—by now an entity in its own right—is being led by "outsiders" who don't share the traditional values of the colony. Whatever audience he is playing to, whatever his other motives, it's surely a tactical blunder to cast the issue in personal terms. Not only does it throw an unnecessary shadow across Paola, Shi Wa, and Edward, but it lays the responsibility at Yori's door for having delegated too much authority to them.

He begins, "Though the new Governor and I agree on many things, we have never seen eye to eye on questions concerning technology. The issue has become important because in the North we are wasting resources on highly inefficient construction methods." He goes on to cite examples of what he regards as mistaken: the decision not to build a north-south service road; the decision to build a useless aqueduct; the decision not to throw all available skilled labor into constructing the village. Then, for good measure, he includes the debates over establishing a mining and production center in the South. His broad face reddens, and his baritone grows stronger as he ticks off the mistakes. While he does not push the issue so far as an explicit challenge to the Governor's authority, the implication is that the Council should have more than an advisory role in such decisions.

Yori does not interrupt. Better to let opposition make its case and use the time to consider his response. It's now clear what the anxiety in the room is about, that barely detectable fragmenting of attention: Lars has taken the precaution of drawing other members into his cause so he may appear to be voicing a general concern.

Conscious or not, the effort is to get a foot in the door, an opening bid for legislative power. Yori sees as much and also sees that his first trial is at hand, especially as others appear to join Lars' cause. But when he listens for the telltale passion behind each speech, he doesn't find it. The support appears to be little more than a mechanical nodding of heads without the conviction that a little thinking might have lent the remarks. Even the energy of Lars' own argument seems to draw its passion from some peripheral source. Not that he isn't serious. Rather that his idea doesn't come across as being his real interest. His words have a polemical edge that sounds more like reprisal for injuries sustained.

What determines Yori's response is less Lars' words than the suggestion of dissatisfaction among members who have not been immediately involved with the settlement. The fact is attested by traces of embarrassment on several faces around the table. What as Governor he must protect against at all costs is this early gesture toward partisan interests. Concede power to opinion, and the very possibility of a polity will gradually be sacrificed to the tyranny of public whim, perhaps for generations.

But rather than joining a debate over his decisions and conceding a modicum of juridical authority to the Council, Yori smiles fraternally at Lars and says, "It is true that Lars and I used to pass the time debating the virtues of technology. In my student days I was wrong to demonize machines. It was like opposing plowshares and pruning hooks. Instead of renewing all that, I want to tell you a story that I have from a variety of sources, most recently from Governor Nasser on his deathbed."

Murmurs of approval are audible and some members exchange glances of relief. The offer to tell a story has also defused anxiety, and the reference to the first Governor has had a still greater effect. Two present members of this group were early colleagues of Nasser and the rest were chosen by him, so the invocation of his name restores equanimity. Those who may have feared an embarrassing scene turn eagerly toward Yori and receive something still more surprising.

"The piece of our history that we must never forget, Governor Nasser said, is the heroic struggle that was lost and then won for this colony. It makes the three who have been called 'outsiders' the most intimate 'insiders' in this community. It's all about the original landing party. Everyone knows a sanitized version of what happened, but what isn't known, except to these three heroic citizens, is that the party of explorers was deliberately liquidated under orders from Starship Command."

This speech sends a seismic tremor and audible gasps through the room, but Yori does not break his momentum. "The Council of Elders on the Galatea always knew such things might happen if the technocracy of the starship were to gain *exclusive* control of a colony, as it had, in part by necessity, controlled life on the ship."

Every eye is on the Governor now except when one or another member casts a sidelong glance in Lars' direction to check his response and find his face wooden.

"If you think technocracy and the worship of goods and services is 'innocent,' then I have another bit of history for you. A quarter of a century ago our three new citizens returned from a research trip in the hills and found their colleagues dead. They could not reveal themselves because First Mate Nasser, as he was then, had headed the party sent to liquidate them. So they learned to survive as they could. All these years later the benefit for us is their having learned to live cooperatively with this planet, while the rest of us turned our backs on the place we were destined to live. No wonder the outlanders should now lead the way as we lounge in our comfortable incubator. It is they who have made the greatest sacrifices for our colony."

Hard words but true. More truth than this gathering has ever heard, and confirmed by a man whose memory is already becoming a legend. Rather like a bomb dropped in the night, it spreads a deeper hush over an already silent room.

Then, as though aside, he adds, "I don't mention this bit of history to cast a shadow across Governor Nasser's memory. He acted under orders and in the belief that he was doing a necessary thing, but after his assignment as Governor he began to see from a broader perspective and to change directions."

Yori stops for a moment to resist being drawn into a confessional mode himself. "The night he died he had me brought to his bed, and in his last breaths he confessed that he had headed that party and had personally killed my father, Akira Kashimoto."

This revelation surpasses all. It stuns the room once more. Akira has not been forgotten by the older members, and the name is legendary among the younger. Revered alongside Nasser as a founding father of the colony and believed to have given his life in the same cause. Only in retrospect will those present realize that the new Governor, with every reason for resentment and revenge, has set aside the personal for the public weal.

"Nonetheless," Yori continues, "I believe Governor Nasser governed well. He reversed the evils where he could, not least by restoring our banished refugees and giving his blessing to the present plan for expansion."

The one person in the room who is not dumbfounded, because she's more concerned with the meaning than the bare facts of Yori's revelations, is Véronique. She sees with admiration that the new Governor is not only judging a matter of highest public concern—even public identity—justly, he's also establishing a touchstone of genuine political conduct. And yet she hides her delight behind a quick hand and a judicious rearrangement of that opportunely disorderly strand of hair. For she also sees, or thinks she sees, the beginning of Lars' self-destruction.

As people begin to absorb the fact that Nasser's personal reformation resulted in political wisdom, they see that he had had the justice actively to track down the outlaws, learn their history, and finally to repatriate them. It was for the good of the colony. His own relation to those unhappy people was at least as complex as Yori's and far more compromised. Yet he had established the benchmark for all futurity of how a governor had to set personal interest aside.

Slowly this revision of history sinks in and the mood of the room changes once more. The meaning of their own experience has just been altered.

Presently Yori draws his conclusion. "What matters now is not personalities but the impersonal forces behind a troubled history that extends deep into the memory of Planet Ulro. There have always been two parties divided over a fundamental difference of understanding. Call them the party of action and the party of wonder. Both are essential. The challenge in every generation is to see that they don't become false rivals. In this forum, our expertise lies in how things are to be done, but there are questions other than the 'how question.' There are equally legitimate questions about what, everything considered, *should* be done? And *why*?"

This moves the disposition of the room toward another kind of deliberation, not least by reminding members of the esteem the older man felt for his successor. Seeing as much, Yori says nothing about Lars' particular complaints but lets them fall away as mere excuses for his protest.

Instead he does something entirely different. "Thanks to Lars' bringing this timely matter to our attention, I want to mention that the members of the Galatea Elders who chose to remain in the colony have agreed to organize themselves as an advisory body along the same lines laid out by the original designers of the mission. I think you will agree that the precedent set by the wise planners of the most successful exploration in the history of the species is a precedent worth following. We need all the wisdom we can get as we begin populating the New Earth, and we could do no better than follow in the steps of so many wise people by establishing our own Council of Elders."

It's a masterstroke. Lars' face positively deflates, but he recovers and, instead of backing off, makes a more audacious attempt. "Why should long-term planning be turned over to people without practical experience? I would think that the people who do the work should have a say in what's to be done."

In setting his own opinion against that long history and persisting in his challenge of the authority of the new governor, he causes heads to turn once more, a few looking with approval but most with simple astonishment. Whatever the merits of his argument, it's a serious practical mistake.

Yori replies in the lightest possible tone and with a smile. "You do have a say! Everybody does. Nothing is 'turned over' to anyone. Our councils are open to any voice in the colony, and we actively seek the authority of experience wherever we can find it. The new Council will not decide what's to be done. In fact they will not *decide* anything. This is not about power in the Corps or in the Council. They're a think tank for deliberation and advice. Nothing more."

Perhaps the most remarkable thing of all in this exchange is that Lars, instead of suffering a defeat, should appear satisfied for the moment with so little, as though he has made whatever point he wanted to make. And so the crisis passes temporarily, and Yori's position appears strengthened.

By way of conclusion, the Governor announces, "In view of these developments and in the interest of transparent deliberations, I'm going to ask you to choose one member of this council to sit with the Elders, and I will ask them to choose one to sit with us here. On this point there is no hurry. We'll settle it later. The idea as always is that the best preparation for good governance is universal education, and second best is open deliberations."

The meeting is about to adjourn when one member proposes that they settle on the representative to the Elders now. "It's a good idea so why dawdle?" he asks. "Let's put somebody in there immediately."

The first person mentioned is Véronique, whereupon one of Lars' allies named Alexi objects. "Since Véronique and the Governor are old friends, maybe we should choose someone more independent."

At that Véronique laughs aloud at him. "Are you listening to yourself, Alexi? You don't doubt for one moment that the Governor or I is capable of setting personal interests aside and acting for the general welfare. If you meant what you said, you'd have no business being here."

This was followed by discreet snickers around the table, especially from the women. But for this attack, Véronique might not have been chosen, but in fact she was immediately confirmed as emissary to the new Council.

28

DEVELOPMENTS IN THE DISTANT NORTH caused little public stir in the colony. Not at first and not directly. People on Planet 2314 had waited so long for something important to happen that they had forgotten they were waiting. Much as if time itself had ended and as if before and after had ceased to matter.

Only slowly did the opening of the North rouse the drowsy colony and shift the tone of everyday life toward expectation. The first hints were hypothetical. Only in retrospect would people see that a new era had begun. Before there was any*thing* to hope for, just the mirage of deliverance, just enough stirring of life to rouse something resembling hope.

Here's how change first appeared. A variety of new activities began to seep into public consciousness and incite curiosity. A murmur of returning life came with the restoration of the "outlaws," but when the call went out for volunteers, it awakened a hunger for "news." News first that teachers were needed for a "grammar school" and that preference would be given to couples with the requisite skills, a sense of adventure, and an appetite for hardship. Rumor said—and rumor got this much wrong—that each person had to be capable of building a house with his own hands from native stone and capable of growing food for his own family, but it was true that each had to be willing and eager. Settlers would be able to depend on assistance from their new neighbors and from the colony, but they went north to build their own lives and to share responsibility for the well-being of others. For those who met the criteria it was time to act, since expansion thereafter was to be by "natural growth," in the full sense of "settling." What few paid attention to was that these rumors were portents of a new public disposition.

It was news when, in response to that first invitation, the line of applicants at Government House extended beyond the building and across the Square. The number chosen would be small but, for more than might have been expected, the slightest chance was worth the wait. In fact, just being there, standing in line, was to have a part in something that mattered. The volunteers felt no anxiety in face of uncertainty. They felt joy in a challenge that gave them a stake in a future.

The beginning of recruitment had other effects. It generated related opportunities. There were production facilities to be expanded, supplies and equipment to be transported, new support services to be established. For these jobs, too, officials were overrun with volunteers. Any work associated with the North, however mean or even dangerous the task, promised an interlude in the dullness of a safe and measured existence. In fact public interest grew to the point that the administrative challenge was to steer all that energy into constructive channels before it waned.

By the time the first volunteers were settled, something else, something invisible and entirely unconscious, began to take root. Everyone with a remote connection to the project began subtly absorbing an alternative political culture. The simple act of describing the selection process to prospective settlers or explaining a problem in the transportation schedule or the conveying of goods—talk of any phase of the project initiated both those who explained and those who listened into new ways of thinking together. Thinking through feasibilities, equities, long- and short-term aims, and a thousand other small connections began forming new mental habits and new modes of social engagement. Yori and the new Elders who watched these shifts in attitude closely knew that if all went right, the settlement might gradually show the South how to turn a zone of biological security into a city.

As the months passed, the mood of the colony continued to evolve. By the time a second, larger group of immigrants were established in the settlement, the landing craft had been adapted to a transport service and some people commuted regularly north and south.

On what would once have been a lazy afternoon spent dawdling at home or in the parks, several dozen people gathered in the heat outside the arcades waiting for the weekly flight to arrive. There was something more than curiosity in it. The spectators, sweltering in the sun, did so gladly just for a glimpse of the lucky few who had been to the mysterious North: Edward Hamilton coming for consultations, teachers and nurses and workers returning for the weekend. People from the colony were also lined up waiting to board for the return trip, mainly students going home to their families and four lucky "tourists" off to have a look at the settlement and lodge in the new Town Hall for two days and nights.

Still more interesting for spectators accustomed to efficiency was the occasion when there was a glitch in the system. It occurred when a first shipment of northern vegetables and fruit was unloaded. Apparently there was no conveyance small enough to transport the produce via the western gate or large enough to haul the shipment around the colony to receiving docks on the eastern side. It was an interesting moment of confusion until one of the spectators had the idea of carrying the goods by hand out of the heat. Without a thought for the discomfort, everyone present sprang into action, and in a few minutes of spontaneous cooperation the perishables were rescued. In short, the once sleepy colonists were becoming greedy for wakefulness. It's the stuff gossip is made of.

In time, public interest would reach a point where if a call for more volunteers were issued and if all volunteers were accepted, the colony would be decimated. Everyone wants to get as close as possible and feel part of the biggest thing that has ever happened. It's enough to remind one that where the artifice of a starship simulates the real, here the real asserts itself directly.

However, all these signs of success do not put an end to Lars' efforts to increase the power of the Corps of Governors. After his earlier setback in the new Governor's first meeting, he does a thing without precedent. He distributes a written appeal to the Elders containing a proposal. In a sense he's putting to the test the principle of openness to outside suggestions. Here's what his document says:

As Head of Technical Services, I have been thinking about the public lethargy. Recent expansion in the North has brought some relief of these symptoms, but it will only be temporary. People are bound to fall back into their old habits. Therefore, I am proposing a permanent cure for the disease of boredom. It is to expand the concept of private property. For example, if people owned their own houses, where now they're owned by "Big Brother," it would create pride and a sense of control. People would take responsibility for their own lives and improve their condition. It is time for us to pass beyond simple colonial life by planning a new stage of development that will ultimately become planetary. Ulro history shows that private property is one of the most dynamic systems ever invented.

And he goes on to cite such corroborating historical facts as might have been collected in a single day of surfing the archives on Alexandros.

This unique document does not say why it's being distributed to the Elders instead of being taken directly to the Governor. It does not admit that it was trading on the success in the North. Nothing about its own provenance: that it contained no recommendations about ways and means, mentions no possible negative effects, acknowledges none of the legal structures that would have to be invented, not even what is meant by "expanding the concept of private property." The last is especially odd since there were no rules governing ownership or exchange of property either on the starship or here. Informal bartering among individuals had always been a fact but hardly ever an issue.

At any rate Lars distributes his document and then . . . silence.

Meanwhile Yori concentrates his attention on the schools. What no one knows, unless Paola knows, is that it is education and the new Elders alone that prevent him from sinking into a slough of despond. They let him feel less trapped by his new responsibilities.

In the schools the sciences have never been ignored, but so little encouragement and support have been devoted to advanced research that it's barely visible. And yet as the site of the presumed future of humanity, the colony must support research with the vigor of the mother planet or complacently watch the decay even of its infrastructure. The less "useful" historical disciplines are in even worse condition, although Hans Rückert and Joseph Kern have done what two people without authority could to ameliorate the situation. As for the arts, except for Sandra Mohr and two or three other young artists recruited a decade earlier from the starship, no attention and few resources have been provided.

It may take generations for new ideals to take root, but it takes as long to uproot age-old traditions, and so Yori's first effort is to revive forgotten sensibilities. His guiding principle is to nurture whatever inclinations may survive and to do so by spreading the widest net. Instead of strengthening the strongest disciplines or concentrating on the weakest, he acts opportunistically and lets contingency choose. The risk is that he might accomplish nothing at all, but since he can rely on Ang Yimou and Edward to keep a watchful eye on the sciences and on Rückert and Kern in the "humanities," he takes on the arts. When opportunity offers in the person of Sandra, he concentrates first on music.

He has seen Sandra Mohr as a natural partner, but there is Lars! Fairness requires him to deal independently with her as an official in the schools. But in this job there is always political realism to consider. So he consults Paola.

When next they are together, he sighs deeply and begins, "You know Sandra Mohr. Tell me about her."

Paola replies, "She's one of the best. Not cut from the same cloth as Véronique, but her character and her position may be just as important to you. Sandra is deeper than her light, cheerful manner may suggest. And she's discreet."

"But there's her relation to Lars. You warned the Elders that the 'Lars problem' will never go away. With or without him, his ideas will always be tempting."

"You're right," she says as an aside. "At the moment he's a loose cannon. But he's also having an even harder time than you adjusting to the new reality." By a gesture she indicates the office where this conversation takes place. "That, too, is political realism. As long as he was in the company of Shi Wa, Edward, and Véronique he was manageable. Now he's mainly with his technicians, but"—she holds up a finger in warning—"he's more complicated. He needs reminding of what he chooses to forget. Where reason doesn't work, seduction may. Sandra might be the ally you need. She may be young and malleable but don't underrate her artistic discipline and strong sense of purpose. For you it would be a delicate move, mainly without words, since she will also be loyal to him."

Not long after this conversation Paola goes north again, and the first thing Yori does is attend a recital by one of Sandra's students. After a rather dull performance he remains in his seat until she approaches him and thanks him for attending. When he compliments her work, she responds quite unlike the person he had observed on the night of his return to the colony. She is reserved, cautious, excessively polite, but in that moment he learns something important: Neither to her nor to anyone else will he ever again be just a friend and equal. As Governor he is first and foremost his position in the public world, however small.

Sandra's reserve isn't shyness or innocence or simplicity. In that moment he can see in her eyes that she fully appreciates the distance between them and the sensitivity of his relation to her dearest companion. Seeing so much, Yori resolves to give her time and win her confidence.

And so he does. Sometime later, after another performance, the two of them sit together for a few minutes in the empty studio. This time she responds with unguarded eagerness. Whatever he asks about the music program, she answers with enthusiasm, confident now that he will not let the conversation take a personal slant. Once again she looks out on the world without guile and her eyes shine with simple cheerfulness. Nonetheless, after some minutes more Yori sees her drifting absentmindedly away from the topic, and he decides to end the conversation on a brighter note: "Did you know the name Claudio Rucai?"

"Paola Rucai's father, wasn't he? I heard his name when I was a student."

"I ask because he once quoted something very important about the role of the arts that applies to what we want to do. He said, 'The poets found us dumb and gave us speech; the painters found us blind and gave us sight; the musicians found us deaf and taught us to hear.'"

She appreciates the point and it encourages her to broach a different topic. "I've had an idea in mind for a while. I'd like to mention it, but I don't have time now. I have students."

"I'm flexible. When do you have time?"

"Tomorrow around noon? But I'd like to meet outside the walls."

Yori stares. "Of course. Where?"

"There's a little seating area in one of the nursery gardens. Véronique designed it for her workers. Let's meet there."

To walk to the nurseries from his office he had to cross a radius of the circular colony from Government House. Rarely these days does Yori leave business behind and enjoy the freedom of a casual walk. It encourages him to consider his situation from outside the constraint of his schedule. Involuntarily his thoughts turn to his impatience with governing. It is one thing to dream about establishing a city; it is quite another to get bogged down in colonial housekeeping.

Governor Nasser had once asked him how a ruler was to find the time for waiting. His easy answer was by disentangling himself from daily operations for the sake of dreaming. And yet here he is, a few months after his accession, already becoming the bureaucrat! If he continues as he's going, he'll soon be going in circles with no ideas left. The realization is startling, and he responds to it by resolving on the spot to make it an inviolable rule of his day to follow a regular course of reading. If he does not challenge what he thinks he thinks, he will sink soon enough into mental torpor and his imagination will run dry.

As he steps through the old airlock into the nurseries, a wall of midday heat hits him in the face with staggering force, and he recoils from the same air he once sought on those long hikes in the hills. The fact goes a long way to reinforcing his present reflections: Is he going soft already? Acclimated again to the life-support system without noticing?

Sandra is sitting alone in a lovely sheltered area that seems designed for conversation. It's a garden niche, a little oasis surrounded on three sides by bamboo that shades two stone benches. They sit down in the arbor vis-à-vis, where she leans forward and launches into what she has come to say.

"My idea isn't about music. It started with Véronique's efforts to get people outside 'the bubble' where they might learn to appreciate the planet."

He returns a smile that may mean more than she knows.

"She has been successful with young students, bringing them out here into the nurseries, even organizing field trips to Paola's gardens. It's slowly making a difference."

"I agree," Yori interjects, waiting for her point. "Though at this rate we'll have to wait for them to replace their parents." Then, as she doesn't go on, "So what's your idea?"

"Well," she sits up straighter, looks shyly away for a moment, then answers a bit hesitantly. "When I think how little people hear in music, how much exposure it takes to love new sounds, that makes me think that if we want people to see the New

Earth, they need more than casual exposure. In most cases we don't even have the casual. We need to set this land in front of people where it can't be easily ignored. We need artists to seduce them into seeing."

He chuckles gently. "So you think, just on the side, while we're turning Intro to Music Appreciation into a conservatory, we should develop a school for the plastic arts?"

"Yes!" she replies. "We need a general assault on narrow experience. We can't wait for everyone to love Bach before teaching them to love Leonardo and the Parthenon."

Yori welcomes her imagination with a warm smile. "So what do you propose?"

"If we had an art program that took students outdoors into the hills, they would learn to see the beauty of the desert, and others would follow. But for that, they need models to learn from."

As she stops there, Yori raises his dark eyebrows encouragingly. "I have a feeling there's more!"

"There is. Remember when the art department at the Galatea Academy wanted to encourage serious painting and they hit an obstacle? The students needed models to study and copy. The result was a way of printing copies from the encyclopedic library of the Ulro arts on Alexandros. They were indistinguishable from the originals. And that was the beginning of a renaissance of art in space."

Without giving him time to breathe, she adds, "We could do the same!"

He studies the idea for a moment. "We use the same basic technology here. I think I see where you're going. That was also the birth of the art gallery, wasn't it?" He doesn't mention that a generation ago his mother had been an artist on the starship.

"Exactly," she replies to the mention of the gallery.

"Eventually," he continues, "a space was adapted and filled with some of the greatest works ever created. Copies—but what does that matter if no one can tell the difference? Anyway, the gallery was opened to the students and the public, with just the result you mention, and you think we could do the same?"

"That's it. Why not? We have the Alexandros library of music remastered from Ulro recordings. Why not art too?"

"I don't have all the technical answers—the paints or inks, whatever they call it, whether they can be matched, and so on—but the rest is commonplace."

"I don't know either. But I was also thinking that if you got Lars interested, he could find out and maybe oversee the project. In about a week he'd come up with the idea of designing a gallery to house such a collection. If you remember, on the ship art was eventually displayed in all kinds of public spaces. Anyway, to get back to the original idea, if our own artists were encouraged to discover this planet, their work might help lure others out of the shell."

Consciously holding the Lars problem at bay, he asks simply, "How would we begin?"

She looks sheepishly at that question for a moment then leans forward, resting her elbows on her knees, and speaks with caution as though taking a precarious step. "What if you asked Lars to look into it? It would give him something to think about besides the settlement. You know he's anxious about the way that project is going. He's too invested in it. He needs a distraction that will dampen his dissatisfaction."

This unexpected depth causes Yori to start because she has described more than Lars. It is his problem too. He needs a distraction. If he's to hold the reins of the colony loosely, it must not be the most important thing in his life. That would be idolatry, and idolatry ends by destroying everything, including itself. He shifts on his seat, feeling his uniform sticking to his body even in the shade.

"Or *you* might broach the subject with him as you've done with me? He's not exactly in love with me, but he loves you. He would take up your dream with a passion, and—I agree with you—handle it brilliantly. Then either you could bring the idea to me or tell me if I should mention it to him. Whatever you think."

Then he sees another way. "Or, have him introduce it in a meeting of the Council! Since it's your idea, why not propose it together as Shi Wa and Edward first proposed the settlement."

She nods agreement and he goes on. "Have you heard Paola mention a book called *Starship Galatea*? It's about life on the ship."

"No, I don't think so."

"Ask to borrow it sometime. There's a dialogue in it you would appreciate. It's Colloquy 3 on the arts and education. It was led by Aurélie Lefèvre, whom you must have known."

"I did know her. We all did. In school she was our guru."

"Good. I think you'll find it more than interesting."

And that was that. Once more the Governor had a path opened to the future by a young person with no political experience. And he had received a major correction in his own course: To listen at the door, he had to get outside the room.

29

MONTHS LATER YORI AND Paola were sitting together in her small courtyard in Government House, nondescript except for a few stones she has brought from the hills to add a touch of home. Much has happened since they last had a good talk and yet they can fall back on the harmony of mood they have enjoyed for many years . . . almost. Even between two who seem to read each other's minds, things unspoken hover in the air as though by the olden-time rule of one question. The question without words this time is not a happy one.

By way of thanking her for suggesting Sandra as a mediator with Lars, Yori recounts the strange meeting in the midday heat under the bamboo, and Paola responds by raising a glass in a toast to recent achievements that are less work done than gifts received. "To the village that's turning a colony into a city."

In turn Yori lifts his glass. "We seem to have been surrounded by disconnected pieces of a puzzle just asking to be assembled. Two operating councils, Edward accepted as a member of the Elders, his DNA project approved with Ang's blessing. It has all been too easy. So far, the way forward seems to be the way back. He raises his glass again: "To waiting for the propitious moment and giving the gentle nudge."

"Also a first challenge survived." She's referring to the event in the Corps of Governors.

"While we're celebrating favorable recent moments, let's remember that first meeting of the Elders months ago. That set the schools on a new footing and will have immense consequences. Also . . ." He takes a moment to consider before continuing, then appears to digress. "Remember what the Governor said in the Chamber of Names about a ruler not being cautious and playing for small stakes?"

She answers, "Yes. He said the ruler is the secret agent of destiny who waits for the moment when the impossible becomes possible." She can see in Yori's eyes that this is all beside the point, that he's avoiding the thing that weighs on the atmosphere of the room. But she gives him time. "He, Nasser, would be proud of the start you've made. It's exactly what he could *not* do: live in suspension, bound to nothing, expecting the unexpected."

"We haven't spoken of the letter Lars wrote to the Elders a while back. Has there been a response?"

"Here it is," she thinks to herself. "The monster in the room." She replies, "I didn't receive a copy, but I have heard about it. It hasn't been neglected."

She summarizes events. Lars' proposal had been read with curiosity by all who received it. But the fact that she, Edward, and Véronique had not received copies signaled the political delicacy of the situation. Essentially it acknowledged the personal tension between Lars and the Governor. And so the Council had taken seriously what might otherwise have been ignored. The decision was first to temporize and let the issue cool if it would cool, then to invite the Governor to meet with them and discuss the matter. "It was decided last night to extend the invitation for next week."

And so it happened that, with this context fixed in everyone's mind, the next session convened, this time in new quarters. Compared with the conference room where the Corps meets, it's a smallish place with windows opening onto a little public square between Government House and the official residence building. There is no table. Just a half dozen straight but comfortable armchairs spaced so people can converse face to face. And when discussion goes on for hours, it's even possible to get up and move around without breaking the chain of thought.

Though Yori had selected the space and suggested the arrangement, this is his first meeting with the Council in their new home. As he evaluates the room in use, he sees that more has been achieved than was intended. It is much more than an appropriate workspace. Somewhere down the years it may be seen in retrospect as having prefigured a subtle mutation in governance itself. Even as Governor Nasser had allowed an invisible slippage from the supreme authority of the starship toward participation in governance, so this room may come in the future to signify an expansion of authority in the direction of "democratic aristocracy." The very materiality of bicameral chambers, Governors and Elders, may prove prophetic.

The members settle into the conversation circle, now become an arc, so that each person has a view of the window. The greenish light from the Square, the transparency of the dome, and the open sky beyond all provide room enough for thinking.

The discussion opens with a brief review of Lars' letter and its context. Then Paola says, "Let's start by remembering that Lars is not the enemy. His ideas aren't *his*. If we didn't have him to set these temptations before us, we'd have to invent someone else to do it. Ideas may be timely or untimely, but they aren't evil. An idea is eternal and awaits an unforeseeable proper context."

As nominal spokesman for a group that hardly needs a spokesman, Hans Rückert is startled by the aptness of Paola's remark and looks up from his musings. "There is no real proposal here. But, motives aside—since we can't reliably know motives—this must be treated carefully or we risk encouraging discontent. Paola is right. Ideas never go away, whether they succeed or fail. Whenever they return, they need to be handled cautiously and on their own merits without respect to persons and opinions. As I see this case, we mainly need to consider how, to whom, and in what form a response should be made."

The Governor asks, "May I get your advice on two procedural questions before you begin?"

All nod consent. And he continues. "The first is to ask if you are willing to send one member to sit on the Corps of Governors as you have kindly accepted their representative to sit with you." He nods toward Véronique. He had not rushed this issue. Though the presence of a representative from the Corps had been urgent for political reasons, the symmetry in representation was not urgent, there being no distrust among the Elders.

The suggestion is discussed briefly and approved with one alteration: Because the Corps meets weekly and their other duties are extensive, they will share the assignment alternately.

Then, the second point, about publishing the proceedings of both councils on Alexandros, taking care that the accounts not be used for public advocacy. "If education is our prime concern all up and down the scale, shouldn't your discussions be available for anyone who is willing to follow them?"

Joseph Kern speaks up: "That comes with a risk of generating hard public opinions and discontent based on soft understanding."

"But aren't the contrary risks even greater?" Edward asks.

Kern answers, "I suppose you mean that secrecy is also a path to the tyranny of public opinion and a step in the directions of both anarchy and totalitarianism. Secrecy certainly encourages infantilism in the populace when we're trying to move in the opposite direction."

"When people are flooded with information," Ava Sarosh adds, "ideas also get hidden in full view."

"But it's still the better choice, isn't it?" Kern replies.

These preliminary matters are soon agreed, and attention returns to the "Hanssen proposal." For Yori's benefit, Joseph Kern explains. "We have a way of approaching a question that we rather like. When a new topic comes up for discussion, each person in turn presents whatever single point he or she regards as most important without regard to what side of the issue it might fall on. That continues until we're satisfied that we have a fair inventory. Then general discussion follows."

By the accidents of seating, Ava Sarosh is Yori's neighbor. She turns to him and adds eagerly, "It helps keep clarification of the issues separate from advocacy. As often as not we don't agree with the points we make for the record." She smiles broadly, affectionately. "Sometimes I'm surprised to hear myself saying things that change my own mind."

Then Kern volunteers the first comment on the issue at hand. His presence—tall, slender, and crowned with a head of wavy grey hair—adds dignity to whatever he says, as does the resonant baritone voice. "The Hanssen document," he begins, "claims historical anecdotes on how successful property and competition have been in motivating people. Of course there's much to learn from the historical record."

He shifts uncomfortably in his chair and crosses his legs one way then the other. "But the document gives no attention to the concept of property itself or to how it consists—or in-consists—with other social phenomena. What it praises under the name 'property' is little more than self-interest. The ancients properly called it sophistry and the moderns called it hedonism."

This was not spoken in the tone of the lighthearted, easygoing Kern, the most clubbable member of the Elders. This was Kern the passionate rhetorician, crying out against evils in low places.

"Once we set the idea of property at the center of life," he continues, "we're not giving our blessing to a little innocent competition. Competition is a separate issue. Siblings are competitive. Students are competitive. There is rivalry for position and rivalry for attention. Sports thrive on competition to be the best. It can serve excellence, be a spur to the heroic, or a cause of war. It's ubiquitous. But do we want to teach the young that the highest ambition is to overreach other people? Give our blessing to it as 'natural' human instinct and rouse a mighty beast that even the great religions failed to curb? At the very least if we're to examine this proposal seriously, we need to review its darker consequences."

Sarosh lays a hand on Yori's arm and remarks aside, "Did you know that the Swiss Kerns included a line of Calvinist ministers? You'll be happy to know that that virtue abounds among us once more. Let us give thanks."

Yori grins and says nothing.

Kern ignores the satire and continues his rhetorical questions. "Still worse is casually to connect competition to the accumulation of things as though this ambivalent force were *civic virtue*. Do we want to teach our children to model themselves on it? Why not make food the highest value and produce a generation of gluttons? Or sex, until we have a city of whoremongers?"

Kern's specialty is literature. He loves old words and absolutely refuses to let language die away like last year's fashion.

After a few moments Ang, sitting on the opposite side of the circle with his back to the window, picks up the idea in a different register. Ang is a short, slender man with a deadpan face, brilliant perhaps but unprepossessing. "I'm a simple scientist," he begins. "I don't have the rhetorical powers of our friend Joseph. But in my humble way I want to mention a symbol for the 'dark consequences' he mentions."

He clears his throat and takes a deep breath. "Remember Robinson Crusoe alone on his island? The one who built a little empire with the help of his man Friday? Friday was a slave, by the way! He didn't even have a name. Just the day of the week when Crusoe found him. This Crusoe-particle, collecting possessions, is a figure we're implicitly being asked to promote as an acceptable citizen of our city. The Crusoe-particle breeds— historically it *did* breed—the tyranny of self-interest. Crusoe was a forecast of what was called *homo economicus*, economic man."

He raises a hand in his only visible concession to rhetorical effect. "I see that no one is explicitly recommending that we understand ourselves as machines of production and consumption. Not yet. But the proposal is a big step in that direction. Even the metaphor in the phrase 'Crusoe-particle' is a warning. What *is* a particle? Is it anything? It took centuries for the physicists to discover that 'reality' is not really real, that subatomic particles are not discrete units. They're more like temporary effects of vibrating energy fields *seen as particles*. Well, individuals are temporary effects of still larger fields. Our sort spent many years learning that we aren't discrete building blocks of a social order. We're transient effects of events larger than ourselves."

If Yori needs confirmation that Ang is not who he once was, *voilà*. He is also surprised by the unity as well as the differences in perspective among these people. Each in turn is reading further implications and driving another stake into the corpse of Lars' proposal. What Kern lays out in the light of prophetic fire, Ang quietly formulates in an image that lets the consequences of self-interest rise up as so many threats to political cohesion.

Sarosh picks up the discussion from still another angle. "I want to add another implication of this document. But first let me say something for the sake of the Governor and our new members." She acknowledges Véronique and Edward, sitting across the semicircle between Ang and Rückert. Like Paola, they have been silent so far.

Turning to Yori, Sarosh explains, "We probably appear to be jumping on this document with both feet. But that's because this is not a new issue for us. We have a long history with it. On the starship the Elders studied versions of it for generations. So the four of us have been considering it for most of our lives. Please don't jump to the conclusion that we're jumping to conclusions."

Yori acknowledges her point by a nod, and she continues. "In the world according to Crusoe people don't grow from embedded codes and forgotten models. He doesn't know all that. His rational competence misses everything except what confronts him as an object of his conscious desire. All the rest—history, education, family, the city—are extensions of his interests."

Yori understands, but he begins to wonder if Lars' pitiful letter warrants such heavy weapons. As he's trying to imagine how he might moderate the strength of these responses, Ang adds an even darker implication.

"Imagine," he says, "if students thought they had a right to learn only what they think they need to satisfy their ambitions! What kind of citizen would those students make?"

"What kind of a *person*?" Edward tosses in the question from the sidelines in a tone of incredulity.

Rückert looks at him and nods. What kind of *city* in a generation or two?"

"The jungle comes to mind," Edward answers. Then as Sarosh doesn't continue, he picks up the topic. "I know I'm new to your procedure here, but may I mention a point in defense of the Hanssen proposal?"

There being no objection, he continues, "Aside from motives and long-range consequences, I suggest the Hanssen proposal gets something right. People need to be engaged. They must have things to hope for and pour their love and their lives into. For a while survival worked but now survival is assured. Once upon a time the religions worked in non-competitive, communal ways, as in building cathedrals or the Hajj, or celebrating common rituals. These weren't illusions, but we are secularists. Individualism has taken the place of the religions. So now, if we don't encourage economic competition, then what is to be the motor of desire? Perhaps even greed can be balanced by other forces. Doesn't this meeting tonight show that we are capable of setting the collective good ahead of the self?"

"Yes." Kern replies, "But we *want* to serve the common good! What about those who don't care?"

Yori is inspired to drop in a single word. "There's always law." Knowing the clarity of Hans Rückert's mind, he's trying to provoke a response from his corner.

Rückert is famous for finding the political essence of any question whatever. Asked *why?* about almost anything, his cryptic answer is likely to be, "Because '*man is a political animal*'—minus the animal."

On this occasion he has been sitting, mainly wrapped in his stolid Germanic solemnity, as though waiting for the whole agenda to unfold before joining in. Now he strokes his chin and directs his words to some point in the floor midway across the circle.

"The Governor is right. Law is important. But where law is concerned there aren't true answers, because the questions have no top or bottom, no front or back, no up or down."

That cryptic remark does nothing to advance the discussion, so he tries again. "Hanssen has bitten off more than he can chew." Rückert stops to select a point or two from many. "The topic is immense but let me offer a footnote to Sarosh's point: Self-interest in Crusoe and self-interest on a collective scale turn out to be the same thing. The second is just a shrewder version of the first. Both demand restraint, so our attention is properly drawn to the role of law. But let's remember that the first impulse behind law is pedagogical. Rules explain sensible ways of doing things. That's not inherently coercive. It's liberating. At least that's where it all begins, but then we get lazy and start forgetting. Good advice begins to degrade into legalism. Then people take law as good in itself, as though without it, chaos would come again."

"But," Yori rejoins, "you've just shown that we don't have to interpret law as rigid command: '*Thou shalt not.*'"

Rückert has been leaning forward with his elbows on his knees, his eyes concealed under the busy eyebrows but directed at that spot of inspiration on the floor. Now he raises his head, meets Yori's gaze, and answers very carefully:

"Think of the effect of individualism on law itself. Individualism is a dogma about what's really real, and it's never so rigid than when it's accepted as common sense. In the world according to Crusoe, law slides into a new role—from teaching to discipline and punishment. Prohibitions are to protect individual interests, and soon enough those interests

morph into a demand for 'rights.' Crusoe's namesakes, like
Lars Hanssen, want to be free of interference but they also
want to be guaranteed the 'right' to life, health, security, and
especially the disposition of 'their goods.' And the legislative
body becomes a battleground for collective interests.

"What happens to truth and living wisely meanwhile? It
all vanishes into getting my or *our* way! It doesn't take genius
to see that, as a slave to self-interest, Crusoe's capacity for
citizenship is reduced to a jungle full of competing desires
or competing tribes. On Ulro that jungle sometimes resulted
from the venerable ideal of 'parliamentary democracy' and the
'democratic republic.'"

"So what do we do now?" Ang asks.

"We don't go down the blind Hanssen alley." Rückert
snaps.

Paola usually limits her role in these sessions to spectator,
and, after all these weighty points, she might prefer not to
add more, but in her ear the discussion sounds a bit too
moralistic. As though they are in danger of demonizing—and
empowering! —property, interest, and economy. Those ideas,
whatever they have meant in history, are fossils that will not
disappear. In a past world, they may have been obsessions that
dissolved everything virtuous and good, but in an unimaginable future they might rise again in ways that are consistent
with the other goods of life.

Thinking all this, she decides to add a note. "This seems
to be a night for footnotes," she begins, "so here's one more:
No one is claiming that owning property is somehow evil.
This is not a moral question. We're discussing what has

worked and not worked for people over the long term, especially what the ethical or character effects have been on them and their institutions. That's why we shouldn't stop on the word 'property' as though it's obvious what it means. We need to search our experience closely to discover how possession alters our relation to a thing."

"For example?" says Sarosh, encouraging her to say more.

"For example, when Planet 2314 was first surveyed, it was assumed—without thinking—that we space wanderers, finding the planet unclaimed, could come down here, plant our flag, and call it ours. And so we did. Then what followed? All but the few who had to work and sacrifice and suffer regarded the planet as a piece of cosmic waste. Most still think of it as either wasteland or raw material. The alternative is *to belong*. That turns the relation around. I mention this as a way of asking about the capacity of Crusoe to *belong* to anything or to *discover* anything except the alien and exploitable object in his face. Ang's particle has a lot to teach about the rewards of overcoming the possessive self if we are to live cooperatively with what cannot be possessed."

Rückert, now leaning back in his chair, runs his finger through his bushy hair. He sighs and adds, "Paola is right. We're exaggerating the problem. The first time we met, the Governor mentioned the idea of doing only what the day requires. The right thing to do now is to lay all this aside and keep the settlement in the North on track. The Hanssen document is a protest against the very thing it advocates. For now the settlement is having the salutary effects on the colonial spirit that this thing"—he waves the proposal in the air—"professes to support. Let's give a respectful and minimal response and concentrate on the schools. Education may not cure all the ills of the spirit, but it can enable the patient to minister to himself . . . if he will."

By way of conclusion Kern turns to Paola with a twinkle in his eye. "In the old days in situations like this Claudio would quote the *Tao* to us. 'Do nothing,' he would say, 'and leave nothing undone.'"

30

THE EPISODE OF LARS' letter passed without further incident, or so it seemed. The issue of property receded. Though, as Yori was quick to see, the fact was not especially encouraging. Lars lay low for a while, but he wasn't idle. He was learning the game of politics, working to sow discontent among others, especially his subordinates in Technical Services. "Property" may have been a smoke screen for something else and shouldn't be judged hastily. Envy? Ambition? Even philosophy? More likely all of these. But leaving motives aside, Yori had to fight the battle on the declared issues, and when it surfaced again some months later, here's what happened.

At the weekly meeting of the Corps, Lars objected strongly to the way settlers were being selected. "It just doesn't make sense to fill the place with amateurs who have to be taught everything from scratch as happened with their aqueduct. My people had to waste time giving instruction when they might have been building infrastructure." He went on to demand that from that moment on, the settlers should be young technicians who could help put the settlement on its feet at record speed. "After that, you can send anyone who wants to go."

Yori ignored the demand by observing calmly that there appeared to be no reason to go against the desires of the settlers. They should solve their own problems in their own way so long as it doesn't run afoul of support from the colony. "Political life is local," he said. "We should not interfere unnecessarily with our grand designs."

Lars erupted, "But it does interfere! That's the whole point. When my people had to teach unskilled people how to use stone and mortar, where to put their pilings so they didn't fall down, it affected morale. And the waste! In the end all they did was build a shell to conceal our perfectly functional system. Let them teach one another if they like, but put competent people in charge to start with."

The Governor replied lightly but decisively: "All that has been settled, Lars. We needn't rehash what's already done."

At that point Lars very nearly lost his temper and brashly threatened to give his people orders not to help on settlement projects. And he gave it an incendiary name: "An old-fashioned work slowdown until we're listened to!"

The room went quiet as everyone waited for what Yori would do next. Presently he spoke with slow, firm solemnity. "Lars, I will give you two answers. First, as your oldest friend I will remind you of a piece of advice you gave me when we were students. You warned me against opposing the only thing between me and oblivion. As your friend, I recommend that you take your own good advice."

Lars, having risked so much already, decided to test Yori's resolve. "And if I order my people to stop work?"

"I think you may have forgotten that we are not just old friends. You are an official of this colony, and I am the Governor. The second answer comes from the Governor. It is this: If you stop work, you will be removed from your position in Technical Services and from membership in the Corps of Governors."

Lars shot back, "If Edward Hamilton can start a new settlement, my friends and I can do the same. We may decide to pack our bags and set up shop elsewhere. There's not much you could do to stop us."

The Governor paused just long enough to break the rhythm of the dispute. "First: If you are mad enough to do what you threaten, let's be clear about the consequences. You will be banished immediately, stripped of citizenship, and given twenty-four hours to leave with nothing but your clothes and whatever food you can carry. Remember, I have been there before! You will be forbidden any contact with the colony or use of its resources and support. That includes Alexandros!

"If you should survive in the wild for one year—and that's far from certain—then you would be allowed to appeal for reinstatement as an ordinary citizen, and the Council of Elders would be asked to examine you and make a recommendation. If they believed that you had learned to accept the conditions of communal life, you might be readmitted on probation for another year. If they did not believe you, you would be banished for life."

This speech was delivered in one uninterrupted gaze at Lars. At the end Yori dropped his eyes to the table in front of him then got up and faced the group. "And now, this meeting of the Corps of Governors stands adjourned!"

31

AFTER LARS HANSSEN'S CONFRONTATION with the Governor in that all-too-public meeting, the oddest thing happened: Nothing! A nothing like the silent scream that fills a void.

For months the event seemed to drop off the radar while never being entirely out of mind for anyone who was there or for some who were not. In fact nothing proved how seismic and epochal the event had been as the silence. As though no one dared speak of a topic that had renewed a fissure in the life of the starship and extended back into the deep history of Planet Ulro. All things considered, Lars' eruption and Yori's response were like a weapon that no sane person dares use.

One way or another the quelling of the storm may have had more to do with Sandra than the public drama. As far as one could tell, several needs converged in an entirely unexpected possibility. Instead of burying his head in the sand, Lars proposed a plan for reproducing paintings from Alexandros for use by the art students. His suggestion was welcomed by all, no less those who cared for peace than those who cared for art.

The results followed apace. Within a year the art department had its teaching aids, and art students were applying new techniques in the studio and *plein air*. Soon thereafter works old and new were beginning to attract attention in public places, and by a further agreement Lars began to make sketches for a public art gallery.

And as for Yori, with the passage of time and the accumulation of duties, one might think he would have no time left over for personal interests. But it is not true. Not only did he keep his resolve to spend a period each day in serious reading, he also devoted time each evening to solitary reflection.

For months those reflections are dominated by one topic: He's a man in love. So? So, he's in love with two women. Even the opposition between two is a shallow analysis.

The old rule of one question, imposed on him by Paola in his youth, has shaped him so thoroughly that part of thinking is holding an issue at bay until it gives itself in sharp outline. But there is no well-formed boundary between Paola and Véronique. He loves them both, and it would be sophistry to say it's with different kinds of love. Another thing he learned long ago is to see particular loves as belonging to a global disposition. That alone saves them from burning out or turning perverse. Even as he held the problem out of mind until it became clear enough to deal with, it wouldn't have been surprising if the other two persons involved had always been aware of the fact in their unique ways.

In this psychic context it happens that on returning from a routine visit to the North, Véronique pays a call on Yori. It's a customary progress report, largely a formality, since there is a monitor on his wall where he can raise the village with the flick of a finger. When she has conveyed what news there is, he surprises her.

"When you first made contact with Paola under orders from Governor Nasser, did she take you into the caves?"

Instantly her face reverts from business to the playful, girlish expression he has always loved. "No. I learned that she lived underground when we first met, but we always met outside. Probably because I was under instructions to avoid you. Later when we started working together, I knew the cave where the cistern is and was in the hearth room a time or two just briefly. I felt like an intruder. There wasn't much there to see."

"Not much. As at Eleusis!" When that means too little to her, he follows it with something that means too much. "Why don't we go there together? I would like to show you where I lived all those years."

The proposal staggers her. She stares wide-eyed as if he's lost his hold on precarious reality. Neither would think for one moment that it was an innocent or a spontaneous remark. They are not simple, and they are ignorant neither of themselves nor of each other. As anything *but* simple people, each—one might say all three—have been living for a long while in that empty place where one is capable of acting or not acting or of choosing to do neither. Yet Yori has just knowingly taken a step, the smallest action. And he knows it as Véronique knows he knows. Meanwhile, without a clue, she has a question to answer.

When she collects herself enough, she responds with a banal counter-question. "How will you find the time?"

He matches the triteness. "With people like you and Lars doing the work, I have less to do than you might think. How about this weekend? We'll take the land rover across the plateau and walk up the riverbed."

She hangs fire, perfectly aware that that dried-up river channel into the hills might thereafter be named Rubicon.

Finally she answers: "When?"

He mentions Sunday and, without another word, having neither agreed nor declined, she smiles and leaves.

On the day not quite agreed to, they do indeed drive to the foot of the hills. They proceed from there on foot up the old stream bed, braving the heat.

"Is this the way you came when you met Paola?"

"No, I've never been here. We always met on the other side of the hill. She warned me that I might meet you on this side. The path around is accessible by the rover, and we always use it now."

To Véronique, the smooth channel of the ancient river ascending between the cliffs is fresh and exotic. Instead of marching straight on to the caves and out of the scorching sun, they take their time, lingering here and there for a few moments in the shade of overhanging rocks as she examines one or another artifact of the rich life of a planet that others regard as a random dead thing stranded in space. At times she lags behind to enjoy the beauty of the black river rocks worn smooth by centuries of erosion, to observe unusual striations in the rock walls or the chemical composition of the stone or the patterns of erosion where she can read the force of the stream. Sometimes it's just a clump of dry weeds with equally interesting stories to tell.

Yori gives her time to explore the little things, wondering how it happens that, among more than a thousand colonists, she alone has been willing to love what others refuse to see. It was different with him, too. He always enjoyed rambling in the hills, but it took Paola a long time to teach him to love this desolate place. Véronique reached that point in a single bound.

As she studies the layers in the old stream banks, he remarks, "I've always thought of this climb from the plateau as more than a physical climb. It seems like a vertical progress from the commonplace to something finer, freer, more related to us."

For him the scene shimmers with memory and pain and joy as he stares at a high peak in the distance above them.

"What do you see up there?"

"Oh," he answers, startled, "well, it's out of sight really. We had a perch up there tucked in under a rock where we used to sit in the evening looking out over the flatlands below. It's where I discovered the Galatea had left. Paola had gone north at the time and I was alone."

Then he wanders back to the topic of the irregular landscape. "The wonderful thing is that we come *up* from the colony and then go *down* into the caves. In *ascending* we learn; in *descending* we are changed. There's more of life in it than a climb in either direction."

Véronique interrupts her examination of the rocks to consider the remark, searching his face in more than silent curiosity. If her feeling at this moment were translated into words, it might be something like this: "Of all the curious and wonderful things to discover on this planet, you are the most curious. You have become indigenous."

But instead she says, "I always imagined you and Paola were lovers."

The remark startles him again, and he hesitates before replying. "We were and, in a sense, we are still. But love goes by many names. Sometimes its horizons are wider than the meeting of bodies and minds. But love still. She calls it Eros, the primal force that binds all things together. So a strange love."

Véronique makes no reply, unless there is a reply in her dropping pensively behind. Her pace becomes more deliberate as they continue up the streambed. Soon they reach the point where a nearly invisible cleft in the wall opens into a narrow fissure. When he offers a helping hand, she hesitates, then decides to accept the hand that she doesn't need, though the rough and winding path is difficult to navigate.

Seeing the exotic landscape through her eyes, he blesses whatever god or random chance it was that first led him into this hidden cleft in the wall and into the darkness of the cave just ahead. It was by pure chance that he had taken the turn that altered his life and so much else forever. Not contingency alone, of course. It takes preparation and readiness even to stumble into the womb of the earth and be reborn.

At the tight opening into the Chamber of Names he draws her through, then, instead of giving her time to accustom her eyes to the dark and explore whatever might be there to explore, acting on some instinct, he advances straight across the room and into the narrow corridor beyond. The ground begins to descend like a mine shaft into the heart of the New Earth, and they are enveloped by total darkness, where touch must serve for sight.

The air becomes increasingly fresh and cool like a breath of life flowing up from lower depths. Still holding her by the hand, Yori leads the way deeper and deeper into the subterranean dark, often by a hand from in front where the way is too narrow, or an arm around her shoulders where the path is wide. On one level stretch he even guides her from behind with his hands on her bare shoulders as though gently pushing her into closer relation with the earth. She spreads her arms in welcome of the drafts of sweet air, and he feels her inhaling deeply as if her flesh remembers a home she has never known. In this cloistral dark the unseeing touch of two persons defines nearness and prepares sight.

At the entrance to the Chamber of the Hearth, light from above reveals a dim world where distinctness of objects depends on the adjustment of the eye. On prior visits, entering from the light, Véronique has seen it in the dim light of utility: the usefulness of the makeshift oven for baking bread, the mushrooms in the wall as foodstuff, the natural light itself as convenient for living here. But emerging from the dark, she sees differently. She examines the particulars of the hearth, not so much working out the means of Paola's life for twenty-five years or of Yori's for ten, as grasping the quality of that life. In those few moments she returns to an almost unthinkable thing that has dawned on her but for which she has no concept. It is that for one who is willing to learn to see, the passage through the dark lets the light be light.

Since Paola has been away in the North for several weeks, the hearth is cold and the room desolate. The gods have departed and left only this trace behind. As Véronique explores, Yori retrieves brush, rekindles the fire, and restores the chamber to itself. Then standing face to face beside the warm hearthstone, he takes her in his arms.

Later they make love, though the word is inadequate. In fact, it will not do. What happens between them on the outcropping of rock that serves as a bed is only a facet of a much larger event. More than two lovers tenderly caressing in the hollow of time on a rock somewhere—or nowhere among billions of galaxies. Yet the joy is not theirs alone. More like the joy of being-itself made flesh in a moment and a place unconfined by space and time.

Later they pass through the cave of the cistern and into the gardens, and for a long, slow time they stroll among the plants, observing with new eyes.

"I see what you did, you know, those times you brought the plants you claimed to have found in the hills." The sparkling eyes and joyous face laugh at him as she continues accusingly. "You traded some of Paola's native species that I didn't have for some of my mutations that she didn't have. I saw it the first time she brought me here."

"Then you see why I couldn't tell." He smiles at the distant memory.

Sitting for a while in the bower in the side of the wall, they watch as the sun moves along the slit between the cliffs. Soon it passes out of sight, leaving them in the shadows of the canyon. Véronique is a quick learner, and she sees now how much she had missed the real life of the caves in her earlier visits. She had seen the deprivation of bare existence but did not feel the pulsing joy of life.

Later as the two make their way up again, Yori carries one of the reed torches without lighting it until they arrive in the Chamber of Names. There he leads Véronique to the wall, lights the torch, and silently watches as she, short of breath, discovers the wonder of the names. He tells the story of his first discovery of the wall, of Paola sitting in the shadows, and of the encounter that she, Véronique, had made possible with the Governor.

She takes her time studying the array of names and then several individual ones until Yori asks, "What do you feel?"

Gazing steadily at the wall, she studies the question before answering. "Curiosity first, and wonder. But there is also a strange attraction. They hold your attention. The ones I know draw me toward them. Each is a window into another world. It's as if we owe a debt to them or as if each is a voice asking us to listen."

Yori gives her a smile that in a brighter light might have conveyed more than admiration, but his reply is on a different topic. "I have a request," he says, drawing her attention to a spot on the smooth wall exactly across the cavern from the names. "If I'm not able to do so, I would like you to see that three names are engraved on this wall, just here." With a finger he marks the exact spot and arrangement.

She stares, startled by the request and its implications. "Of course, if you like. What names?"

"Akira Kashimoto, Paola Rucai, and Governor Talib Nasser."

Véronique, still more mystified, "Certainly, if I can." After some moments trying to make sense of his request, she asks,

"But why? And why here?" She points to the wall opposite, "Why not with the others? And why them?"

"I'll tell you all that another time."

But she will not be put off. "I see the obvious. They are the founders. But the Governor alongside your father and Paola? The Governor was their deadly enemy."

"If what the founders have to teach is forgotten, it will throw humanity into peril once more. It's not about remembering three people. The individuals don't matter. What matters is as much about forgetting as remembering."

"They're symbols?"

"They're names. Which is much more. It's about what the three names, taken together, may inspire forever after."

She nods as though she understands what no one understands very well. "I see why you might isolate them on the side opposite the Ulro names, but why together?"

"For those who come here to remember. A few will learn that life is always strife, that sometimes one must act with hope for more than life, as my father did. Some will learn that sometimes one must give oneself to an unknown destiny, as Paola has. A small number may even learn that sometimes one who has been terribly wrong can be transformed, as the Governor was. All that adds up to what we may hope many will learn from the three standing together: Forgiveness relieves the burden of the past."

With that Yori takes her hand and leads her out into the late afternoon light. Nothing more is said until they're making the gradual descent toward the plain. Eventually, he lays a hand on her arm to stop her. Making a sweeping gesture across the plateau, he asks, "Did you know that this was once a freshwater lake? I used to sit up there on the ridges thinking of it as a dead sea and that someday it might be resurrected."

"Wouldn't it be wonderful if we could do like Edward and release water from the hills to restore this stream?"

"And let it flow across the plain."

32

WHEN YORI ANNOUNCED FORMAL recognition of the Elders, not all members of the Corps of Governors were pleased. It was more the idea of the thing than the fact. It rankled some that the Governor had changed the game without consulting them when all he was doing was recognizing the difference between theory and practice.

Within a few months, however, the bicameral advisors were operating as smoothly as could be where the purpose was to explore alternatives and find the best way forward. And it helped to have each deliberative body represented in the other. This is not to say that all went smoothly on the New Earth or ever would. Not at all. What people had come unconsciously to call The City was no Arcadia. Here, too, people came crying into the world, struggled together and apart, and, as often as not, left it all behind in tears. A polity is not a place where problems yield to final solutions, and a single instance shows as much.

Contrary to what Yori might have expected, on one important knot of issues he found himself almost of a mind with the Corps and at odds with the Elders. The issue was law. The New Earth—to him still P2314—had been settled by people who had lived under a central command structure for three centuries. Governor Nasser had made that tradition a bit more generous but without weakening authority. As in much of collective life, legislation and written laws were unnecessary. But inevitably time and complexity put such simple ways at risk. Meanwhile there were those who, for quite different reasons, were eager for the security of a fixed code.

For a long while the idea was little more than a verbal gesture in the meetings, and Yori let it pass without remark. But it didn't pass. It slowly gathered momentum until allusions to written laws became too common to ignore. Sometimes he pointed out that where things work, fixed rules would have no effect other than to compel the future to repeat the past. Usually that curbed the impulse and the Corps ended up doing only what was necessary.

But these are exactly the points that keep a governor on his guard. At such moments he listens for what is not said or even thought, searching for dispositions and passions that are warning signs of trouble. He must see what fits the city and imagine what may come to fit or not to fit by unforeseeable mutations. So Yori waits for the now proverbial quiet knock on the door announcing the time for change.

Complexity increases as the technological bio-system inches toward a polity, and it increases with improvement of the schools. As the young learn to think in new ways and imagine life in different modes, change becomes the one thing that doesn't change. Likewise, the first settlement and the possibility of more to follow begin to weaken the force of inherited mores and acquired civic habits. Still, because the issue is complicated and the risks of getting it wrong are great, Yori stalls and ponders the question of how to provide consistency and relative stability without risking the stasis of "statism." Codes will come, but they will come at the price of reducing life to a map.

What he does regard in a favorable light is a written constitution describing the broad purview of the councils, the terms of appointment, the authority of The City over satellite settlements, the means of selecting governors, and the like. In truth he has—and knows he has—an unacknowledged personal stake in the idea in that a constitution might provide him an eventual way out of the governorship. In the occasional moments when he dreams of returning to the hills and his books, he imagines that others might do his job as well as he. Then he could devote himself to writing his history of the last days of Ulro. At such moments he is inclined to forget that because ruling is not the thing he most wants to do, he may be the right person in the right place.

Some change is ubiquitous, and because timing is all, he decides to put the general topic of codified laws on the itinerary of the Elders. If, having explored the present need, they resist, that will support his sense that the time has not come.

When next they meet and the topic is raised, Véronique, as representative of the Corps, is asked to summarize the sentiment of the department heads. She turns a winning face on all alike and spreads goodwill by a buoyant manner that contrasts with the Governor's seriousness.

"I don't see that the issue has become sharply focused. So far no one has proposed anything that requires a decision one way or another. But the disposition seems to be growing. The Governor is probably bringing it to you for exploration in order to stay ahead of sentiment. Some feel that the city needs a general document describing how things are actually done. Others want written laws. I, for one, paid relatively little attention to any of this until the Governor decided to raise the issue."

Ava Sarosh, who appreciates Véronique's levelheadedness, asks, "What do you think is the state of mind behind the sentiment? For example, is it real foresight? Ambition? A sense of danger? Play for advantage? What is your reading?"

Véronique, though no longer in her bubbling twenties, gives Sarosh a mischievous grin and answers cheerfully, "All those probably figure in, but mainly it's male paranoia."

Everyone laughs. It was an old game between the women and the men on the starship Council to claim, and to refute the claim, that men have limited capacity for reading other people's dispositions. This time it falls to Joseph Kern to match the women's lightheartedness.

"Let me guess. The females of the species—without self-interest, mind you!—are so attuned to the dispositions of others that they can intuit what people mean before they know themselves. Whereas the males of the species are trapped in the net of logic and reasons and live in terror of feelings, especially their own. So the male invents machinery like codes of law to grind the life out of contingency." His glance at Ava Sarosh is mocking if affectionate. "Have I got that about right, Sarosh?"

She responds gleefully, "Yes. That's about as far as the male of the species is likely to get."

Véronique resumes, laughing. "I'll bow out of that debate and suggest a general paranoia instead. As in the way we parked and huddled together in our shell on this plateau even after there was nothing to fear. So long as we can imagine anarchy, we hang on to the status quo by our fingernails. Something like this is probably at work."

Sarosh wants to know what supporting evidence she sees. "Mainly the fact that it's all trumped up. We're afraid of the dark, so we hear ghosts knocking on the wall. It's mysticism! Rationally, why regulate what's working perfectly well? When something needs regulating, we regulate it. When it no longer needs regulating, we neglect the rule and it drops away. It's curious to watch rational beings—scientists, engineers, managers—anxious to control everything in sight. It's compulsive."

"And where is the Governor in all this?" Sarosh asks Véronique, even though he's sitting right in front of her and might speak for himself. "What does the Corps see?"

Véronique understands and returns a slightly ironic smile. "He pays attention when people mention the subject and appears to be sympathetic. But sometimes he warns against limiting flexibility. Where some members think governance is about control, he thinks it's about choice."

Yori is amused at the exchange. Delighted, in fact, by the ability of this group to make a game of serious thinking. At that moment he's wondering if that's why people speak of the "play of mind." Does it, mind, work better at play? Meanwhile as the others seem to be waiting for him, he comments briefly on the possibility of writing a constitution and postponing the machinery of legislation.

"There is an ancient argument that law is a curse. Given our disposition to control things, I hope your discussions will examine the case against law. Is it always a good thing? If not, when and how is it not?"

The topic is so familiar to most of the people in the room that it creates no immediate excitement. Not, that is, until Yori casts a shadow across law in general. Then one person catches fire.

Edward Hamilton has not spent his years in philosophical dialogue, but he has learned from hard experience to be suspicious of rules. He responds to Yori's skeptical note with some force. "I can tell you exactly why we should be in no hurry to make rules. When you sent the engineers to us in the North, these arrived with their heads full of rules about how to build a village. The problem was that their rules didn't fit our circumstances."

"Of course," Kern adds with a vigorous nod. "Rules are general, but conditions are unique. When they don't match, you get injustice rather than justice. And yet there must be rules."

It's Ang who picks up this theme and causes Yori to wonder if the scientist is aware of how far his horizons have extended over the years. Ang says, "Of course there's a gap to be bridged between the general and the particular, but that's what judges are for. Their business is to discover—or invent—connections between laws and acts. A clear code would certainly simplify the duties of teaching every individual personally . . . and repeatedly!"

Sarosh responds almost caustically, "So would replacing teachers with instructional technology, but it would destroy the social bonds at the very point where they are most important." This comes close to saying that law is a lazy way of teaching. But the moment passes with no harm done.

Rückert takes up the challenge. "Rules, like writing, weaken the necessity for thinking. You don't have to assimilate things into your own habits. You just look them up in an authoritative source. There in one gesture the meaning and purpose of education is surrendered."

The subject here is vast, and it's becoming more unwieldy by the minute. All the more reason to put down a few markers for later consideration. With that aim in view, Rückert adds, "And yet we learn from one another about better and worse ways of doing things by formulating rules. It's how we learn a game. The crux is that the rules don't create the game; the rules report on how the game is played. When *de*-scription devolves into *pre*-scription, teaching becomes policing. When this happens, counterproductive impulses are loosed in the world, and the rule of law begets disorder. This is another reason not to write laws so long as the mores of the people are sufficient."

"You mean, I suppose," Sarosh says, "that when social cohesion has to be guaranteed by wide enforcement, cohesion is already on the wane. Then it's time for invention rather than punishment."

"Perhaps. But right now we're a long way from the descent into the savagery of power politics. The iron hand of the law is too remote to worry about at our stage."

Joseph Kern takes exception to Rückert's last remark. "I think the Governor is asking us to be clear about the foundations of law along with possible lines of development.

Sometimes the great betrayal begins at the origin. You, Hans, have just alluded to my modest point. It's less about *making* laws than about *writing* laws. Even if you could define a rule in perfect, static clarity, conditions would change, and the meaning would erode. So if law is fundamentally pedagogical, then political life is perpetual re-education. Not in the sense of propaganda or the repetitive conditioning of prisoners in a Soviet prison or of rats in a maze, but the polity must never tire of explaining the rationale for necessary rules."

"Exactly," Rückert replies. "The choice is, law as persuasive authority or law as power to compel? When we imagine that the purpose of law is to make people toe the line, we set obedience above understanding. I need to be strengthened by the advice of my neighbors. That will make me strong where I am weak. I don't need the police. There's no place for violence here."

Edward objects, "Except, Hans, you are *willing* to learn. There's a devil in that little word 'will'! How do you persuade a person to *want* to be persuaded? We must infuse discipline into the habits of the young by persuasion rather than force. And the 'unlawful act' should face benevolent correction from our neighbors. But what I can't see is how you avoid force when people resist re-education. What's to save us from another descent into the politics of power?"

At this point there is a pause in the discussion until Ava Sarosh casts an ironic glance up and down the line of participants. "Remember how Elena Bart used to find theological paradigms buried in our discussions? You, Hans, used to hate that. Well, I'm going to do the same. Almost everything we're saying was discovered in Saint Paul's epistle to the Christians in Rome."

"Oh my god," Rückert groans. "The curse of the eternal return!" And he crosses himself.

Everyone laughs but she goes on undeterred. "I once heard you make the very point with the example of setting a cookie jar in front of a child and forbidding it to eat. But you neglected to mention the theological origin of your discovery."

He interrupts roguishly, "That's because nothing that isn't a secular truth first can make theological sense."

She ignores that. "If you had consulted the original you might have found that your cookie jar also contains an argument *for* law. Provoke desire and you rouse vitality. Forbid the cookies and you provoke deliberation: our ability to act or not to act."

"But," she waves Rückert's attempt to answer aside, "I only want to say when prohibition creates desire, the temptation is not all bad. It shows our ability to be responsible. That's why Adam's"—she brushes an objection aside with another wave of a hand —"yes, I know, it's just a myth—it's why Adam's fall is a good thing."

Paola has said nothing so far, and Edward pointedly asks her what she thinks. She reflects a moment before answering, "I've been thinking about something else Hans said many years ago. He called the ideal city 'a city without walls.' It's in a colloquy in *Starship Galatea*. His point was that human beings are exceptions who may be *included* in the city and governed by the city but who can't fully *belong* to the city. Cities and laws, he said, are only possible because we belong to the excess. I think he meant that law belongs to *play* rather than work. To *grace* rather than necessity. Unless law is free like play, always evolving and devolving, it becomes deadly. So we have to be vigilant, which means stay awake!"

In her less than limpid way, Paola had gathered up the anti-law sentiments along with the intuition that there might be a law that is neither static nor repressive.

Rückert, clearly pleased by her recollection of his discussion years earlier, responds, "Imagine approaching law as play! Isn't that why carnival is important? Or the medieval feast of misrule? And it's why celebrations must be excessive and why at times of mourning customs are suspended. We are not just creatures of order. We need disorder. We live *between* rule and contingency."

He looks at Yori. "That's the foundation of the city, and it's why the wise ruler has to carve out a space between rules and anarchy."

So it went, this prologue to another endless conversation, on and on until, at some small hour of the morning, Véronique Dumas got up the courage to ask, "So what are we recommending to the Governor?" But as even Paola couldn't reduce the unwieldly discussion to anything more than a prohibition against prohibition, the Elders decided to adjourn and reconvene the next evening.

In fact the discussions expanded exponentially and continued every night for a week. Yori wisely attended only the first, but at the end of the week he received a statement that might have been read as parody, illustrating all the hazards of written laws. This is how it went:

(1) Since stories rather than legislation describe who people are and since stories are the business of education, the city should legislate only when it's unavoidable.

(2) We should use personal persuasion to draw people to a standard rather than set them against it by rules.

(3) When laws become necessary, they should be descriptive and based as closely as possible on prevailing mores.

(4) Since no law is sacred or sovereign, the city should provide for the occasional suspension of laws as well as for their expiration and reinvention.

Having invited, not to say incited, a week-long seminar on law, what did the Governor think when he received this simple and bland recommendation? Certainly not that the time had been wasted or that nothing had been accomplished. He admired the Elders' will to think on the broadest speculative scale, yet to counsel minimal action. The result was that for now he would do nothing and do it with his eyes open. But that wasn't what captivated him.

The idea he couldn't get out of his mind, more a scent in the air than an idea, was Ava Sarosh's obscure allusion to a law beyond the law. He had not understood what she meant, yet her remarks connected in some way with, of all things, an unrelated private dilemma he had refused to think about. Like parallel ideas in non-coinciding universes. It was his sore conscience about loving two women. In spare moments thereafter, he revolved the mystery in mind and made no progress. At last, frustrated by failure, he did the opposite of giving up and moving on. He parked the idea in midair and, like a good ruler, waited for it to take shape on its own.

33

FROM THE MOMENT YANG Shi Wa first proposed the northern settlement to the Corps of Governors, a few recognized it as an unforeseen impetus for the transformation of the colony itself. What no one recognized at the time was how extensive that influence might become.

Just as colonial technology supported the settlement top-down, so to speak, so the settlement, without any guiding intention, inspired political development in the colony from the bottom up. Viewed from the distance of "Edward's Town," the colony was regarded as the center of public activity with the result that the place without a name for a generation acquired one. "The City," they called it, and The City it became.

But there were more tangible influences. The one that had the greatest effect on public spirit was the controversial aqueduct. Despite Lars' initial resistance, it became the source of his passion to release water high in the hills above the colony and let it flow down the old riverbed into the channel of eroded bedrock at the bottom of the prehistoric lake. The stream that would come to be called "The River" was allowed to cross the plateau in a long curve ending in a manmade lake at the nurseries on the west side of the colony. Along each side of the channel, Véronique's department drilled hollows in the stone floor, filled them with manufactured soil, and planted trees that were expected to form a ribbon of green and shade from the western wall to the hills.

In a related development close to the south end of The River, adjacent to the nurseries, one wall of The City was torn open and a City Art Gallery built just beyond the line of the wall. On entering from the arcades, the effect is of being both inside and outside the old colony. Farther on, between the museum and the river, Véronique designed a green park that uses water from the new reservoir so that three new magnets for public interest are collected into one.

People who want to enjoy the only open water or outdoor green space they have ever seen must pass though the rooms of the gallery to get to the outside. At first, predictably, people make for the river as straight as the winding design of the building allows, but as the scenes both inside and out become more familiar, the pattern changes. They linger in the climate-controlled gallery or, mornings and evenings, lounge in the garden before reaching the park benches under the trees beside the water. In a related but less conspicuous development, Yori has had portals installed at the ends of all the arcades to facilitate easy passage to the outside. So far that effort hasn't paid off, but its day, too, will come.

During this period Paola tolerates the colony without feeling at home in it. Her gardens in the hills console her less since they have become an experimental annex of the Agriculture Department. Even in the Chamber of the Hearth she feels a bit exposed to the public eye. For these reasons she prefers spending as much time as possible with Shi Wa and Edward in their cave opposite Edward's Town, commuting from there to The City for the meetings of the Elders, the company of Véronique, and of Yori when he isn't otherwise occupied.

On one occasion—the last occasion—he finds her visibly altered. In a long evening together, he sadly sees that age has touched the roots of her life and sooner than it ought. Not age exactly. She's in vigorous middle years and good health, but the path of the human spirit does not quantify as organs and systems do. He sees at once what is happening and at once resists. In a reflex of self-interest, he resolves not to let her give up and not to let her go.

What he doesn't see—and doesn't want to see—is that when a person devotes herself body and soul to a worthy task, the time may come, and sooner than expected, when she sees her work done and finds joy in a race well run and a course honorably finished. There need be nothing sad in that. Isn't it even a condition to be wished? To make a good ending to the strivings of a worthy life blest with success? On this particular evening she subjects herself to his all-too-visible distress because there remains one point on which her service to him, hence to the Galatea mission, is incomplete.

Her years working with Véronique—it must have been ten by now—have been a happy time, sharing their love of growing things. The friendship is of a kind that Paola has known only once before, with Shi Wa before their separation and before she had a family. Their time together has also been a bit like the years of Yori's novitiate, in that Paola has conveyed a lifetime of experience on a basis of equality such as she could not enjoy with him at first, and Véronique has absorbed it all. Now, moved as ever by a secret love of her own, Véronique is ready to assume the role that Paola has played for ten years and more: supporting Yori.

Now Paola's flame is out and her time is short. In the middle of the expansion of Edward's Town and evolution of The City, she has come with a message for "her Governor." She knows what his loss will be when she is gone, but her purpose is not to prepare him for losing her. More is at stake than his comfort or his peace of mind. By now the person who wears the name Yori Kashimoto has been renamed by a public task: He *is* the Governor. As she had first taught him to say until the remark had become a cliché, "It's never about us. We are whoever we are by the place we have been given and what it has fallen to us to do." The danger now is that when she is no longer present, he might lapse for one reason or another into private feelings. That danger she must prepare him to withstand.

In this first face-to-face encounter in months, they devote a long time—more than is needed—to public business before she shifts to a distant key: "I have told you before that Véronique is in love with you. You must know she will never accept another man."

"Yes. But I've been in love with you for years. How can I love you both?"

"I think you have heard that love has many names . . . You love Véronique, too, in your own way. Love isn't a category with multiple instances. It is always singular and incomparable. The two need not be inconsistent. How many members of a family can one love at the same time? How many stars?

We're finite, and there are organizational problems, but love can no more be standardized than a city can."

She goes on to say that the law of love does not work by constraint but by declaration and fidelity and, in understanding that, he will also understand The City. "I'm only asking you to recognize a truth. The rest will take care of itself. Véronique is right for your work as I no longer can be. She is right in unforeseeable ways and you'll be cheating her, yourself, and your task if you refuse to accept it." She stops a moment and adds, "Cheat your task and you'll even be cheating me."

He forces a smile that only shows melancholy. "I will not let you go, if that's what you're thinking. You will always remain my beloved guru-in-chief."

"Yes. Just not present in the room."

"Now you're going to speak of the hollow of time!"

"If so, it would also be the triumph of a full life."

"I will not let you go! That's the end of it."

Once upon a time when he had protested in the face of grief—on first learning of his father's death, or when he was banished—she had let the topic pass and waited, but this time she has no time left for waiting.

Gently but without compromising the hard lesson, she leans forward, takes both his hands in hers, and says, "Try to hold on and you hold nothing. So we hold our loves like our pleasures, lightly, and bless them as they fly. It must happen to us. You must accept that my work is done as yours is beginning."

He frees his hands, gets up, and paces back and forth across the floor. Eventually he grows calm and stops, stands in front of her, looking down. "Through loving you I learned to love all things, visible and invisible, even banishment without hope." He does not add, though he must have wanted to, and in that he would have been wrong: "And now you're asking me to give all that up."

Most of the conversation that follows is like so many they have had in the hills, without words but no less understood. Reluctantly he sees that if the man who had been bred to wise Taoist governance, first of himself and then of others—if he were to slip back into the adolescent demand that reality conform to his will, he would prove not a blessing to The City, but a curse.

Paola smiles. "I have come to speak to you for the last time in what you used to call the sibylline voice. We know that I am no prophet and there is no such voice, but three things were given to me: our fathers' book *Starship Galatea*, twenty-five years of exile to pore over the wisdom of the past, and a young novice to pass it on to. Otherwise, my life would have been a bleak stretch."

He is quiet for a moment, then asks with a shrug close to renunciation, "So what do you want me to do?"

"The time has come to let me go as I must let you go. As you must let me let you go so that we do not bring ruin on the world."

At that moment even Paola may be tempted by impulses less than noble, by things that she must not say, as she does not say, "I've always known this moment would come, the last temptation, but I didn't know it would come so soon or how hard it would be."

She does not let herself even think, "Now I must willingly give up the dearest thing in my life to a rival whom I also love." And another thing buried too deep for thought: "I have loved him as I should, even loved in him his love for her. Now I send him to her, and he makes it as easy for me as he can by not asking me to console him for my sacrifice." And one last thing she *does* think without words: "Somehow I will bear this, too, and learn to love it, since the love that passes is no less loved."

She gets up from her seat in his small parlor, where they have spent the evening. "You must go back to your vocation and I must go back to the hills." With these benedictory words and no gesture of parting, she leaves.

As she passes across Government Square, Véronique is watching from a park bench where she has spent a miserable evening, torn between the two people in the world she most loves. In the oddest of love triangles, she remains devoted absolutely to two whose love for her is the joy, and whose love for each other is the bane of her life. She rises to call out to her friend until something in the bearing of the older woman, whether the detectable weariness in her step or the ashen face, prevents her. Sitting down again she whispers audibly to herself words she can't fathom: "She has given him up and broken her heart! She has given him to me. What can possibly come of such a gift?"

34

AFTER HER LAST VISIT with Yori, Paola is rarely seen in The City. She does not neglect the meetings of the Council, but when they are at night, she stays in her room in Government House then leaves before dawn for home. If meetings are during the day, she returns the same evening, always on foot. Yori would gladly provide a land rover, but he knows her too well to offer. Out on the plateau so early or so late, an observer might see a woman wrapped in her eternal homespun, shuffling along like a person half again her age, through the trees by the river, until the path around the hill diverges westward.

In this period Yori sees her infrequently except when he meets with the Council. Not that either avoids the other. Just a tacit understanding that the glory of the past exists only in its having-been. Yori is compelled to accept her judgment that her work is done, and he never speaks, even to Véronique, of his sadness in seeing her so diminished.

A time eventually comes when she does not appear at a scheduled meeting. Nor does she send a message. Véronique promptly passes the news to Yori, who is somewhere on an exploratory mission in the wild. Then she sets off for the caves. There she finds Paola in the Chamber of the Hearth on her "bed" waiting peacefully to die. Some days before, she had stopped eating and now quietly declines all efforts to feed her.

For two days she lingers with Véronique at her side. The mind and the dark all-seeing eyes remain clear but she rarely speaks. At the last moment she fixes Véronique in a benedictory gaze, gives her hand a faint squeeze, and passes.

Some things end in that moment and some things begin. The unfinished work named Paola Rucai is finished. The evidence is all in, and it's possible for the first time to know who she was and will always be. In this moment Paola Rucai becomes an eternal exemplary Idea. If life itself were extinguished and the stars were to die, her name, spoken or not, would stand as durable as love or triangularity or light. An immortal configuration in a possible universe and a beacon for any who could find it. A summons even, for those who care.

What surprises everyone is that without anyone noticing, the eccentric woman from the hills had become a fixture in the colony. A reference point now disappeared, leaving a gap in nature. As if a cathedral at the center of town had unaccountably vanished or an element in the air one breathes were subtracted or a starship where one was born went missing—so the death of the outlander has left a hole in the essential measure of things.

As news of Paola's death spreads, Yori is quick to recognize the need for some ritual to mark an event that has touched everyone. In consultation with the Elders, it is decided that her urn will be brought back to Government House for a public memorial in the Square. The event is announced for the evening of the third day. If on that day any public interest whatever is a surprise, how much greater the surprise in finding Government Square packed with people. First Sandra

Mohr plays a movement of a Bach cello sonata. Then Yori and several others pay brief tributes. It is a solemn but almost happy celebration of a life that few had known or cared to know until it disappeared. Afterward, by plan, the Council and the few who were close to her follow the Governor, urn in hand, in procession through the new art gallery and beyond the park to the river.

But there is more, quite unplanned. The sun having just set, torches are distributed for the long walk up the riverbank to the hills where Paola is to rest in her beloved caves. What makes the event extraordinary is not the personal but its spontaneous public character. To one watching from the hills it might appear that the cortege included the whole colony, as flickering lights define the long, slow curve of the channel across the plateau. Once at the caves, there is room only for a few in the Chamber of Names, but hundreds wait outside as the urn is placed on the rock where Paola used to sit. Then a cloth marker is removed from the wall, revealing three names freshly carved into the rock wall:

Paola Rucai
Governor Talib Nasser
Akira Kashimoto

Founders of The City

After the unveiling and a few moments of silence, those in the Chamber leave so that the ones waiting can enter. The line is so long and the deference so great that it goes on into the night. For the occasion the cave has been artificially lighted so that people who know nothing of the place and have never been underground are awestruck by the scene and the hundreds of names spread across the opposite wall. For hours that night the observer from the hills might watch a serpentine line of people making their way along the river and under the stars back to The City.

Thereafter, no effort is made to give importance to the place, especially not to make the Chamber of Names into a memorial to the past. Yet something of the sort happens. Paola's Caves becomes a kind of pilgrimage site. One who knows that causes are deductions from effects will understand how the Chamber of the Hearth also comes to be regarded as something like the womb and birthplace of the New Earth. For generations to come, and in spite of causes, the caves in the hills will incarnate the mission of Starship Galatea and the spirit of The City that were once a mere glint in the eyes of a few desperate dreamers on Planet Ulro.

After Paola's death Yori's coherences become a bit shaky without quite dissolving. In his youth the kaleidoscope of life turned often, and its elements shifted to new intensities. It's easy for the young to champion contingency and criticize the fear of change. But this is different, as though nature itself were capricious. If experience is an arch "wherethrough Gleams that untravelled world," then the capstone that once held the ensemble together has gone missing. He may no longer need Paola to teach him to think, but he clings to the habit of her confirmation. Having yet to learn that not Paola, but only her presence in the room, is missing, he feels more than a little adrift.

Whatever difference Paola's death makes for Yori the man, the Governor gives the appearance of being unchanged. Not that appearances matter much to him. He is descended from an ancient culture of honor in which the chief desire is to uphold an inherited ideal or feel disgrace in betraying it. His bonds to other people are therefore not of the ordinary kind. If he is tainted by the Ulro culture of the spectacle, the infection is slight, and the older he becomes, the better defined is the boundary between the public and the private. Ordinary relations are more structural than personal, and only a few people in his life have become part of his flesh and bone: The father whom he lost as a child never ceased to be that; Governor Nasser who was more enemy than friend had been that; and Paola was preeminently that. Now the one person remaining with whom he has such a bond is Véronique.

And yet there is something alarming in his state of mind: He has lost interest in ruling. The feeling is not unfamiliar. Much earlier he would gladly have "returned to the hills with Paola and lived like the gods." Now he would prefer to keep company with the Elders and give his days and nights to exploring the twilight of Ulro. Although he confers regularly with Rückert and the others, he cannot be one of them. The exception once again: included, not belonging.

It is in this state of mind that Véronique finds him in his office one evening soon after Paola's memorial. There is nothing unusual in her coming, but it is unusual to arrive uninvited and unannounced. She has hesitated to come. In part it's a lingering sense of responsibility for her role in Paola's sacrifice. In part it's uncertainty about Yori's state of mind, but at such times people who live largely in their thoughts especially need companionship, and she knows it.

When she enters, he sees something more in her face and eyes than the usual affectionate light and is grateful that she doesn't try to pry into his condition.

She asks, "Am I intruding?"

"Yes. But it doesn't follow that it's unwelcome."

They sit down on the side of the room, away from the flickering monitors where Yori had begun his history with Governor Nasser. It's where Paola had always been uncomfortable but where Véronique is perfectly at ease, in the middle of colonial business. Though they have not been alone together since Paola's death, by mutual consent they accept each other's company without awkwardness and settle down comfortably more like old friends than recent lovers. For a while they chat in a key that is new to them, about affairs in the North and developments in The City, like intimates who have finally reached the quiet comfort of middle age. So much "world" lies behind them on the way to this moment, from childhood on the starship to their first day together in the caves until now. Yet nothing hangs in the air to be clarified, nothing of particular interest to be said or avoided, no mention at first of Paola or how much her absence will alter their life. The extraordinary thing is the ordinariness, he and she communing without speaking.

Eventually she asks about his research. It's a question he generally brushes aside as if it were a slightly absurd hobbyhorse.

"It's just a game, you know."

She accepts the dodge with a touch of mockery, "Like Rückert's idea of law as play? Correct me if I'm wrong, but isn't every inventive act essentially play?"

"Meaning?"

"I once heard Paola try to tell Lars that he didn't know how to play, only how to work. I often think about that conversation, if you can call it one, when only one person was listening. Anyway, she went on to say it was because he didn't understand time."

"That's too simple for people like Lars, who are accustomed to complexity!"

"Now, what do *you* mean?"

"Sometimes the clues we need are lying all around us unnoticed." Yori sits comfortably, leaning his cheek against one hand as the Japanese eyes become at once warmer and more concentrated. "You know the feeling when you're designing a square or a park and lose track of the clock? You forget to eat or to quit work 'on time.' When I'm occupied with my Ulro project, I often don't know how long I've been at it. It's like being outside any time that can be measured and counted—even consciousness of time. We aren't *working* in the sense of producing something. It's play. It's being possessed!"

Then Véronique remembers a similar moment. "Once when we were working—or 'playing' together!—in her garden, Paola remarked that it was like being in eternity."

"Yes. She was always searching for a way to say that more clearly. Once she said, 'It's the moment in the day that's hardest to find, yet always there *to be found*. Like names on a wall. In a time between times.'"

344

Both turn these sibylline expressions over in mind quietly, affectionately, until Véronique says, "I've never told you the thing she said the day she died. She was lying on her stone bed in perfect tranquility holding my hand. She moved her eyes to mine and fixed me with that clear, dark gaze. In the quiet voice you could not help believing, she said, 'We were mere mortals born in a machine and we have ended up living like the immortals on the New Earth.'"

Véronique waited a full minute or a little longer for Yori to comment on the remark. When he didn't, she added, "She wasn't delirious, but she seemed to be denying death even as she was willing it."

For a full minute or a little longer he still didn't answer, appearing to study that dying remark as though it contained a legacy. Eventually he answered, "She spoke in riddles so we wouldn't think we understood and promptly forget."

Nothing more for several minutes as Yori sat staring out the door on the other side of the room into the little rock garden Véronique had designed for the Governor's office. Meanwhile she merely watched him, wishing there were a window through which she could see his thoughts.

Then he repeated himself as though trying still to get his inheritance from Paola right. "I think she meant something she learned from her father: If we learn that we are not objects but ways of being—events of feeling, imagining, knowing—we can grasp our highest capacity. We're unique, if we are, in having crossed the galaxy and discovered the eternal moment just where we left it: in the present where we confront the *'Nothing that is not there and the nothing that is.'*"

345